# Robert's smile was devastating.

It transformed his face and most of Genevra's apprehension disappeared, only to be replaced by an embarrassing awareness of the dazzling attraction he held for her. He represented the epitome of every chivalrous dream her girlish heart had ever cherished, a man possessed of every knightly virtue and every courtly grace. But she was old enough, mature enough, she hoped, to chide herself for behaving like the heroine of some minstrel's tale.

She forced herself to breathe again. She swallowed. 'God's greetings, my lord,' she said, her voice unusually husky.

**Sarah Westleigh** has enjoyed a varied life. Working as a local government officer in London, she qualified as a chartered quantity surveyor. She assisted her husband in his chartered accountancy practice, at the same time managing an employment agency. Moving to Devon, she finally found time to write, publishing short stories and articles, before discovering historical novels.

**Recent titles by the same author:**

A HIGHLY IRREGULAR FOOTMAN
SEAFIRE
THE OUTRAGEOUS DOWAGER

# JOUSTING WITH SHADOWS

Sarah Westleigh

MILLS & BOON®

First published in Great Britain 1997
Harlequin Mills & Boon Limited,
Eton House, 18-24 Paradise Road, Richmond, Surrey TW9 1SR

© Sarah Westleigh 1997

ISBN 0 263 80214 0

Set in Times 10 on 11½ pt. by
Rowland Phototypesetting Limited
Bury St Edmunds, Suffolk

04-9709-75161

Printed and bound in Great Britain

# Chapter One

Ignoring her uncle's murmured admonition, Genevra leant forward in her seat near the Earl, the blue silk of her skirt sighing against the grey squirrel fur lining the rich brown velvet of her mantle. The previous jousts had been of marginal interest to her as she waited for this moment. Now, at last, she could catch a glimpse of this baron, this Robert St Aubin of Thirkall Castle, situated on the border of Suffolk.

Two knights waited, one at each end of the lists, armoured, armed, mounted on huge, lavishly caparisoned war horses. The Heralds, their array brilliant in the brash April light, rode out to announce the contest.

The great Earl of Northempston, host to this extravagant St George's Day tournament, sat on red velvet cushions, fringed and tasselled in gold like the festoons of scarlet silk draping the balustrade before him. His loge, at the centre of the lists, was covered with striped Alexander in his livery colours of azure and silver and decorated with sparkling imagination with the painted masks of animals, mythical creatures, devils and angels.

The Heralds halted before him. With a colourful flourish, embellished with yet more bullion gleaming in

fringes and tassels, they raised their horns to blast the
air with sound.

Their attention captured, the crowd who gathered in
the spacious outer bailey of Ardingstone Castle, the huge
grey pile forming the battlemented backdrop to the day's
events, fell quiet. The voice of the first Herald rang out,
reciting the long list of his knight's achievements in
the field.

Genevra peered, in the glare of the sun, at the knight
who was still waiting, motionless, to run his course. The
distance was too great for her to see detail, but she could
tell that his stature was large, his horse and accoutrements
magnificent, and glimpsed a wisp of green silk fluttering
from his sun-spangled heaume.

She had supplied the green scarf. It had been demanded
of her by her uncle, who had said that St Aubin wished
to wear her favour.

'Why?' she had asked, frowning.

Only then had she been informed that she had been
chosen as Lord St Aubin's bride. She had never set eyes
on St Aubin.

She had met few men other than farm hands and
menials, consigned as she had been to a nunnery on the
banks of the Derwent at the foot of the remote, rocky
but beautiful hills of Derbyshire. Her uncle, Gilbert
Heskith, and his wife Hannah, would have preferred to
leave her mouldering there for ever. Had tried to persuade
her to become a nun.

But she had not felt called to the religious life and,
supported by the Mother Superior, who recognised her
lack of vocation, had steadfastly refused to renounce her
inheritance and take her vows. At Lammas-tide, when
she would be one-and-twenty, she had planned to claim
her inheritance and order her own life. But her uncle had

sent for her and had her brought here to Ardingstone. A marriage had been arranged.

Not through any wish of his, even now. He had brought her here by order of the Earl himself, to wed a man chosen by his lordship. Her uncle, who had been her guardian since the death of her grandfather ten years since, had studiously neglected his duty to find her a husband, either before or after she had reached marriageable age. He had preferred to keep the tithes from her mother's manor under his own control for as long as possible.

Now, just as she had begun to anticipate her coming of age and to make plans, she found herself, by order of the Earl, destined to wed a stranger, this knight now thundering along the lists on his huge chestnut destrier, lance levelled, to the frantic cheers of the crowd. Once wed, her possessions would pass from her uncle's control to his. Her disappointment and apprehension were palpable.

He was an accomplished jouster. Even she could appreciate that, and the acclaim of the spectators confirmed it. He was favourite to win the tournament. He had fought in France and Spain, distinguishing himself at Najera. But she knew no more about him or his family, except that his father must be dead for him to have inherited the barony. He did not look old, because of his bearing and strength, but to have achieved so much Robert St Aubin must have reached full manhood.

What was he like? Would she approve of him and his looks or be repulsed and come to hate—even to fear—him? Would he be kind or cruel? These were the imponderables that tightened the grasp of her gloved fingers on the balustrade and gripped her stomach with churning, anxious excitement.

She longed for love. To love and be loved. But it was the lot of women of her station to wed men chosen for them by others. She had no mind to rebel. She would make the best of her marriage, whatever befell. She hoped at least for felicity, for a brood of children to bring pride to their father and joy to herself.

She prayed that no adverse circumstance would ever have the power to turn her into a shrewish, disgruntled woman like her aunt Hannah, sitting on the padded bench on her uncle's other side. But then, Hannah had always been a shrew; marriage had simply made her worse. It had been at her insistence, though it had suited Lord Heskith, too, to have the ten-year-old Genevra, natural daughter of his dead sister, sent away to a remote nunnery, ostensibly to further her education. Which in truth it had done, more thoroughly than they had intended.

'Sit back, Genevra,' hissed the acid voice across her uncle's broad, velvet-clad chest. 'Behave as the lady your misguided mother claimed you to be!'

Slowly, reluctantly, Genevra obeyed the hated tones. She did not wish to cause a commotion on this day and in this place. Soon, soon, she would be free of her aunt's persecution. And she had seen enough for now, had noted the huge spread eagle embroidered in gold across the bright green and murrey of his parti-coloured jupon, and on his horse's matching caparison.

But most impressive of all was the winged eagle, wrought in gold, cresting his tourney helmet, his heaume. No wonder the crowd was shouting for the Golden Eagle! Closer inspection must wait until later, when she would be formally introduced and betrothed to Robert St Aubin.

'For a child born out of wedlock, you have been remarkably favoured,' went on the remorseless voice of her aunt. 'We had despaired of finding you a suitable match. Why Northempston chose you as the bride for his protégé, I cannot fathom. How he knew of your existence—'

'His Lordship visited the Convent six months since. He is one of its benefactors and has paid several visits over the years. I was introduced to him then, as was everyone else. When last he came, he spoke to me kindly.'

'Ha. You never said.'

'It seemed of little moment.'

'Well, it is strange that he should choose you, of all people, to wed his favourite. It is not as though you can lay claim to any beauty.'

Genevra flushed. She did not need her aunt to remind her of her plainness.

'It is her dowry he covets,' interjected Gilbert sourly, his voice almost drowned by a renewed burst of cheering for the Golden Eagle as St Aubin won the bout.

Genevra said nothing. The visiting Earl had spoken with her for some time on his last visit, his manner abrupt yet in some indefinable way approving. He had subjected her to a thorough scrutiny; she had thought she had seen appreciation in his eyes, despite the drabness of her clothing. She had liked him, although he was plainly a forceful man who would brook no challenge to his authority.

Afterwards, bending over her embroidery, she had wondered why the mighty lord had spent so long talking to her. She had thought it perhaps because she was able to discourse with him in Latin and Greek as well as in French and English, which had seemed to please him, and to discuss mathematics and science.

'I pride myself on being a man of refinement and education,' he had said as he took his leave. 'I admire your mind, mistress. You have not wasted your years

here, but have used the time wisely in studying the philos-
ophers and scholars of old.'

But, of course, whatever the Earl might think of her,
it must be her dowry which had influenced St Aubin to
agree to the match, for he knew no more of her than she
did of him.

She watched as he left the field, still mounted, to the
continuing acclaim of the spectators, while his opponent
limped off on foot. A faint stir of pride lifted her spirits.
It should not be so bad to be wedded to a man of such
outstanding prowess. He would rest now, and prepare to
take to the field again against future challengers.

Hannah sniffed, loud enough to be heard over the
surrounding bustle. 'You think a poor inheritance like
hers would sway him?' she asked her husband. 'The
tithes barely brought in enough to pay for her keep, and
that of her servant, at the convent!'

Gilbert glanced at his wife sideways. The colour in
that part of his face not hidden by his large floppy cap
and dark beard deepened. 'You know better than that,
wife. Except in the plague years, it paid well enough.
And Merlinscrag suffered less than our own barony, and
quickly recovered.'

'Indeed? Then why was I not informed, pray? What
did you do with this largesse, my lord?'

'Much as you would like to do so, you do not hold
the purse-strings, wife,' said Gilbert bluntly. 'I spent it
as I thought best. But how do you imagine we managed
to live as befits our rank? You must have known that,
with all our villeins dead or absconded and with day
labour so costly, the tithes and rents from our lands could
not support your extravagances. I fear we will not live
in so fine a style in future. Genevra's revenues have
helped us over some lean years.'

'And would have gone on doing so without the interference of the Earl.'

Gilbert shot an anguished glance along the row to where the Earl sat in state. 'Be silent, woman!' he hissed.

'Not for much longer, madam,' interjected Genevra, seething with anger at hearing how she had been cheated. 'I should have taken control myself come Lammas-tide.'

'You?' snorted Hannah. 'What do you know of running a manor?'

'I helped the nuns—' began Genevra, but they had stopped listening.

'Northempston has made it worth my while,' said Gilbert.

'How?' demanded his wife.

Gilbert shrugged. 'How do you imagine?'

'Money? Land?'

'Another manor to add to the barony,' he admitted.

'Then your talk of us having to live in poverty was all lies!'

'No. The new manor will only partly make up for the loss of Merlinscrag's revenues. But had I not agreed, we would have had nothing at all to take their place, since Genevra was determined to claim them for herself.'

Ignoring Gilbert's implication that, once of age, she would have acted selfishly, Genevra then let their quarrel pass over her head. Naturally the deal included some profit to Gilbert. Genevra doubted whether he had even now owned to the whole extent of the settlement or of his thieving from her. But the manor bestowed upon her mother as a reward for her services at Court must be rich.

Hannah was lavishly gowned, as was she, in one of Hannah's fine wool kirtles and rich silken surcoats, hurriedly altered to fit. She herself wore a modest maiden's caul upon her head, which tidily gathered up her long, bark-coloured hair, but Hannah's greying locks were hidden by an elaborate concoction of wire and gauze formed in the shape of horns, which Genevra thought appropriate.

Plain veils, it seemed, were no longer favoured on occasions such as this, while wimples were worn only by old ladies, nuns and widows. Fashions had changed in the ten years she had been cloistered. Some of the ladies had their hair gathered into great boxes worn over their ears.

Hearing her uncle and aunt bickering over the money they had or had not had from her legacy, Genevra wondered whether mayhap she had been better off in the kindly, gentle atmosphere of the nunnery, where she had been free to indulge her love of study, than living at Bloxley with her uncle and his uncongenial family.

In her early years, secure in the love of her mother, she had not realised that she was different from other children except that she lacked a father, whom she presumed to be dead. Not until her grandfather died and Gilbert inherited the barony had she been brought face to face with the irregularity of her birth.

Her grandfather had always treated her with a distant kindliness, although as she grew older she had noticed that the serfs, the retinue, the house carls, even the meanest scullion, had shown her less respect than they did her imperious cousins, whose cast-off clothes she wore. All except dear Meg, who had been the only person, apart from her mother, ever to show her love.

Gilbert, her new guardian, had told her that her mother, at seventeen, had been sent to Court to serve Queen Philippa. A year or so later she had returned home pregnant. She had refused to say who the father was, but had insisted that he was of noble birth and wished to wed her. He would come for her ere long.

'Of course,' Hannah had said spitefully, 'he did no such thing. So you were born a bastard, my dear Genevra—for all we know, you may be the get of a serf. I will not tolerate you living permanently under my roof.'

'It is not your roof,' Genevra had protested, quashing her dismay at those cruel words. 'It is my uncle's.'

'He thinks as I do. You will be better off in the Convent of St Mary the Virgin. You will have every comfort, the chance to learn how to be useful, and you will not be under my feet.'

'But, Aunt—'

'No argument, if you please. Our minds are made up. You leave on Monday. So Meg will pack your things and her own, for she will go with you, and your uncle will provide an escort to see you safely there.'

She had cried herself to sleep for weeks: but, at ten, how could she resist? And later, grown to womanhood and longing to taste its fruits, she had still been helpless, for the Baron had sent no money to her personally, only transmitting to the Reverend Mother the sums the Convent demanded for her and Meg's keep and her education. Only at Christmas did they send a small sum to be passed to her as a gift.

She believed that, for the last few years, she had been living to some extent on the charity of the sisters, for what Gilbert sent could not pay for the new kirtles she had needed as she grew. But, for good or ill, she had left the Convent now.

As the tournament progressed, Genevra's anticipation quickened. The Golden Eagle was undoubtedly the darling of the crowd, a glamorous figure, the epitome of knightly prowess. How fortunate she was to be promised to so splendid a personage! He had already won a mountain of armour from his beaten opponents and now he was riding forward to receive the ultimate accolade, the Earl's own prize.

As he approached, she could see that a smaller version of the eagle featured in one quarter of his shield, too. The spread eagle had formed part of his family's arms for generations.

He drew his mount up before the Earl and raised his visor. The Earl, built solidly like an old oak, leaned forward to present the costly golden salver, handing it to a page to pass to St Aubin.

And then, 'Methinks you should return Mistress Genevra's favour, my lord,' pronounced the Earl in his carrying tones. He indicated Genevra, suddenly frozen into immobility, sitting nearby.

Keeping his mount under control with his thighs, the knight dropped his reins while he detached the green silk from his heaume. Taking his lance from its bracket, he lowered the sharp end, protected by a crown-like coronal, and draped the scarf on it. Then, sidling his horse to stand before her, bowing from the waist as he sat in his saddle, he thrust it forward so that she could retrieve her property.

Confused, Genevra reached out for the silk, at the same time forcing her gaze up to meet that of her prospective bridegroom. She could see little of his face, just two vivid blue eyes inspecting her without expression, separated by a beaky nose.

His voice came muffled from behind the metal of his heaume. 'I thank you, demoiselle. Your favour brought me good fortune.'

Then he wheeled his horse and rode from the field, to the continuing sound of tumultuous cheering.

*          *          *

Genevra sat quietly while Meg brushed her hair. She must look her best for her betrothal ceremony. She wanted to impress. . .

'He looks to be a fine figure of a man,' said Meg, as though she had read her mistress's thoughts. 'You'll find no difficulty in doing your duty by him, I'd say.'

'No,' agreed Genevra, wondering precisely what her duty would involve. She had to share his bed and allow him to mate with her, that she knew. Exactly what mating entailed, apart from engaging in the undignified antics she had observed among the servants and squires, who indulged their appetites in dark corners and under hedgerows, she did not know. But coupling was as natural as life itself and they seemed to find it highly enjoyable, since they did it so often.

Besides, as it was a necessary act to maintain life, God would not have made it unpleasant. And she had to admit that the sight of Robert St Aubin stirred aches and longings inside her that made the prospect of doing her duty exciting. For years she had itched to *know*. Within days she would.

'I hope I shall learn to love him,' she said suddenly into the silence which had fallen.

'Aye, God grant you may, for love between man and wife eases the burdens of life.'

'He may not love me.'

Genevra's wistful voice brought the steady brushing to a stop. Then Meg's arms were about her, holding her tightly, as had been her wont when Genevra had been a child in need of comfort.

'He will be a difficult man to please and a fool into the bargain an he does not,' Meg declared. 'You are young, lovely and of a sweet disposition—'

'Am I?' asked Genevra ruefully. 'I am no longer very

young, the mirror tells me I am not pretty, and I do not feel my disposition to be sweet when I wish to strangle my Aunt Hannah the moment she opens her mouth! And I have little love for my uncle or cousins, either.' Genevra turned suddenly in Meg's arms to return the embrace. 'You are the only one I love, dearest Meg!'

'But if your husband is a good man, you will love him,' predicted Meg with certainty. 'As for your looks, you have no need to fret over them, my duck. Your bones are good—'

'Especially my nose!'

''Tis not so bad. No worse than his, at all events.' Meg had taken care to examine her mistress's future husband as closely as she could and spoke from superior knowledge.

'Think of our poor children!' lamented Genevra, but she was smiling. The dimples at either side of her wide mouth were showing and tears wet Meg's eyes as she saw them.

'All either of you has to do is to smile,' she sniffed. 'His face would pay for it, just like yours. But, poor fellow, he looks as though it is many moons since he had occasion to be merry.'

'Yet he won the tournament.'

Meg resumed her brushing. 'That seemed to give him satisfaction, but not pleasure. He acknowledged the crowd, but if he smiled it was hidden behind that heaume of his. Later when I glimpsed him, he wore a fierce frown on his face.'

'Mayhap he does not wish to wed me.'

Genevra's voice betrayed her uncertainty. Meg gave a cluck of disapproval.

'Then why did he agree to the match? Men do have a choice in these matters. He may have doubts—like you,' she added, taking a rare dig at her mistress. ''Tis natural enough under the circumstances.'

'I suppose. Oh, Meg, I pray he does not intend to withdraw!'

Meg finished the brushing, parted Genevra's hair down the centre of her crown and began to weave one half into a plait. 'You've naught to fear, Mistress Genny. He is a man of honour and has given his word. One good look at you will convince him to keep it.'

Meg had called her by her old nursery name. A comfortable feeling swept over Genevra, dispelling her doubts. Of course things would be all right. And if all else failed, she would still have Meg with her, to love and understand her and to be loved in return.

Her serving-woman had finished the other plait and now coiled both over Genevra's ears, holding them in place with a jewelled fret. Then she reached into a carved wood box and brought out a golden circlet which she placed on top of Genevra's head.

'There!' she said fondly. 'The green of your kirtle matches the colour of your eyes and the rust of the surcoat brings out the lights in your hair. I rejoice to see you at last gowned as befits your rank.'

'More borrowed and altered gowns,' said Genevra ruefully. 'But, Meg—' she touched the gold band crossing her forehead with reverent fingers '—where did you get this circlet?'

'The Baron brought this box with him. Look, it contains all your mother's jewels. I suppose he lacked the gall to sell or to keep them. But I'd warrant that her ladyship has been flaunting them these many years.'

'Then she will miss them sadly,' murmured Genevra, delving into the box to bring forth a gem-encrusted gold bangle which revived dim memories of her mother's tending of her, the jewels flashing in sun or candlelight as her arm moved.

'I shall wear this,' she pronounced softly, working the hoop over the sleeve of her shot-sarcenet kirtle. 'And this brooch. Pin it on my surcoat. I remember clutching it when I was young.'

'So you did,' said Meg, doing as bidden. 'Fancy you remembering. It caught your eye. The lady Margaret would be glad to see you wearing her jewels now. Poor lady,' she added softly.

'Tell me about her,' prompted Genevra.

'She was a sweet lady, fairer than you, unspoiled by her time at Court, which was short, in all conscience— she was only there for a little above a year. But she had nursed the Queen after a distressing and dangerous miscarriage and had had Merlinscrag bestowed upon her in recognition of her services. Unhappily, she returned to Bloxley in disgrace and it was then that I became her tiring-woman. I watched her become increasingly saddened by separation from the boy she loved. She confided in me, when you were born, that he had been a squire of noble birth, expecting to be knighted forthwith. She said that they had wed in secret, but bound me not to tell a soul. I was about the same age, you see, and she thought I would understand.'

'Why did she not tell my grandfather?'

'To shield her lover. She dared not claim or name him for fear of his father, a powerful and hard man who would probably have disowned his son had he discovered the truth, or sought to have the marriage annulled.'

'How could he do that if it had been consummated?'

'He was a powerful man with influence in the highest circles. And they were both so young. Holy Church can find a reason to dissolve any marriage, given enough incentive.'

'Money, you mean,' said Genevra sourly. 'My father seems to have lacked spirit. He should have defied his father!'

''Tis easily said, and the boy was maybe a little weak, but he went to try to win his father's consent before admitting to the marriage. He thought he might, since he was not the heir.'

'But did not in fact succeed and so never came to claim his wife and child?'

'So it would seem.'

'You are too generous, Meg. He was a coward.' Genevra paused a moment, fingering the brooch and contemplating the distinctly unwelcome conclusion that she was the daughter of a man who lacked courage. Then she asked, 'She did not tell even you who my father was?'

'No, my duck. And when he failed to come to claim her, she seemed to lose interest in living. She caught a fever one winter and simply faded away.'

'I wish she had not. I needed her. Did she not think of that?'

'She loved you, Mistress Genny. Her little love, she used to call you, and said you had inherited much of your father's looks.'

'My nose, I suppose,' muttered Genevra, picking up her polished steel mirror and inspecting the offending feature anew. It was still humped and bony.

'No, not your nose, my duck. That came straight from your mother. She had it from hers.'

'Uncle Gilbert didn't inherit it.'

'No.'

'So what is in me of my father?'

Meg inspected the delicacy of the fine-boned face

before her. 'Your colouring, though he was more red than you are. You have his green eyes. And his square jaw. So your mother said.'

'I wish I'd known him. But I still think he must been a coward. How could he abandon us?'

Meg shrugged. 'His love could not withstand his father's fury, I'd guess. Or mayhap something else happened to prevent him.' She sighed. 'They were both so young.'

'Well, it seems Robert St Aubin is not too proud to marry a bastard.' Genevra straightened her shoulders and heaved a sigh. 'Am I ready?'

'Aye, Mistress Genny. You look a real treat. They can come for you at any time.' Meg cocked her head. 'I hear a footstep on the stair. Probably someone come to escort you to the chamber where the ceremony is to take place.'

Genevra was sharing a room in apartments added along the walls of the inner ward long after the original keep had been built. The two other young women and their serving-women were, fortunately, absent. Her uncle and aunt had been lodged on the floor below. She was not surprised to find that Hannah herself had come to fetch her.

Dutifully, she rose to endure her aunt's inspection.

'You wear your mother's jewels, I see.'

'Yes, aunt. I felt bound to try to impress Lord St Aubin.'

'Indeed,' agreed Hannah sourly. 'Well, you'll do, I suppose. Wear your cloak. Follow me.'

Hannah had brought a page with her. As Meg put the cloak about Genevra's shoulders, giving her a reassuring squeeze as she did so, Hannah made an imperious gesture and the lad led the way down the spiral stair to the floor below and then out across the inner ward towards the keep. They climbed the stone stairs to the door and the passage behind the screens. From there they entered the Great Hall, which teemed with life as the tables were erected and laid for the banquet.

A group of people had gathered on the dais at the far end. She recognised her uncle and the Earl of Northempston. Two of the other men waiting there were clearly notaries, present to oversee the legalities. But there could be no mistake as to the identity of the tall, glamorous figure standing beside his mentor.

Genevra, as she walked steadily towards him, her skirts rustling over the rush-strewn floor to raise a pleasant waft from the scattered herbs, took the opportunity to further study the man with whom it had been decreed she should spend the rest of her life.

Unlike the other men, he was bareheaded. His hair shone like pale gold in the light from the numerous torchères, cressets and candles illuminating the Hall. He was richly but sombrely dressed in black, that most expensive of dyes, with but a touch of silver-grey decoration.

His mantle, trimmed with white miniver, was clasped on his shoulder with a large brooch sparkling with gemstones, and a richly jewelled, knightly belt lay around his slender hips. From it hung a long dagger, with an exquisitely wrought hilt, sheathed in matching silver.

All this she could see through the smoke haze as she approached. But it was not until she mounted the steps to the dais and trod towards the group waiting for her that she was able to see his face clearly.

A strong face, with lines of hard experience etched on it. The blue eyes which had met hers before were veiled as he bowed in greeting. His firm, finely moulded mouth did not smile. His nose—Meg had been right. It was not a pleasing feature, it was too hooked. Yet, overall, his appearance did not strike her as displeasing. Distinguished was mayhap the word she was seeking.

As he lifted his head and she rose from her curtsy, his features relaxed. He smiled. And Genevra fell in love.

# *Chapter Two*

The sounds of bustle and chatter, the yap and snarl of
a dog, the crash of something dropped as the squires,
pages, grooms and other attendants went about their
tasks, dimmed to nothing as Genevra gazed at Robert
St Aubin. His smile was not spontaneous, she realised
regretfully, he was merely exerting himself to be civil.
The expression in his eyes remained cool, watchful, even
wary. And yet that smile's effect was, for her, devas-
tating.

It transformed his face, deepening the long lines scor-
ing his cheeks, the weather-drawn crow's-feet about his
eyes, reducing the apparent age of his clean-shaven vis-
age by at least ten years. Whereas before she had credited
him with some five-and-thirty years, momentarily he
appeared no more than twenty-five. Yet too much hard
experience was written on his face for him to be as young
as that. He was probably somewhere between the two.

The mere fact that he made the effort to force a smile
caused her heart to swell in gratitude, so fragile had
been her composure. And although his eyes remained
watchful, the brilliant blue of his gaze softened slightly
as it rested on her, as though he appreciated her nervous-

ness and was trying to set her at her ease. So he must be a man of some sensibility and understanding.

With his corn-coloured hair and beak of a nose, he could be likened to the golden eagle that was his emblem, but he was no fearsome bird of prey, like the hooded peregrine, jessed and chained to its perch behind Northempston's carved and padded chair.

Most of Genevra's apprehension disappeared, only to be replaced by an embarrassing awareness of the dazzling attraction he held for her. He represented the epitome of every chivalrous dream her girlish heart had ever cherished, a man possessed of every knightly virtue and every courtly grace. But she was old enough, mature enough, she hoped, to chide herself for behaving like the heroine of some minstrel's tale.

She forced herself to breathe again. She swallowed. 'God's greetings, my lord,' she said, her voice unusually husky.

Robert St Aubin bowed before the girl his lord and mentor had chosen for him. Quite why the Earl had determined that he should wed Genevra Heskith was unknown to him, but whatever that most puissant lord, William Egerton, the Earl of Northempston, wished, Robert St Aubin would grant, were it possible.

His lordship, in the far-off days when Robert had been his page and then his squire, had seemed to possess all the parental virtues his own bullying father had lacked, treating him in some respects more gently than his own sons, both now regrettably dead, leaving Northempston without an heir.

They, although already almost grown to manhood when Robert joined the household, had been intimidated by the strength of their father's will while he, even at

the tender age of seven, had not. He had never bowed
his head to his sire's tyranny and Northempston, although
a hard man, had in comparison seemed an angel of
kindness.

He had, Robert considered, mellowed considerably
over the years and particularly since the death of his
remaining heirs during the last visitation of the plague.
Mayhap he had come to regret the harsh treatment he
had so often inflicted upon his children.

The lord William had saved his life more than once
and extricated him from numerous scrapes, for in his
earlier days he had been prone to disregard prudence or
safety when engaged on some youthful enterprise. With
the years had come responsibility and disillusion to temper his unruly ways.

He was now his own master, a knight of some renown
and a baron of consequence since his father's death five
years since. Now, knowing he wished to wed again and
beget an heir, the Earl had suggested he wed Heskith's
bastard niece and thus bring Merlinscrag Castle, somewhere in the far west of England, into the hold of the St
Aubin barony.

To please his lordship he had agreed, determined to
wed the girl of Northempston's choice at whatever cost
to himself. To his profound relief it seemed that the cost
would be slight. The maid was not ill-favoured, she kept
herself clean and had been gently reared.

Slurs concerning her ancestry could be ignored by a
man of his stature. Her mother had been of noble birth,
chosen to serve Queen Philippa, who had died only
recently, at Court. And by inference her father, too, had
been a courtier. It was only the spiteful who suggested
otherwise.

As he lifted his eyes to meet her wide clear gaze and

saw reflected there the nervous anxiety with which she was scrutinising him, St Aubin felt a sudden sympathy for his future bride, a convent-bred maiden, fully faced for the first time with the man chosen by others to be her husband. He had the advantage. He had been able to examine her face as he returned her favour at the end of the tournament. He forced a reassuring smile.

Immediately, a flood of colour rose from her throat to invade her cheeks. She greeted him, her voice throaty with emotion. She did not smile, though she essayed one, which only resulted in a small quirk of her generous mouth. He allowed his eyes to dwell upon her features and watched the colour flee as fast as it had come, leaving her creamy skin dappled by the flickering light with golden tints and mysterious shadows.

She lowered her lids to cover the confusion in her unusual eyes, more green than grey, and the fans of her lashes drew dark crescents on the tender skin above her high cheekbones. Her jaw was too wide and square, yet this only served to emphasise the fragility of her bones. Her nose, narrow, high-bridged with a neatly rounded tip, fascinated him.

Overall, her face held character rather than beauty. His first wife had been beautiful. She and the child who had not been his had died ten years since, in the second visitation of the plague. He gave thanks that his new wife would, by all accounts, possess integrity rather than looks.

His lordship, Robert thought, had chosen well for him. But then, he would expect nothing less of the man whose judgement he had trusted since a child. Mayhap, this time, his bride having been selected by his lordship rather than by his own careless and grasping father, he would enjoy the felicity of a sound marriage. This time, he would ensure that his wife bore him a true heir. He would not leave her, as he had left Jane, before his seed had taken firm root.

As the train of his thoughts brought back painful memories his smile faded and his gaze became distant. He needed to find this girl pleasing, for he had to get an heir on her, but emotion must be carefully governed. A mere stripling at the time, he had been foolish enough to fall in love with his first wife, who had betrayed him. He had no intention of allowing his feelings to again lead him into such painful paths.

Genevra watched the smile fade and the bleak, almost hawkish expression return to his face. A little shiver ran through her. Yet she had glimpsed what he could be, had seen the sympathy in him, and she hugged the memory to her. Once they were wed, she would do her utmost to discover the depths of her husband's nature and to bring him joy.

Romantic she might be, but sensible, too. She did not delude herself into thinking that her love would be instantly returned. His would have to be won: and the wariness in those azure eyes told her that her task would not be easy. There must be a reason for the reserve, which added an enticing mystery to his character. But one thing was certain. This was the man she loved, and no other. Therefore she was content to make the promises demanded of her.

The betrothal was to be enacted in a chamber behind the dais, a sanctum from which the Earl normally emerged to take his place at the High Table in the chair of State. Those invited to witness the handfasting now followed his lordship into the small, sparsely furnished chamber,

its spartan atmosphere relieved only by a couple of tapestries which partially covered the stone walls.

Genevra, grave, the colour returned to stain her cheekbones, indicated her willingness to continue with the
betrothal, as did St Aubin. Her hand trembled as she
placed it in his, her whole arm quivered. Robert's
response came as a surprise to them both. He squeezed
her fingers reassuringly and smiled at her again, this time
with genuine warmth.

The overwhelming surge of empathy he felt for his
young bride-to-be astonished him, yet why should it? He
could scarcely fail to appreciate how diffident a young
virgin must feel, faced with uniting her life with that of
a complete stranger, older and more experienced than
herself.

The colour flooded back into Genevra's face, her nostrils flared, her lips parted, her breathing quickened.
Robert drew a quick breath. No stranger to women or to
desire, he recognised that his prospective wife would
bring to their marriage bed the gift of innocent, un-
awakened passion.

But she commanded herself quickly and was composed
enough, her gaze steady on his, as she plighted her troth,
clearly and steadily stating that, of her own free will, she
consented to take Robert St Aubin as her lord and husband, and promised to espouse him on the Sunday
following, in the face of Holy Church.

The die was cast, her future determined. Short of death
or some other calamity, neither of them could break the
solemn agreement they had just entered into: it was as
binding as the marriage itself. Genevra felt certain she
could look forward with confidence and hope.

Despite the general austerity of his manner, St Aubin

had been aware of her nervousness. What else could that
squeeze of the hand that had so overset her mean? He
must now also be aware of the disconcerting effect his
touch had on her. Her reaction had brought a new look
into his eyes, a look that had set her insides quivering.

She was not given long to ruminate in peace. While
her newly betrothed turned away to receive the congratulations of his friends, the Earl of Northempston joined
her, cutting out her aunt, who had been moving resolutely
to her side. Thwarted, Hannah diverted her steps elsewhere, to Genevra's relief.

Northempston took her hand and leant forward to kiss
her forehead.

'I am delighted that our acquaintance has resulted in
so congenial a match, demoiselle.'

Genevra returned his salute with a small curtsy. To
many people this lord appeared formidable, but Genevra
had never found him so. 'I trust it will prove to be
so, lord.'

The Earl patted the hand hc still held. 'I can see no
reason why it should not. Lord St Aubin received an
excellent education in my household and is a man of
honour and refinement.' He smiled. 'With your own high
degree of learning, you should find that you have much
in common.'

'I shall do my best to serve him as he deserves, lord.'

'I should expect nothing less of one so highly recommended by your Mother Superior. Robert needs true
companionship and love, my dear.' Genevra blushed but
did not reply. Northempston appeared to hesitate before
he said, 'You may not know that St Aubin married young
and that his wife and young son died of the plague ten
years since. He has not, until now, sought to wed again.
I would wish to see him well suited.'

Now Genevra, her eyes clear, said, 'Indeed, lord, I did not know. I thank you for telling me,' and thought how much St Aubin must have loved his wife to remain so faithful to her memory.

''Twas something you should be aware of. Ah! Here he is!' Northempston paused while St Aubin joined them. 'Robert, my boy, I pray you may both find felicity in your forthcoming union.'

'Thank you, my lord. I am sure we are both grateful for your mediation in the matter. After the nuptials, I intend that we should travel immediately to Merlinscrag. I need to acquaint myself with the manor my wife brings under my dominion.'

'Indeed you must.' The Earl, smiling benignly, turned to Genevra again. 'The gown the women are sewing for your wedding, it is to your liking?'

Genevra, attempting to hide the glowing happiness which had invaded her being, made another small obeisance. 'Indeed, my lord, your generosity overwhelms me. A new wardrobe was more than I expected.'

'But new apparel was necessary, I believe. You owned nothing suitable with which to begin your new life and your uncle has his purse-strings firmly drawn. Your convent gowns would never do!'

'No, lord, and what I wear now is my aunt's discarded apparel altered to fit. Although,' she added with a small, impish smile, 'if we are to travel to Merlinscrag, I doubt there will be much occasion to wear anything too splendid. The castle is isolated on a windswept cliff.'

'You know it?'

'I visited it as a young child, lord, before my mother's death. I cannot really remember it at all. I just retain an impression of wild seas and wind. But others have been there since and have told me of it.'

'Well, Robert!' Northempston clapped his protégé on the shoulder. 'You will have to see that your lady wife is provided with a suitable wardrobe for every occasion!'

'Indeed, lord. You have been most generous in the matter, but I have wealth enough to ensure that my wife lacks for nothing.'

Genevra expected Northempston to take offence at that stiffly proud assertion, but he did not. Instead he chuckled, as though in admiration of St Aubin's independent stance.

He clapped a beefy hand on St Aubin's shoulder. 'Splendid! But do not delay the getting of your heir, my boy. Once your wife's belly is full, you must return to your major hold of Thirkall, so that the child may be born there.'

Genevra's colour rose again but, despite her embarrassment, she managed a smile. 'We may have a daughter, lord.'

'So you may, indeed. But, boy or girl, do not neglect to let me know of the birth!'

'Should she not be present at the birth, you will be second only to my lady mother in being informed,' promised Robert.

Northempston nodded benignly and passed on. For a moment they stood together in isolation.

'Your mother is not to be here for your marriage, my lord?' asked Genevra.

'No. Travelling is a burden to her and my sister Alida is blind. The arrangement was made hurriedly. They do not yet know of my intention to wed.'

'They do not know?' repeated Genevra, incredulous.

'I thought it kind not to burden them with the need to make the journey,' said Robert abruptly. 'I shall send to inform them immediately after the ceremony.'

'Lady St Aubin would surely wish—'

'Undoubtedly,' cut in her son austerely. 'I have saved her the trouble of feeling compelled to make an arduous and unwelcome journey.'

Genevra eyed him through her lashes. It was almost as though he did not wish his mother or sister to be present at their wedding. Was he ashamed of his bride? Or was there some deeper, family reason she had yet to discover? Was he ashamed of *them*?

'You have no other close relations?' she asked tentatively.

'A brother, Drogo.'

'Can he not be here to support you?'

'I am perfectly capable of marrying without the support of any member of my family!' snapped St Aubin irritably. 'My brother is as yet equally unaware of my intention to wed.'

'When shall I meet them?' asked Genevra a trifle apprehensively. St Aubin's mood had changed completely. If he considered them unacceptable. . .she could not believe that he would cast his mother off without cause. . .

Robert's brooding gaze rested on her. 'I do not know. Does it matter?'

Genevra's hesitation was almost imperceptible. 'No,' she said. 'It is you I am to wed, not your family. I can wait until you are ready to travel to Thirkall. The match was arranged by Lord Northempston and his presence will suffice.'

St Aubin nodded. 'And so. . .you are content, demoiselle?' he asked.

Dismissing her doubts, Genevra smiled and the dimples bracketed her mouth. 'I am content,' she averred.

And she was. Whatever had made St Aubin reluctant

to have his family present at their nuptials was of no immediate concern to her. Families did not always agree, as she knew only too well.

She would be best pleased if her uncle and aunt decided to leave before the ceremony, but there was little chance of that. They would enjoy the lavish hospitality of the Earl for as long as they were able. But—if St Aubin was at odds with his family, life at Thirkall might prove difficult.

A groom came to inform Northempston that the banquet was ready to be served. The Earl indicated his readiness to proceed with the meal and called the others in the chamber to attention. A flourish of trumpets heralded his entry into the Great Hall at the head of a procession of his guests of honour.

Pages knelt with bowls of water, towels draped over their arms, ready for the ritual cleansing of hands. Genevra dipped her fingers in the water and dried them on the proffered towel while at her side St Aubin did the same.

He was seated at the Earl's right hand, with Genevra next to him. The trencher they were to share, a thick slab of specially prepared bread, lay before them on the linen-covered table. A mazer, wrought from maple wood and rimmed with silver, rested empty beside it. Platters and dishes of gold and silver bearing bread, butter, preserves and other cold food were already set upon the cloth, together with small wooden boxes, exquisitely carved, containing herbs and spices.

Down in the Hall she could see the other trestles similarly set, though the dishes there were of wood or pewter, occassionally silver. Most magnificent of all the silver utensils were the huge salt cellars, set to mark the divide between the nobility, the knights and the distinguished guests, and the lesser orders lower down the tables.

At the far end of the Hall, crowded benches held the retinues and servants of the knights and noblemen present. Meg would no doubt be there somewhere, but Genevra could not spot her.

The assembled guests, attired in their most lavish costumes, heavily bejewelled, glittered in the smoky atmosphere engendered by the central fire and made worse by the the burning torches and candles illuminating the feast. Some of the merchants, sitting below the salt, were more extravagantly gowned and bejewelled than the nobility. They took little note of the sumptuary laws, which laid down what materials of what colour they were entitled to use, Genevra noted.

Each nobleman and knight, some accompanied by their ladies, had at least one badged squire standing behind him ready to serve him, and many also had a page, wearing a livery with his master's insignia blazoned across his breast. A great many hounds lay at their masters' feet or snapped at the servants' heels.

The knights' banners and pennants hung from the rafters in muted glory and swathed the columns in shimmering silk. Tapestries and murals decorated the walls. All in all, it was the most fabulous scene Genevra had ever witnessed. She gazed in awe at all the splendour displayed before her.

Grace was said by the Earl's resident priest. The minstrels in the gallery began to play. As the servants, resplendent in the azure and silver of Northempston's livery, carried in the steaming cauldrons and dishes, Genevra turned to her betrothed and addressed him in a voice full of wonder.

'Bloxley was never as sumptuous as this. And although

the nuns kept a good table and possessed silver on which
to serve their food, a feast of this magnitude was beyond
their means or desire.'

St Aubin smiled indulgently. 'This is your first great
feast? You will attend many more. We must mount them
ourselves in due course, but do not fear. I have an excellent steward at Thirkall and my mother is a competent
châtelaine.'

So he was ready to give his mother praise. Relieved,
for she did not wish to find him at odds with his dam,
Genevra tucked the knowledge away in a recess of her
mind. 'I am not afraid, my lord. I received excellent
training in all facets of housekeeping at the convent.'

'In addition to your scholarship? His lordship informs
me that you are well read in the Classics and have studied
mathematics and science, too.'

'There was little else to do in the convent, lord, since
I had no desire to take the veil.'

'Most ladies would have been content to concentrate
on more domestic tasks, like embroidery and sewing.'

'I did my share of that, and learned something of the
healing arts from the sister apothecary and the sister
infirmarian.' After a slight pause, 'The musicians are
making excellent music,' she remarked, for sweet strains
of viol and flute floated down, counterpointed by harp
and tabor. 'His lordship can no doubt afford the best. I
can play a psaltery a little, though I am not a talented
musician.'

'You amaze me, demoiselle. I had not anticipated
being wed to so learned a wife. Your arts, I fear, put
mine to shame.'

He did not sound best pleased. Genevra nibbled
thoughtfully on a piece of the roast suckling pig placed
on their trencher by St Aubin's squire, a dark-haired,

fine-looking lad of some seventeen years called Alan of Harden. To her secret amusement, Alan regarded her with a youthful mixture of admiration and resentment, the latter occasioned by her intrusion into the intimacy he enjoyed with his lord.

Genevra could appreciate the wisdom of soothing St Aubin's male ego. 'My accomplishments are as nothing to yours, lord. You are versed in the arts of war and can command not only the praise of soldiers but also the adulation of the crowd. And his lordship informs me that you, too, are fond of studying the classics. It is his hope that we shall find much in common in discussing them.'

Robert grunted as he handed her the silver-rimmed mazer, now filled with ruby-coloured wine. He waited while Genevra drank, then retrieved the cup and emptied it.

He indicated to Alan that he wished it refilled, then said, 'Mayhap we shall. I can pick out a tune on the lute. As for my knowledge of war, my fighting days are over. I shall not take up arms against the King's enemies again. I have given fifteen years of my life to defending Edward's possessions in Aquitaine and fighting in France and Spain. Now I intend to retire to my estates and raise a family in peace. If called upon, I shall pay my shield money, my scutage, and leave the fighting to others. I am weary of the soldier's life.'

Genevra's spirits lifted. He would not lead his men into battle, leaving her, alone and anxious, to defend his properties at home. Not that lawlessness was as rife as it had once been, but a few renegade lords still sought to enhance their own fortunes at the expense of others. No lord's domain was ever quite safe from attack even now, which explained why some chose to fortify their houses and others either lived in the castles their ancestors had built or constructed new ones.

She spoke eagerly. 'It gladdens me to hear you say so, lord. But you will surely enter the lists again as you did today. 'Twould be a pity to retire from the field altogether. And how, then, would your squires learn their trade?'

'Do not fear, I shall practice my skills and teach others, including my sons, how to fight. Such knowledge is necessary in order to defend one's life and one's possessions. If I or my family are attacked, I shall take up arms, never fear!'

'I do not, lord. And I doubt not that, taking part in any tournament, you will continue to engage in combat as worthily and with as much success as you did today.'

Now he smiled, a ruminative smile that caused Genevra's heart to lurch and her hand to shake as she plucked a slice of chicken breast from the trencher Alan kept well supplied with choice morsels.

'Aye, I enjoy the challenge of a tournament. And it is an excellent way to practise one's skills with a minimum of bloodshed. It is also a way to achieve glory while running little risk,' he added somewhat deprecatingly, as though that aspect did not please him. He actually frowned as he took another draught of wine.

''Twas a pity about Sir Piers. Poor fellow, he carried too much weight and is past his prime. He fell awkwardly from his saddle and broke his back. He is paralysed and cannot live.'

This sobered Genevra. She reached for a crisp white roll and broke it absently. The sport was dangerous. St Aubin could be injured or killed during the course of a tournament. But a man was not a man who lived wrapped in swaddling bands. The risk was no greater than many others. He could equally well die of a sickness or of a

fall while out hunting. Life was so often short, death
stalked them all at every turn.

She herself must face the perils of childbirth. But it
would be stupid to allow such thoughts to depress her
on this joyous occasion. They were both fit and healthy.
God willing, they would enjoy many happy years
together.

She spread butter on the soft white bread and popped
some in her mouth as another flourish of trumpets
heralded the bringing in of the next course. As before, a
steward tasted the food his lord would eat. This was a
ritual observed in most households. An enemy bearing a
grudge or lusting for power was yet another threat to any
lord or man of wealth. It was so easy to poison the food.

Yet, she mused, refusing to be daunted by her previous
sombre train of thought, most men of consequence survived to a reasonable age unless they were born sickly
or killed on the field of battle.

Or became the victim of some pestilence like that
which had demonstrated God's wrath with the world
three times in the past five-and-twenty years, reducing
England's population so drastically that there were not
enough people left to grow and harvest the crops. The
land was almost denuded of its villeins so that the strips
they had tilled lay waste.

Even great houses like that of Lancaster had suffered
bitterly, yet Lord Northempston, who must be sixty at
the least, was as hale and hearty as any man. His surviv-
ing children and grandchildren had died, St Aubin had
lost his wife and son, but both men had lived through
the worst the Lord could throw at them and would, she
prayed, continue to do so.

Meanwhile, her attention had been caught by a dish
being set before them.

'Lord, I have never seen so fine a swan!' she exclaimed. 'It seems a pity to remove the feathers and carve it, yet I long to sample its taste!'

'And so you shall! I note that you have already tasted every unusual dish, from the doves in aspic through sturgeon to all the tarts, syllabubs and custards in sight!'

Genevra dimpled again. 'An I did not, how would I know whether I liked them?'

This childish delight in discovery amused St Aubin, she noted, who took the trouble to ensure that she received a portion of everything for which she asked. Her greatest admiration, however, was drawn forth at the end of the banquet by the elaborate sugar confection, the marchpane. It had been formed to represent a pair of jousting unicorns, one flying the Northempston pennant in full colour and the other that of St Aubin.

'Oh, it is beautiful!' she breathed.

'Clever,' agreed St Aubin, 'and judicious in its design. It looks to me as though Northempston is about to emerge the winner!'

Genevra giggled. She had eaten and drunk far too much, enjoying the pleasures and liberty afforded her by her new status. If only the nuns could see her now! But she must not lose her dignity. She straightened her shoulders and nodded wisely.

'They do well to flatter their lord. But see, here come the mummers and jongleurs!'

Before the company became too rowdy, Genevra prepared to leave the Hall. If she drank any more wine, she would do something she would regret afterwards. Men and women were embracing all around the Hall. Even her aunt was leaning on the shoulder of the knight sitting beside her while Uncle Gilbert was openly fondling his buxom neighbour.

In such company, it was tempting to throw her arms about St Aubin's neck, for she longed to be held close to him, but that might betray the fact that she had fallen in love with him.

Dignity, she reminded herself severely. She was not quite drunk enough to lose all sense of propriety. At all costs she must retain her dignity.

She smiled sweetly at her betrothed. 'My lord, will you send Alan to find Meg for me?' she asked carefully, for her speech tended to be slightly slurred. 'It is time I returned to my room.'

St Aubin, who seemed able to imbibe quantities of wine without showing any signs of drunkenness, gave Alan the order and then reached unexpectedly for her hand.

The alcohol had mellowed him, she could see that by the expression in his eyes, but there was no trace of slurring in his voice. 'Demoiselle, will you ride with me before dinner on the morrow?'

'I should like to, lord, although I have no mount but the poor hack my uncle sent to carry me from the convent— unless, mayhap, I could borrow one of the Earl's?'

'You ride well, I hear. I will arrange a suitable mount for you. Does your woman ride?'

Genevra shook her head. 'She sits a led horse to travel.'

'I see. Your aunt, then?'

'Yes. . .but. . .'

'You would rather not have her company? Just so. Then will you trust to me and my escort to keep you safe?'

'Indeed, lord, why should I not? In but a very few days my entire life will be in your safekeeping.'

'And my happiness in yours. Sleep well, mistress. I will see you anon.'

They arranged a time and Genevra went off with Meg, her mind in a whirl not entirely caused by too much wine.

He had sought her company for the morrow. Above everything she loved to ride freely through the countryside. She had much to make her happy.

# *Chapter Three*

'You look happy,' remarked Meg as they made their way back to Genevra's chamber, led by a page with a flaring torch. 'I trust you've not been drinking too deeply of the wine cup,' she added, the uncertain light giving her a glimpse of her mistress's brilliant eyes and the little, secret smile touching her lips.

'We are riding together in the morn,' Genevra explained her high spirits away. 'You know how much I enjoy a gallop.' Even to Meg she was not prepared to confide her present euphoric happiness. It was too new, too precious to be shared.

Back in her room, still devoid of its other occupants, Meg chattered about the betrothal and the feast. Genevra gazed absently at the candle on the prie-dieu, fickering fitfully in a draught, making the statue of the Virgin in its niche above appear to move, even to smile.

'He was pleasant enough,' was all she would say, though she did admit that her fear of his misliking the match appeared to be ill-founded. 'I think we shall deal well enough together. And now, Meg, I must sleep. I must be fit to ride on the morrow!'

Dismissing Meg to her pallet in the adjoining antechamber, Genevra, having offered up her devotions as usual at the prie-dieu and thanked the Holy Virgin for fulfilling all her dreams, composed herself for sleep. But the excitement was too high in her. Slumber was further delayed by the noisy arrival of the two other young women to share the cosy seclusion of the large bed.

Pulling the curtains back to tumble in, they allowed the draught in, too. Then they chattered excitedly for what seemed like an eternity. Genevra feigned sleep to avoid questions about her betrothal. When at last they did drop off, one of them snored.

Genevra tried not to toss and turn and disturb them as she sought sleep. Instead, she attempted to picture Merlinscrag and to fill her mind with visions of the future. She imagined standing on the vaguely remembered cliff top beside St Aubin, gazing across the tossing sea towards the strange lands which lay beyond the horizon.

And then the castle's grim granite walls seemed to move closer so that its long shadow encompassed her. The sun no longer warmed her and she shivered. A distance away, out in the sun, stood the Golden Eagle, his face hidden by his visor. But as she began to run towards him, her legs heavy, her feet moving as though they were stuck in deep mud, he turned away. Genevra gave a strangled cry of despair and woke up, her body bathed in perspiration.

She had not disturbed her companions, who were both still deeply asleep. Despite the perspiration, she was shivering. A peep through the crack in the curtains told her that it was already light. Knowing she would not sleep again after that disturbing dream, Genevra slipped from the bed and, clad only in her linen smock, padded through to rouse Meg.

'What is it, my duck?' asked Meg, waking from her

own deep sleep to sit up on her pallet and then struggle
to her feet.

Genevra nodded towards the other tiring-women and
put a finger to her lips. 'Hush, Meg. We do not want to
wake everyone. But I need warm water to wash before
I dress to go riding.'

Pale shards of light penetrated the horn shutter protect-
ing the window of the ante-room. Meg saw Genevra
shivering and reached out to lay a concerned hand on
her damp forehead. 'Are you sickening, child?'

'No, I had a bad dream, that is all. Quickly, Meg,
before the others wake.'

Meg who, like the other tiring-women, had slept fully
clothed, insisted on returning to the bedchamber and
wrapping her mistress in a mantle before she left to make
her way down to the kitchens where great cauldrons of
water would be heating over the fires.

Genevra clutched the garment about her and sat on the
low sill of one of the windows. She propped the shutter
open so that she could see the limited view of the surrounding countryside afforded by the narrow opening,
little more than an arrow slit.

Grooms and other menials were already stirring in the
courtyards below, but beyond the great outer curtain wall
the peaceful view, a feast of brilliant sunlight glinting
on a meandering river and throwing shadows to bring
fields and trees and distant hills into stark relief, began
to dispel the feeling of gloom left by her dream.

There was no accounting for it. In the bright light of
day the nightmare seemed foolish and unreal. She seldom
dreamed and she had no idea whether it meant anything
or not. But she did not intend to allow it to mar her
present happiness. Once she saw St Aubin again, and

especially if he smiled at her, she would be able to forget it.

St Aubin sent his squire, Alan of Harden, to fetch her. He made obeisance and said, 'My lord is waiting in the courtyard, Mistress Genevra.'

'My thanks, Alan. I am quite ready, as you see.'

She had donned the old riding clothes she had worn at the convent, including leather breech hose hidden beneath her skirts to protect her thighs from chafing. She had begged this spare garment from one of the men sent to escort her to Ardingstone, paying him with the last of her scant hoard of silver. This had enabled her to ride the long distances necessary in greater comfort.

Meg had made do with padding stitched to her underskirt, as she had done in the past, but the breeches were far and away more comfortable, so she intended to continue to wear them and risk the scandal were she to be found out.

She had no other gown to ride in, a fact she had overlooked the previous evening when accepting her betrothed's invitation to accompany him. She trusted he would disregard its age and the drab material from which it had been made. There was, after all, no point in trying to dazzle him with fine clothes when soon he would see her in nothing but the gathered and tucked lawn smock she would wear in bed.

That thought brought a blush to her cheeks, giving her features a bloom that had been lacking. Her brown hair was plaited and tied with a green ribbon, and hung heavy down her back beneath the hood of her cloak.

She picked up her gloves and whip. 'Lead on,' she invited Alan.

As they trod passages and stairs Genevra attempted to

make conversation, partly to hide the nervousness which had overtaken her as a result of her dream. Alan was younger than she, but had a bouncing assurance which betrayed his self-confidence. Since his eyes held nothing but admiration, Genevra deduced that her poor habit did not detract unduly from her appearance. He was a well set-up, honest lad, and she discovered a definite liking for Alan of Harden.

'How long have you been in Lord St Aubin's service?' she asked.

'I joined the old lord's household as a page, mistress, and he put me to serve the lord Robert from the start. The lord Robert made me his squire when I reached the age of fourteen, just before he became the Baron. I've been with him twelve years altogether, and accompanied him on all his campaigns,' he told her proudly.

'So you are well travelled,' remarked Genevra a little wistfully. She had never been further from Bloxley than the convent in Derbyshire in her life. Ardingstone was somewhere between the two. 'Have you fought beside him?'

'Nay, lady, not in a true battle. I was merely a page at Najera. But I have lately stood at his side during a skirmish in Aquitaine, opposing rebels who would wrest the dukedom from His Grace the King.'

'And you will become a knight soon?'

'I trust so, mistress. I am St Aubin's senior squire, though I shall still remain with my lord, an he will grant me a fief within his barony. I have no land of my own until my father dies.'

Genevra regarded him quizzically. 'This although he intends to fight no more except on the tourney field?'

Alan grinned in response. 'I should rather serve him than any other lord I know. I shall challenge him to break a lance with me in the lists and hope to beat him. But I should gladly remain in his service. He has need of knights to furnish his retinue and garrisons.'

This brought them out into the inner ward, where St Aubin stood by a mounting block with his own and a spare horse. A couple of huge wolfhounds lolled at his heels. An escort of men-at-arms wearing his eagle badge waited to accompany them, their horses caparisoned in the St Aubin colours of emerald green and murrey, a mulberry red.

Alan moved off to mount his own, rather more elaborately arrayed horse, as Genevra exchanged greetings with St Aubin.

He doffed his pleated and feathered hat.

He was without armour. He wore a murrey cotte-hardie of finest saye with silver buttons fastening the front and others decorating the sleeves to the elbow. The brooch of yestereve was now pinned to his hat and he wore his richly jewelled belt and a dagger.

A short, dandelion-coloured, dagged cloak lined with dark green watered silk swung from his broad shoulders. Dark green hose encased his horseman's thighs and calf-length boots of finest cordwain shod his feet. He stood straight and tall. The sun glinted on his hair. He looked superb.

His smile, though, was perfunctory as he said, 'God's greetings, demoiselle.'

Last evening the austerity had been in both his dress and manner. Today it was concentrated in his demeanour, for his attire was far from sombre. 'I have selected a palfrey from Lord Northempston's stable which I hope will suit you,' he went on without further preamble. 'She is young but, I am told, sweet-tempered and biddable.'

'My thanks, lord.'

Genevra had been too busy studying her betrothed to
do more than glance at the young horse clearly intended
for her to ride. She moved to its neat head and stroked
it between its flaring nostrils.

It was a young mare, a pretty creature, a reddish-brown
bay with a white blaze and socks on three feet, richly
caparisoned in Northempston's livery of azure and silver.
The creature responded to Genevra's advances by nodding her dainty head and shaking the bells attached to
her headstall, nudging Genevra's hand with her nose and
giving a whicker of pleasure.

'She pleases you?'

'Aye, lord, and it seems she likes me.' Genevra gave
the palfrey a final pat, gathered the fancily cut and silver-
studded reins in her hand, and prepared to mount. 'I look
forward to the ride.'

Grooms sprang forward but St Aubin waved them
away and helped her to mount himself.

'They call her Chloe,' he said as she settled into the
costly lady's saddle and arranged her skirts while he
spread her cloak over the filly's rump. He had not, she
hoped, noticed her man's breeches.

'Then come, Chloe,' murmured Genevra as St Aubin
sprang into the padded and decorated riding saddle of
the extravagantly caparisoned black stallion he called
Prince—he was not riding his destrier or using his
fighting saddle, Genevra noted—without assistance. 'Let
us enjoy our outing.'

They trooped through into the outer bailey, the hounds
gambolling alongside. From there they crossed to the
gatehouse, passing under the portcullis and over the
drawbridge spanning the stinking waters of the moat
and so through the barbican defending the approach to
the castle.

Side by side, with a Herald and half the escort riding ahead while, behind them, Alan and a falconer, who rode with a bird perched on his wrist, led the remainder, they progressed sedately through the village. Nevertheless, they scattered the geese and yapping dogs foraging among the huddle of half-deserted villeins' and cottars' dwellings before passing on to skirt the fields of cultivated strips where man and beast were already labouring.

Day labourers worked the lord's demesne and many of the other strips now, St Aubin told Genevra, for few villeins had survived the pestilence which had visited the country three times in his lifetime. In order to keep as much land as possible under cultivation, many lords had freed their serfs to discourage them from fleeing to the sanctuary of the towns.

Freemen could leave the land to which they had been tied or remain to become yeomen farmers, as they willed. Northempston's land was now entirely worked by freemen or by day labourers, who exacted high wages.

''Tis what Lord Heskith should have done,' said Genevra. 'There are no villeins at all left at Bloxley. Many died and the remainder simply left. The lord my uncle has great difficulty in keeping his lands in cultivation now.'

'The plague has changed much. It was no respecter of persons and many great lords and ladies died too. Whole families were wiped out. Northempston lost his heirs. I fear that England will never be as it was. Like those attached to your brother's land, many serfs whose lords will not grant them freedom are simply leaving to hide and find well-paid work in the towns. The feudal system is dying.'

'They owed their lords labour and the lords owed them protection,' mused Genevra, patting Chloe's neck soothingly as the palfrey shied and tossed her head in agitation because a coney suddenly darted from its burrow to be chased by the hounds. 'But now the land is quieter again, mayhap they value freedom above the security their lords can afford them.'

St Aubin glanced at her, a strange, considering look on his sombre face. 'You think so?' he asked, with that in his voice which made Genevra think that he did not agree with her. 'For what would they crave freedom?'

'The ability to move away an they wish without being hunted as criminals, and to wed their sons and daughters to those from outside their lord's lands without having to pay a crippling fine, mayhap,' said Genevra flatly.

'Oh, that!' His tone was half-amused, half-dismissive. 'Most villeins are still quite prosperous and can afford any merchet demanded when a child desires to leave his lord's land to wed.'

'Those who have large holdings, mayhap—I agree that they are often prosperous. But they and their families remain completely at their lord's mercy in every respect. They are bound to pay their tithes and give their labour to him, they must pay to have their grain ground into flour in his mill, their bread baked in his ovens and must ensure that their children remain attached to his land or pay the merchet. . .I cannot think theirs a happy existence,' said Genevra.

'Were these ideas put into your head by those at your convent, demoiselle?' demanded St Aubin with what sounded to her like arrogant displeasure. 'I cannot think that you bred them yourself.'

'Nay, lord.' Genevra quickly denied the charge for fear that the convent might suffer. She should think before she spoke so freely! 'We gave thanks to God that the convent was so little touched by the plague. It still has villeins working its lands. They do not yet seem infected by the craving for freedom. But I had time to study and to think. Tied to the land as they are, villeins have less control over their own lives than even I have over mine.'

She spoke softly and a little defiantly, for this morning the effects of her dream still lingered. The fact that she had fallen in love with Robert St Aubin did not make her marriage any the less one arranged without her agreement.

In silence, St Aubin reached out for her bridle and drew both their mounts to a halt. Behind, Alan and the men with him scrambled to bring their horses up behind, amid much jangling of harnesses, shouts, snorts and stamping of hooves.

His eyes narrowed on her. Ignoring the commotion his sudden action had caused behind, St Aubin said coldly, 'An you did not wish for this marriage, mistress, you should have said so at the betrothal.'

Genevra, shocked by his reaction, tried in vain to keep her voice steady. 'I did not say that the arrangement was distasteful to me, my lord, merely that I was not consulted in the matter. I consider myself fortunate to have received Earl Northempston's favour,' she went on more calmly.

'Daughters are reared to expect to wed a man of their father's choice and to be forced into subjection should they dare to protest. Love, even affection, does not enter into the arrangement. Merely lands, money, power. Women are seldom given much say in anything. Just like villeins.'

His grip on her horse's bridle visibly tightened, making the jewels in his glove flash. 'Ladies are raised to run great houses and bear children for their lords. That is their accepted role. Unless, of course, they prefer to retire to a nunnery.'

'With never a thought given to their happiness, lord,' rejoined Genevra with spirit. 'An they dare to protest or disobey, their liege lord may beat them as he would his horse, his hounds or his servants and his children!'

St Aubin studied her, his brow creased into a frown. 'You think I would beat you, madam?' he inquired austerely.

Genevra gazed back steadily, although inwardly she was quaking. Whatever had possessed her to challenge him in this way, and him so severe-looking this morning, unable to raise more than a token smile? Was it because his withdrawn demeanour had shattered her dreams of yestereve? If so, then she could count her provocation a success. Even his anger was easier to bear than his polite indifference.

'No, lord,' she said honestly. 'As I have said, I consider myself fortunate in the choice made for me.'

Nodding abruptly, St Aubin released her bridle and squeezed his horse's flanks. Genevra said no more, but urged Chloe forward by his side.

Soon they reached the common land, where the villeins' pigs, sheep and those oxen not working in the fields, rooted and grazed with their lord's. Already some new-born lambs skipped at their mother's sides and the hounds, amusingly named Cain and Abel, had to be called to heel.

Once they had passed beyond the cultivated land surrounding the castle and reached open countryside, the pace quickened. Soon, at a word from St Aubin, the company rose to a canter, the hounds loping easily alongside. Genevra's cloak caught the wind, her hood fell back. She freed her plait from beneath her cloak, relishing the keen air streaming past her head.

St Aubin's cloak was flying too, the feathers in his hat

riffling in the breeze. But his face was set. He appeared to be using the exercise to relieve his smouldering displeasure rather than for enjoyment's sake.

Despite her lord's mood, Genevra could not but enjoy the ride. It was years since she had been on the back of a mount of Chloe's quality. The little filly carried her as though she rode in an armchair, so smooth was her gait. When St Aubin called ahead for the escort to make way and set his horse to gallop across a stretch of wild land strewn with scattered bushes, Genevra had no hesitation in following.

Chloe stretched her neck, lengthened her stride and eagerly sought to overtake St Aubin's Prince. She was game and Genevra gave her her head, but Prince was truly a prince among horses; the little palfrey fell ever further behind, as did the rest of the party. Once or twice St Aubin glanced over his shoulder to see where she was but he made no attempt to slacken his own pace to accommodate hers.

Eventually St Aubin reined in and began to walk his stallion, giving it time to recover its breath and her to catch up. Steam rose from both animals' necks and flanks, bringing with it the strong odour of horse. Genevra drew in the familiar scent and, previous discord forgotten, a wide smile of content spread itself over her glowing face.

'I have not enjoyed a gallop so much since I was a child at Bloxley,' she remarked cheerfully, ignoring St Aubin's mood. 'The mounts at the convent were poor creatures with little speed in their legs!'

At least the bleak grimness had left St Aubin's expression. He did not often smile, Genevra suspected. 'You approve of Chloe?' he asked.

'Oh, yes!' Genevra slapped the steaming neck. The

escort had caught up and was falling into place around them again. 'She is the best horse I have ever had the pleasure of riding!'

St Aubin bowed from the waist as he sat in his elaborately decorated saddle. 'Then I shall buy her for you, an his lordship will part with her. Your nuptial gift, my betrothed.'

'Oh!' Genevra caught her breath in delight and her colour mounted. 'Oh, thank you, my lord! You could not have chosen a gift I should have appreciated more!'

'Not even jewellery?'

Genevra caught the faintest sign of a twinkle in his eye and her joyous laugh rang out. 'Not even the most expensive jewel in the world, my lord!'

A reluctant half-smile touched his lips. The blue eyes rested on her kindly. 'I am pleased that you ride well and appreciate good horseflesh, my lady. We may, perhaps, enjoy exploring your hold of Merlinscrag together.'

'Indeed, lord. The lands are quite extensive, I believe, and the tithes of some considerable value.'

'So his lordship informed me.'

Of course, it was for her lands that St Aubin had agreed to wed her. The flush of pleasure left her face. Yet for what other reason did any man of St Aubin's rank wed but to increase his wealth?

Thinking back to their previous discussion, she remarked, 'Farming in the West Country is mostly organised differently. The villeins dwell within their holdings, cultivating some fields but using most of their land to graze sheep, for the selling of wool is their chief means of livelihood. What of Thirkall?'

'There remain few villeins at Thirkall,' St Aubin responded curtly. 'Those that do still cultivate strips.'

His tone warned her not to pursue the subject. She had

been unwise to argue——no, not argue, discuss!——the issue
with him at all, let alone raise the matter again.

At this point St Aubin took his hawk on his own arm
and flew it successfully after a series of small prey. After
this diversion they continued at a steady trot along a
bridle path through a large copse of scattered trees and
emerged to find Ardingstone Castle in view again, the
tall keep, higher even than the towers which punctuated
its several curtain walls, glowing softly in the morning
sunshine.

As they approached more closely Genevra, scanning
the battlements, caught glimpses of metal helmets in the
embrasures and knew that guards walked the allures,
keeping watch. The men stationed high on the keep
would be the first to trumpet a warning.

Their own return had been noted. As they drew near,
St Aubin's Herald sounded his horn, an answer came
from the watchman in the gatehouse and they all clattered
over the drawbridge. St Aubin's men made for the stables
while he and his squire escorted Genevra to the door
leading to her chamber.

Meticulously courteous, St Aubin assisted her from
Chloe's back. He had no need to take her by the waist
to help her down, but he did. The brief clasp of his strong
hands sent shivers of feeling through Genevra's body.
To hide her confusion she concentrated on rescuing her
skirts from the mire of the courtyard and stepping carefully around a pile of steaming dung.

'Thank you, my lord,' she murmured, her eyes on the
ground. Were she to look at him, he must see the turmoil
his touch had wrought.

'I will attend to the purchase of the palfrey and its
accoutrements, demoiselle. You will be able to ride it to
Merlinscrag. We shall meet again at dinner.'

Genevra had broken her fast in her chamber to the accompaniment of the other two girls' chatter, for they had woken while she made her toilet and risen at once to prepare to depart. They had had many words of wisdom to tender before bidding her farewell. Both, although no older than herself, had been wed for several years.

Genevra had not considered much of their counsel useful. Neither had been wed to men of their choice and their advice, like that of her aunt, was chiefly to obey her lord in everything, without question.

Had they but known, in their view she must have made a bad start, thought Genevra wryly. It was not in her nature to accept the wisdom of others without question. She had learned a degree of obedience in the convent, but known she could never accept the strict adherence to the Order's rule demanded of those who took the veil.

But, although stern, St Aubin did not strike her as cruel. He would surely not punish her for holding opinions of her own. Except, mayhap, by withdrawing his goodwill.

She could not forget those smiles he had given her last evening. If she could win more of those, her heart would be content.

Many of the other guests who had come for the tournament left that day too. The Hall was less crowded when the Earl's party took their places on the dais.

Most of the rubbish resulting from last night's debauch had been cleared, but the rushes and herbs covering the floor, so fresh less than four-and-twenty hours since, had now been trampled and fouled to resemble the marsh they were sometimes named.

Dogs rooted among the debris searching out scraps of meat, gristle and bone, but adding their own droppings to the malodorous mat underfoot. As they took their places at the High Table, Robert's hounds dropped down at his feet. Last evening they had been banished to the stables with his grooms. They were splendid animals, ready to be friendly. Genevra scratched one behind his ears.

'Which is Cain and which Abel?' she asked as he turned away from speaking with Northempston.

Robert was uncomfortably aware that he wished the fingers teasing the hound's ears were fondling him. He thrust down a thought which so roused his libido. Time enough for that after the wedding. But her close presence was becoming increasingly disturbing and her fine understanding a mental challenge he had not anticipated. Against the odds, he found her company enjoyable, although he attempted to hide the fact.

He was in grave danger of allowing his emotions to become involved, a circumstance which must be resisted. Yet he had never known a woman like her, one lacking in true beauty yet so attractive and at the same time so stimulating to be with. He could begin to think of her as a worthy companion, a helpmeet for life. But his emotions must be kept out of this relationship, for the sake of his own sanity, at least until he was sure he could trust her.

Not wishing his momentary lack of grip on his physical and mental condition to give a false impression of his immediate intentions toward her, he spoke with deliberate dispassion. 'The grey-coated brute receiving your attention is Cain and this is Abel, not his brother but his son. You will note that Abel's shoulders are slightly brindled, which distinguishes him from his sire. Abel's mother, Delilah, is soon to whelp again, so I left her behind at Thirkall.'

Abel was now jealously demanding Genevra's attention, trying to push between her and the older dog. She said a few soft words of reprimand but stroked him just the same. Robert managed to keep his tone bland as he asked, 'You are fond of dogs?'

'Aye, lord, as I am of all animals.' She abandoned the dogs to turn to him, her delicately moulded, square-jawed face alive, though it held a wry, wistful expression. 'Before I was sent to the convent I had a pet dog, a small terrier which delighted in catching rats.' She laughed deprecatingly. 'I cried myself to sleep at having to leave her behind.'

Robert threw a scrap to the dogs, who quarrelled over it until he threw another. 'Mayhap you would like one of Delilah's new litter.'

'You are more than kind, lord.' Genevra looked down fondly at Cain, who, having swallowed his gristle, sat watching her with large, hopeful eyes. She patted his head and ran her fingers through his rough coat. 'I should delight to have another pet. Will Cain be the father?'

'Aye. He and Delilah have produced some fine specimens between them. I sell the puppies I do not wish to keep.' He hesitated a moment before adding, 'I use my stallions as studs. Breeding dogs and horses is something which interests me and lies well with the necessary rearing of farm animals and the tilling of the land.'

She did not look shocked or disapproving of his words so he gave her a teasing, warning look before saying, 'Do not tell his lordship, but that is one reason why I was so keen to purchase Chloe for you. She will make a fine dam one day.'

Genevra's eyes lit up. 'He has agreed to sell her?'

'Aye. And do not fear—although I would like to breed from her, she will belong to Lady St Aubin. Yours will be the final decision. I will not use her unless you are agreeable.'

'I believe I should like her to produce a foal one day. But not just yet! I wish to enjoy riding her first.'

'Naturally. We will not hurry the matter.'

He dared not, for decency's sake, mention the breeding of children, but that was also in his mind. He would chose a moment early in his wife's pregnancy to have Prince cover the palfrey. Genevra would not wish to ride much once the child was in her belly, or for some time after the birth. That would reduce the period when she might wish to ride Chloe and be unable to do so.

His plans ran comfortably through his head. He could imagine a household swarming with youngsters, both his own and those of other lords sent to him for training. Genevra, he thought, would make full use of her undoubtedly superior intelligence in their raising. She would be ideal to supervise their book learning and could teach the girls the feminine arts while he taught the boys the tenets of chivalry and trained them in the use of arms.

On the morrow she would be closeted with the women supervising her wardrobe and toilet, while he was to join the Earl's hunting party, so they would see little of each other, except at meals, until the nuptials the following day.

His future wife would not have the advantage of living under his roof for a while before the wedding to learn the ways of his household, as was the custom. This was by design. He had good reason to avoid such an eventuality and had persuaded Gilbert Heskith to speed the negotiations and agree to an immediate union.

Sunday. He looked forward to his marriage with an agreeable degree of anticipation and hope. Were she to prove a faithful and fruitful wife he could see little reason why they should not live in amity together. He offered her the refilled mazer and watched complacently while she drank.

# Chapter Four

Genevra, attired in fabulous, costly fabrics heavy with embroidery, her long brown hair hanging straight and loose down her back under a simple golden circlet, as befitted a virgin bride, was escorted to the chapel door by her uncle and aunt, with Meg following watchfully behind.

Next to her skin she wore the softest lawn. A linen undergown stiffened the soft sarcenet of her peach-coloured kirtle. Over this she wore a heavy samite sleeveless surcoat, made of dark green silk interwoven with threads of gold and lavishly embroidered round the square neck and armholes with gold thread.

The skirts of kirtle and surcoat trailed at the back in a long garnished train which she picked up and hung over her arm as she trod carefully across the cobbles to the chapel, situated on the far side of the inner ward. This took most of her attention, for she was desperate not to mire her new kid slippers or her finery. The gold thread on her train alone must be worth a fortune.

Thus it was not until she entered the porch that she saw St Aubin waiting there in the shadows. The dark russet of his brocaded and lavishly embellished cotte-hardie clung to his broad shoulders, swept down to his waist and hugged his narrow hips. It suited his colouring. He was one of those fair men whose complexion did not turn red in adverse weather or heat but retained its shade of pale golden brown.

Below the cotte-hardie and the jewelled knight's belt slung about his hips, silver-grey silken hose swathed his shapely legs and fine leather, jewel-encrusted shoes ending in long, curled points at the toe, shod his feet. His head was adorned with a pleated cap in grey velvet, jewelled and feathered. The gold buttons fastening the cotte and some of the jewels set among the embroidery caught a gleam of light and flashed as he stepped forward to greet her.

Genevra's heart began to pump erratically and, after that first, all-embracing glance, she dared not look at her bridegroom. His attire proclaimed him as immeasurably rich. She could scarce believe that she was about to be irrevocably united in wedlock to the lord making his bow before her.

Calmly impassive, he did not look as though he knew what it was to be nervous. As usual, his face remained grave, while his eyes were narrowed against intrusion. Even her new finery had no power to impress him.

His squire was in attendance behind him and the Earl of Northempston stood by his side, a witness to the marriage he had contrived. And by the chapel door stood Northempston's stout, jolly priest, to whom she had confessed small sins of commission and omission earlier in the day.

All manner of people—remaining guests, officers of the household, servants, house-carls and scullions—had gathered in the courtyard. The priest, slightly drunk, the colour in his round face high, eyed the expectant throng, cleared his throat and launched into the marriage ceremony.

After a few preliminaries he solemnly addressed St Aubin.

'Hast thou the will to have this woman to thy wedded wife?'

Genevra held her breath. St Aubin seemed so remote for all he stood so close. Her aunt's frequent and scornful references to her base birth rang like a knell in her mind. Did he regret his decision? Would he withdraw at this eleventh hour?

'Aye, sir,' responded the bridegroom gravely.

Genevra's heart lurched, then settled. She relaxed marginally. He was not going to shame her by reneging on the binding betrothal contract. But even if he wished to, how could he, now, without being condemned by Mother Church and damaging his honour beyond repair?

'Wilt thou do thy best to love her and hold thyself to her and to no other to thy life's end?'

'Aye, sir,' said St Aubin again, his dispassionate voice unraised but clear.

'Then take her by her hand,' instructed the priest, 'and say after me: "I, Robert, take thee, Genevra. . ."'

St Aubin reached for her cold hand. Astounded, Genevra realised the the strong fingers grasping hers were trembling. So he was not quite so calm as he appeared. Her hand shook and her insides fluttered in response to his touch as her heart began to pound again.

'I, Robert, take thee, Genevra,' St Aubin repeated.

'"In form of Holy Church,"' went on the priest, '"to my wedded wife, forsaking all other, holding me wholly to thee, in sickness and in health, in riches and in poverty, in well and in woe, till death us depart, and there to I plight thee my troth."'

'And there to I plight thee my troth,' finished St Aubin firmly, having repeated each separate phrase in a toneless voice.

Then it was Genevra's turn to repeat the vows. Bolstered by a new assurance, aware only of the man at her side, she spoke the words softly but clearly.

At the priest's command St Aubin placed a heavy wrought-gold ring on her finger. It looked old, as though it had been in his family for years. It fitted tolerably well.

'Then I declare thee man and wife,' declared the priest in ringing tones.

A stir went through the watchers, who began to press forward to enter the chapel, jostling to find themselves a favourable place from which to watch the nuptial mass.

It seemed to Genevra a time for dedication. She vowed, as the mass proceeded, to remain true to her lord, to love him and to care for him, to serve him to the best of her ability. And prayed for the gift of felicity, and of children.

What her husband was thinking she could not tell. His face remained inscrutable throughout. Yet Genevra could sense the emotional strength held within him. He was capable of love, if only she could find the key to his heart.

Afterwards, the priest made a record of the marriage on a scroll and sped them on their way to the wedding feast with his blessings.

Genevra sat quietly throughout the festivities, which surpassed even those following the joust, sharing St Aubin's mazer and picking at the food set on their trencher by young Alan.

She had been placed next to Northempston, in honour of the occasion. He addressed her from time to time but there was little need for conversation, for he had ordered entertainment during the meal and this was provided by his fool, an itinerant jongleur, a team of acrobats and a wandering minstrel who sang sweet songs of love, accompanying himself on a lute. Any momentary lull was filled by the pleasant sound of the castle minstrels playing in the gallery.

The songs of love stirred her senses, already swimming with excitement in an atmosphere made heady by candle grease and wine fumes. She glanced at her husband. He had drunk rather more than was his wont. Knowing what lay before them, she herself decided to accept what courage alcohol could give.

And so when, later, a shout went up and parties of ladies and gentlemen came to lead away the bride and groom in order to bed them, Genevra left the Hall in a rather distrait mood, prepared to endure the embarrassing custom of the bedding without undue apprehension. She had her heart's desire, she was wedded to Robert St Aubin, and she did not care if the whole world shared her joy.

The noisy escort to the chamber Northempston had allotted them, the undressing, the ritual cleansing, the anointing with dried rose petals and the combing of her hair, the settling of her into the big bed, the chaffing and the bawdy jokes thrown about with startling abandon considering the company, had no power to disquiet her. Her expectations were high and she would meet her groom with love and willing obedience. Every other consideration floated over her head.

Predictably, her aunt sounded the only sour note, one which pierced through Genevra's calm like a dagger through butter.

'I trust you have thanked God on your knees for this good fortune,' declaimed Hannah, catching the attention of everyone in the room. 'A bastard is rarely so blessed. Never forget the favour Lord St Aubin has done you at

our host the Earl's behest, my girl. Be submissive, obedi-
ent, remember that even if you are base-born, the good
name of Heskith still rests somewhat on your shoulders.

'An you bring dishonour to your leige lord, or are even
so undutiful as to displease him, your uncle and cousins
will suffer the slur of association. Northempston would
be outraged on St Aubin's behalf. They would be angered
to find themselves in his disfavour.'

She had not mentioned herself, but Genevra knew full
well that Hannah's motives were always selfish, though
since she considered her children extensions of herself
she could be mercenary on their behalf. Shaken from
her cocoon of alcohol-induced complacency, Genevra
shuddered.

She felt demeaned, embarrassed, humiliated that her
doubtful birth should be flaunted at this delicate time in
front of strangers, for no one in the room apart from Meg
and her aunt was more than a passing acquaintance. She
was suddenly very sober. And very angry.

'Thank you, my lady aunt,' she said coldly, straighten-
ing her slender shoulders. She must keep her dignity at
all costs, despite being caught standing before them in
nothing but a fine lawn smock which did little to conceal
the pink skin beneath. 'Be assured that I shall do nothing
to disoblige Lord Northempston who, in arranging this
match, has afforded me the only true kindness and security I have known since my grandfather died.'

Hannah reddened and gobbled in an effort to speak.
'No security!' she managed to say at last. 'When we
have paid for years to keep you at the Convent of St
Mary the Virgin!'

'You forget that I was sent there to remove the con-
tamination of my presence from Bloxley, my lady, and
that the convent was paid from the revenues from my

legacy of Merlinscrag. The Reverend Mother asked but
a small portion of the whole and you profited from the
remainder while I remained unwed and under age. I will
thank you not to lecture me on the niceties of decent
behaviour, Lady Heskith!'

At this, before Hannah could find her voice to reply,
the Earl of Northempston's sister, a childless widow who
was acting as his hostess since he was a widower three
times over, intervened.

A stick-thin woman with a raddled face in which shone
two bright, kindly blue eyes, she took Genevra by the
arm and led her to the bed, saying, 'Be still, my dear.'

With Genevra under the covers she turned and spoke
with the authority of superior age and rank.

'This is not the moment to rake up old family skel-
etons, Lady Heskith. Your niece is wed now and her
future no longer of concern to you. An my lord the Earl
and Lord St Aubin himself consider her worthy of this
match, then few will quarrel with them. Unless, of
course,' she added with the sweetest of smiles, 'they
happen to be dam to a daughter of marriageable age and
inclined to envy Lady St Aubin her good fortune.'

That would be partly it, thought Genevra as she smiled
gratefully at her benefactress. Aunt Hannah's eldest
daughter must have seen some fifteen summers by now.
Genevra had not heard that she was as yet betrothed.

She settled gratefully into the swan's-down mattress.
A fat bolster supported her back as she sat with the bed
linen and embroidered blanket pulled up to cover her to
the waist and just above. Nervous she was, but of all the
emotions tumbling through her the dominant one was of
excitement. Soon she would know what it was to be
intimately touched by her lord and husband.

She became acutely aware of her breasts beneath the

thin material of her gathered and ruffled smock, the darker flesh at the peak of the mounds quite visible and, horror of horrors, her stiffened nipples almost poking through the lawn! Why they should react in this stupid way she had no idea, but it was not usual and she was excruciatingly conscious of the phenomenon as she tried to control the beat of her racing heart.

As she waited, she smiled and nodded but heard little of the lively chatter indulged in by her companions. Gradually, her high pitch of excitement cooled. Nerves took over as she tried to reassure herself that St Aubin would find her pleasing.

Northempston and a party of barons and knights had taken St Aubin to an adjoining room to disrobe. Just as Genevra had convinced herself that the delay was due to her husband's reluctance to join her, the raucous, half-drunken party entered the bridal chamber and thrust the bridegroom towards the bed.

He wore a blue velvet dressing-robe, which he discarded at the last moment. A linen smock covered his nakedness, but as he took his place beside her in the bed Genevra was acutely aware of his presence, of the mixed odours of human skin and the herbs and spices with which it had been anointed. She shrank away slightly, afraid he would notice how his close presence made her tremble.

But even so, the heat of his body reached her, inducing a liquid warmth in her own limbs which made it almost impossible for her to grasp the loving cup handed to her. But his hand was strong and no longer trembled. He took the cup and, as Northempston gave the toast, he leaned towards her to hold it to her lips. Then he drank himself and handed the cup back to his mentor.

The vessel passed swiftly from hand to hand while

two young ladies, little more than children, strewed the bed with primroses and herbs said to aid fertility. Then the priest, swaying slightly, blessed them and everyone trooped out, taking most of the lighted candles with them.

At last they were alone. Yet it was too soon, too soon! She had not yet accustomed herself to the presence of a man in her bed, a man who held rights over her body she could only guess at. One of the young ladies she had shared her bed with for the last few nights had shrugged and been dismissive of the necessary intimacy.

''Tis soon over,' she'd said. 'Just let him do what he wants, do everything he asks you to do and think of something else.'

The other, wed to a slightly younger and more pleasing man, had said, 'You are more fortunate than us, your husband is young and handsome. You might well enjoy it. Many women do. Even I do not find my lord's attentions disagreeable. And 'tis the only way to beget an heir. I have given my lord two,' she said with self-satisfaction and went on,

'Once your belly is full, he may well be persuaded to leave you alone. On the other hand, if you insist on that, he may turn to another woman for consolation.' A slight shrug of her narrow shoulders accompanied this observation. 'You may not care, of course, but with his looks, his rank and his reputation, there will be plenty ready and willing to supply it. I dare swear he could bed any woman he might choose.'

The first young woman, more stout and matronly than her companion, sighed. 'We already have an heir and I shall be brought to childbed again in seven months. If my lord chose to satisfy himself elsewhere meanwhile without troubling me, I should not complain.'

'Oh, surely not!' Genevra had exclaimed. 'You cannot

wish your lord to sin, to be unfaithful!'

'Most husbands are,' she observed matter-of-factly. 'And why should it trouble me? They are nothing. I am his wife.'

'But yours may not wander,' quickly interposed the other, seeing Genevra's troubled countenance, 'an you are welcoming to him. Any man would be satisfied to bed one so pleasing as you, Mistress Genevra.'

The conversation had unsettled her. She had grave reservations over the other's accuracy in assessing her attractions, but had not pressed the matter further. She knew she must chart her own path through the unknown hazards of marriage. But now the moment was upon her, she did not know where to begin.

St Aubin moved to lean over her, propped on one elbow. She could not determine his expression in the flickering light of the remaining candles and the single cresset on the far wall. But then she caught the gleam of his eyes, darkened now to a deep blue by an intensity of feeling he no longer chose to hide and which shook her heart, making it leap into her throat.

'Don't be afraid, wife.' His voice sounded husky. 'You know it is my duty to consummate this union. I shall be condemned as impotent an the sheets are not soiled on the morrow. I shall try not to hurt you.'

'I am not afraid, lord,' murmured Genevra resolutely, and found it to be the truth. She was merely so nervous she could scarcely speak. 'I, too, am ready to do my duty, an you will but show me what it is.'

He did not speak again but put his free hand out to touch her breast. It seemed to spring into his palm. Genevra's breath quickened.

Her husband grunted with something that sounded like satisfaction and stroked his thumb across her nipple. It

had almost retreated to its normal position since that
embarrassing moment earlier, but now it thrust forward
with even greater urgency. He continued the breathtaking
caress for a little longer then, through the lawn of her
smock, took it between his fingers, rolling it gently.

'Is that pleasant to you, wife?' he murmured.

Her limbs were already melting in his warmth, but
now new spears of exquisite pain shot through her body,
rendering her helpless. Her gasp, the only reply she could
command, appeared to give him satisfaction. A slight
smile touched the chiselled lips approaching hers.

She waited in an ecstasy of sensation for his kiss.
When it came it was gentle, a mere touch. He brushed
his mouth over hers with delicacy, kissed the corners
in turn, then transferred his attention to her wondering,
greeny-grey eyes and finally her despised nose.

His fingers continued to manipulate her nipple. Wave
after wave of exquisite sensation flowed through
Genevra's helpless body.

He shifted his hand to cup her breast. 'Open your
mouth,' he murmured against her lips.

Having been well instructed in the matter of obedience
Genevra complied, while wondering at the command.
Next moment she almost choked at the hard invasion of
his probing tongue. She gave a small gargle of protest
before she realised that after that first stab of possession
he was exploring her mouth with a flexible instrument
capable of exciting intense pleasure.

His mouth tasted of wine, as, she supposed, did hers.
Tentatively, she began to return the caress, their tongues
tangled, danced, parted as he lifted his head again. She
had not wanted the kiss to end.

'Lie still,' he ordered. He shifted his position, freeing
both hands to play with her breasts. His mouth found the

throbbing pulse in her neck. Aeons of pleasure later he shifted again to reach down for the hem of her smock. 'You don't need this,' he told her. He sounded so calm. Strange, when she felt as though she were drowning in a wild sea of sensation. 'Lift yourself up.'

Embarrassed now, wondering still, the stormy waves of feeling subsiding to a gentle rocking motion, Genevra nevertheless did as bidden.

He undressed her like a doll. The garment came off over her head and was thrown to the floor. His own nightsmock quickly followed. Heated naked skin touched naked skin. Genevra shivered, but not with cold. He was stroking her now, long, slow sweeps of his hand which travelled the length of her body, while his mouth claimed the peak of one of her breasts.

She gasped and wriggled helplessly as he first gently bit and then suckled. She had never imagined that he might do that! Suckle her like a baby! All kinds of sensations had her in their thrall, strange things seemed to be happening to her body. And then his hand stopped stroking and instead his fingers began to explore the secret place between her legs, where the sensations had centred.

Momentarily affronted, for this was too much, she tried to clamp her thighs together, uttering a faint moan of protest.

'Relax, my wife,' came the calm voice from the region of her breast. His warm, steady breath chilled her damp skin. 'I have licence to touch you so and it will do no harm. You are not quite ready for me yet.'

Ready for him? Genevra was lost in a confusion of instructions and new sensations but she did not wish him to stop. His fingers were working magic and her body was crying out for something but she was not sure what.

She had to trust Robert St Aubin to show her.

The excitement built in her. She found herself responding to his touch, moving spontaneously under the invasion of his fingers. And then, just as the feelings threatened to swamp her, to drown her in some region as yet unexplored, St Aubin moved swiftly above her. She felt the momentary heat of hard flesh against her thigh before an agonising pain made her cry aloud.

St Aubin lay still, breathing fast, but she could feel him throbbing inside her. 'Hush, wife. It will not hurt again. That was your maidenhead breaking. You are no longer a maiden but a woman who has known her husband. Be still.'

Tears ran from the corners of Genevra's eyes but although begun in pain they continued in happiness as she welcomed him inside her. Was this the intimacy some women found distasteful? This delicious friction of his thrusts inside her opened body? But so much must depend upon the man. . . She stopped thinking in order to enjoy.

He moved steadily at first but soon his drive became fast and urgent. Genevra's mounting excitement had been cut off by that shaft of searing pain and had no time to build fully again before he grunted, shuddered and collapsed on top of her.

Only at that last moment had he lost control. Before that his actions had been deliberate. He had known exactly what to do to please and rouse her and had done it. But in the end the desire she had glimpsed in his eyes at the outset had overcome him.

At least she had the comfort of knowing that, however much he might disguise it, he had desired her. Consummation of the marriage had not been entirely a matter of cold duty. Genevra linked her arms about his shoulders as shudders racked his body. He seemed, strangely, against all she knew of him, vulnerable. She was not sure what else to do while he recoverd himself.

Men, she had heard, were easily and quickly satisfied by the most ugly of women, bawds and tavern wenches, almost any female willing to lift her skirts. She prayed that her husband's present helplessness meant that he had found her a more pleasing bedmate than women like those.

But the marriage act was by no means as distasteful as she had been led to believe. Her husband's demands, though strange, had been undeniably enjoyable. She had experienced a rising tide of exquisite enchantment until that searing pain had shocked her back to reality.

His passion spent, her husband did not take long to recover. 'It is accomplished, wife,' he murmured as he rolled aside. 'You did well.' He placed a light kiss on her lips. 'Now sleep.'

Wide-eyed and wakeful, Genevra was surprised at her deep sense of disappointment. There should have been more. More sharing. More...what? The mating had left her sore and sticky. She would have liked to call Meg to attend her. But she could scarcely do that while her husband lay beside her, eyes closed, breathing evenly, apparently fully sated and already asleep.

She prayed that she had pleased him. He had not said so in so many words, only that she'd done well. That should be reward enough, she supposed. He had done his duty and so had she.

But because she loved him and had found such pleasure in his arms, she had not expected it to end so abruptly, leaving her aching for something more. Next time, she would know what to expect. Mayhap, then, she would find what she sought. She almost envied her husband, who had so easily forgotten everything in sleep.

But not quite, for she had all her new experiences to savour.

She must not be jealous of his first wife or of any of the doubtless numerous women he had bedded since. She must concentrate on winning his love so that he would keep himself only unto her.

She could not know that her husband was not asleep but lying still beside her, refusing to acknowledge the tenderness his new wife roused in him.

He had set himself to bed her with a cool, calculated ardour which would keep emotion at bay. The result had been unexpected and stunning; she would have climaxed beneath his hand had he not quickly entered her, more roughly than he had intended, and so hurt her. Even so, once the shock was over she had begun to respond again; but he had been unable to control his own body and so had made a precipitate end.

He had made a botch of it, like some ill-disciplined, callow youth. Her innocence, her loveliness, her responsiveness, had contrived to make him too eager, to lose control. He knew that, in his dismay at so doing, he had been less than kind afterwards.

Yet experience should have told him that a high degree of physical response, though necessary to experiencing a satisfactory union rather than a perfunctory release, did not equate with the deep passion and emotion he had expended on his first wife and intended to deny to his second. Years of assuaging his needs on women for whom he cared not one jot had taught him that.

He need not have been so abrupt with Genevra. As he fell into the deep sleep which normally followed completion, he did so with an uneasy sense of guilt.

\*     \*     \*

By the time Meg, with several older ladies led by
Northempston's sister, entered the chamber next morning
to wake her, her husband had gone. Genevra experienced
an instant of alarmed disappointment before she dismissed his absence as of no account. He, no doubt, was
an early riser and had not wished to disturb her from the
deep sleep induced by the exhaustions of the previous
day and its enervating climax last night.

Last night! Colour flooded her cheeks as memory
returned. But beneath the embarrassment lay a new joy
in being a woman and being alive.

Meg dipped a curtsy. 'I've brought ale and a biscuit
for you, my lady.'

'Thank you, Meg,' she murmured. 'God's greetings to
you, ladies.'

'And to you, Lady St Aubin,' said Northempston's
sister, speaking for the others. 'We trust the marriage has
been consummated?'

As Genevra nodded an affirmation, a frisson of new
excitement went through her, banishing embarrassment.
Lady St Aubin! She liked the dignity of her new title.
Another reason for being happy to be St Aubin's wife.
An she needed one.

Her aunt was there, and although she did not push
herself forward as Genevra might have expected, she did
audibly murmur, 'Her lord was not disposed to tarry abed
this morn, it seems.'

Genevra ignored the slur and spoke to Meg. 'Pray
procure me a tub of hot water. I wish to bathe.'

A nod, however, was not good enough for her visitors,
who gathered about the bed.

Northempston's sister, who dressed sumptuously and
walked with all the dignity and assurance of age and

rank, spoke again. 'We must remove the sheets, my lady. An you will rise. . .'

New embarrassment gripped Genevra. Her smock lay in a heap where St Aubin had thrown it. Meg had disappeared in order to relay Genevra's order for water to a loitering page. Genevra met and held her aunt's eyes.

'Since my tiring-woman is not here, would you hand me my mantle, my lady?' she enquired sweetly.

Hannah, scowling, could scarcely refuse. She handed her niece the new, flowing garment of bleached wool edged with miniver, designed to be wrapped around its owner to keep her decent and warm in the privacy of her chamber.

Genevra accepted the service with a gracious smile, pulled the mantle around her shoulders and left the bed. She sat down on a cushioned chest while the ladies busied themselves eyeing the evidence of her lost virginity and then removing the sheet. This ritual performed, they trooped out, leaving Genevra alone with Meg, who had returned.

Except that Hannah lingered to remark, 'He is no soft boy, your husband. Do not expect him to pamper and cosset you, Genevra.'

She smiled, unable to hide her malice. 'I saw your disappointment when you discovered that he was not still by your side, my girl. What did you expect? A puppy dog to fawn at your heels? He is a hard, fighting man with needs and desires to match. Do not expect a gentle courtship, for you will not receive it from a knight possessed of Lord St Aubin's reputation.'

Genevra, glad that the deliberately upsetting and frightening words had been spoken after rather than before her bedding, lifted her chin and her finely arched brows. 'You say so, my lady? But how can you know how joyous was my initiation into the mysteries of the marriage bed, when mayhap you have never experienced such felicity yourself?'

Hannah paled. 'You impudent slut! How dare you speak to me in that manner?'

'I outrank you now, my lady,' Genevra reminded her quietly. 'The St Aubin's barony is more senior and its holdings more extensive than that of Heskith. Northempston is his patron but Baron Heskith's overload. The King himself is Lord St Aubin's liege lord, as Lord St Aubin is now mine.'

Hannah could do little but splutter, 'Mark my words, pride goes before a fall, my lady!' as she left the chamber.

# *Chapter Five*

Once her aunt had left, Genevra gave a rueful smile, although she could not regret her words. Aunt Hannah had been asking to be set in her place for as long as Genevra could remember. She turned to Meg in relief.

'How glad I am to be free of Lady Heskith's spite at last!'

Meg knew better than to acknowledge her mistress's confidence in words and thus criticise a member of the nobility. 'You are happy, my duck?' she asked instead.

Genevra's face lit up. She scarcely needed to speak. 'Yes,' she confirmed with a conscious smile. 'I found the marriage bed much to my liking. I cannot imagine why some women view it with distaste.'

Meg's wise face broke into an answering smile. This was a confidence she could respond to. 'Mayhap because they are not wed to so perfect a knight, my duck. He looks stern and has a reputation for severity, but you have found him kind, have you not?'

'Kind? I do not know, Meg.' Genevra picked up the mug and took a draught of the ale. 'Considerate, mayhap. He is certainly not intentionally cruel, he hurt me only when he broke my maidenhead. Otherwise—well, his use of me was gentle and roused such feelings in me. . .'

She could not go on to describe the sensations that had flooded her being under the touch of her husband's hands, even to Meg. Or the mounting joy she had known as she sheathed part of his strong hard body in the softness of hers. Meg could never imagine such a thrilling thing. She munched her biscuit dreamily.

But Meg was smiling and nodding. 'And you love him, my duck. When a woman loves, the man can give her exquisite joy an he takes the trouble. And if he loves her, too, then what otherwise is simply a matter of need or lust becomes something of a sacrament, a representation of the true attachment which exists between them.'

Genevra convulsively swallowed the food in her mouth. 'You are so wise, Meg! How can you know all this?'

Now it was Meg's turn to blush. Her still-youthful face became suffused with colour. She delved into Genevra's travelling chest to hide her confusion. 'Although I never wed, I once had a lover, my lady.'

Genevra studied the woman who had been a second mother to her all these years with new eyes. She had taken her for granted, seeing her as a rather dumpy person, now approaching her fortieth year, with threads of grey in the brown hair hidden beneath her veil. She had never noticed or remembered what she had been like in the years when she herself had been too young to understand. She had simply been there.

'You did?' she asked in astonishment. And added uncertainly, 'Without being wed?'

Meg, her voice muffled by exertion as she searched through the contents of the box for a suitable gown, admitted as much.

'But who was he, Meg? Why did you not wed?'

Meg stood up and faced her mistress at last, a gown clasped defensively in her arms, her stance rather defiant. 'He was a groom, my lady. He was already wed but his wife was an invalid, confined to her bed.'

'And. . .you loved him?'

'We loved each other, my lady. But it was not to be. Your grandfather died and you were sent away to the convent. I chose to stay with you, my duck. I knew you had need of me.'

'Oh, Meg! You should not! You should have taken your happiness instead of shutting yourself away with me!' Genevra jumped to her feet and ran across to Meg, ignoring the new and expensive gown and taking the careworn hands into her own. 'But I am glad you did not! And now, God willing, you will met another man you can love.'

'I have met my Bernard again, my lady. He came in Lord Heskith's train.'

'And?' demanded Genevra excitedly.

'His wife is dead. He has not wed again and we still feel the same way about each other. But my duty is to you, my duck. I could not possibly leave you now.'

Genevra's eyes were blazing. 'I would not wish you to. But he could leave my uncle! Ask him, Meg! I am certain the lord my husband will engage him as my groom!'

Meg's face was a picture of confused delight. But before she could answer, a string of pages and scullions arrived with a large banded wooden tub and buckets and pitchers of hot water to fill it.

It was not until she was sitting in the lemon-balm scented water soaping herself that Genevra was able to return to the subject of Meg's love life.

'You will ask him, Meg, won't you? I have my own

palfrey now and shall need an escort when I ride out. It is quite providential!'

'But you may not like Bernard, my lady,' objected Meg half-heartedly.

'If you love him, then I shall certainly like him!' asserted Genevra. 'Once I am dressed, you must go and seek him out, but hurry! I believe my uncle leaves later this day.'

At that moment a stir at the door to the adjoining chamber heralded the return of Lord St Aubin. He strode into the room with all the vigour of a man of action, smelling strongly of horse and fresh air. He must have been riding. Genevra automatically shielded her breasts, which had taken on a life of their own. She crossed her arms over them and hoped St Aubin would not notice how her entire body, already pink from the hot water, blushed to an even deeper shade.

But he scarcely looked at her. Instead, he strode to the window and stood gazing out over the bailey while he spoke. 'We leave after dinner,' he announced abruptly. 'I wish to make a start on the journey to Merlinscrag as soon as possible. Lord and Lady Heskith are leaving within the hour. We shall not be far behind them on the road, but I shall not attempt to catch them up.' He looked at her suddenly. 'Unless you would welcome their company for part of the journey?'

'Oh, no, lord!' Genevra forgot her embarrassment and raised herself a little in the water. 'But Meg has just been telling me that she has renewed acquaintance with one of my uncle's grooms. They wish to wed. Could you speak to my uncle and request that Bernard be allowed to leave his service and enter yours, as my personal groom? An you approve of him, of course,' she added quickly, seeing a dark frown appear on her lord's face.

But it seemed that the frown was one of concentration rather than anger.

'Bernard, you say?' He addressed Meg. 'He is a man who has given long service to the Heskiths, I surmise?'

Meg curtsied. 'Aye, lord. Bernard of Lincoln. He has remained with Lord Heskith the ten years I have been with my lady in the convent.' She blushed. 'Awaiting my return, he tells me, my lord.'

'Then we must see that his devotion is rewarded. If he seems an honest, useful fellow I have no objection to taking him into my service. No doubt I shall find him in the stables?'

'Aye, lord. I am most grateful.'

'Well, wife, I shall go and see to the matter. Meanwhile, perhaps you will make ready to leave. I shall see you at dinner.'

With these words he was gone. Genevra slowly rose from the water and took the linen cloth Meg handed her to dry herself on. Meg's hands were shaking.

'What if they have already left?' she said worriedly.

Genevra wrapped the cloth about her and trod to the window embrasure. The opening was wider than that in her previous chamber and she had quite an extensive view of the inner court.

'They have not,' she told Meg. 'See, the escort is gathering and the horses are being brought from the stables. Can you see your Bernard?'

Meg peered down and gave an excited cry. 'Aye, there he is! And his lordship has just crossed the yard to find him!'

Both women squeezed into the embrasure together and Genevra observed, 'He is asking one of the other men. Yes, he is being directed to a man who must be your Bernard.'

'Aye, that's him, my duck! The tall thin one with red hair, what's left of it, and if you can see it under his cap.'

'My lord has taken him aside. Now my uncle has appeared. I pray he will allow Bernard to leave his service.'

'Bernard is a free man, my lady. He can scarcely prevent him.'

After that remark Meg remained silent while the conference continued and the pair were joined by Heskith. At last the scene resolved itself. St Aubin led Bernard away from his former workmates amid much shouting of farewells and the pair, Bernard shouldering his pack, disappeared in the direction of the stables.

'He has done it,' cried Genevra excitedly. 'Oh, Meg, I am so happy for you!'

'And I for you, my duck. Your lord thinks highly of you to be so ready to fulfil your wishes.'

But later that day when, in the dying glow of the sun, they arrived at the manor house where St Aubin had decided to seek shelter for the night, Genevra was not so certain of his desire to grant all her wishes. For he did not join her in the chamber allotted to her but sought a pallet in the Great Hall with his men.

As the journey progressed, one obstacle after another, some real and some, she suspected, manufactured, prevented his bedding her again.

The first night, luxuriating in a chamber to herself, apart from Meg, who could have been banished, Genevra decided that his absence from her bed was due to his wishing to enjoy his host's company and reminisce, since they were old friends. He could have joined her later, but mayhap he did not wish to disturb her.

That he might be too inebriated to climb the stairs and

slept slumped over the board or collapsed on the floor did occur to her, but she dismissed the idea out of hand. The Golden Eagle, a knight dedicated to physical prowess, had a large capacity for wine, but compared to others was abstemious. She had never seen him more than slightly hazy.

The journey took over two weeks. They had passed through Oxford and Bath, cities which had awed Genevra by their size and beauty. From thence they had traversed hill and dale, had skirted to the south of the wastes of Exmoor, barren apart from grazing stock and deer, to arrive at Barnstaple. After that they had clung to the coast where the Severn Sea met the great Western Ocean, another sight which had delighted Genevra, reviving childhood memories, until at last they had reached Merlinscrag.

During that time they had lodged in an assortment of manor houses, castles and monasteries where privacy was almost impossible. She had slept in chambers shared with daughters or other guests, in women's dorters attached to monasteries and even, on occasion, had lain on a pallet in a corner of some Great Hall with St Aubin and his squire nearby.

Sometimes he had lain in a different part of the building altogether, which had been preferable for, while he had slept so near, frustration had built in her. As her impatience to lie with her husband again had grown, so had her sense of guilt. It was unseemly for a young woman, so newly wed, to ache for her husband's attentions. She had prayed for grace and had prayed, too, that he would not detect her indecorous eagerness to bed with him again for, if he had, he must think her immodest.

Despite her frustration Genevra had enjoyed the ride through the delightful, budding countryside where

primroses had often swathed the banks beside the road.
Her initial weariness, induced by long hours in the saddle,
had soon passed. The spring days followed one upon
another with only the occasional shower of rain to
inconvenience them.

When St Aubin had ridden beside her or had sat with
her to eat, they had discussed all kinds of matters, from
religion and politics to animal husbandry and medicine.
She, eager to discover his mind, had treasured these
moments despite the fact that they had often argued. The
conversations had been friendly, never acrimonious. He
had seemed, now, to accept that she should be free to
express her views. She had thought that mayhap he had
enjoyed the stimulation of a good debate as much as
she had.

But much of the time he had not ridden beside her.
Often he had left her with Meg, sitting like a sack on
her led horse, while he had ridden with Alan or the
captain of his escort.

So mayhap she had been deceiving herself. Perhaps
he had not found her to his liking in bed. Mayhap she
should not be so free with her arguments, mayhap he
had not enjoyed their debates as she had; on occasion he
had seemed to listen with impatience, at other times with
amused indulgence, as though she were a child to be
humoured, not a woman whose views counted.

She could come to only one conclusion. He had bedded
her to consummate the marriage, but had no great desire
to repeat the experience. Since he did not often seek her
company, she could only conclude that when he did it
was from courtesy.

This was normal between man and wife but Genevra,
having fallen so precipitately in love, had hoped for more.
Just as she had hoped for more when he bedded her.

That had been a physical lack. This was an emotional void, an essential feeling of loneliness despite his being near. Her happiness began to erode.

'Do not fret, my duck,' counselled Meg, who was likewise parted from her Bernard for much of the time. 'Have patience until we reach our journey's end. All is new and strange, but I dare swear that things will right themselves once we reach Merlinscrag.'

The evening before they anticipated arriving at their destination, alone together in a small chamber, Meg stroked a bristle brush through Genevra's hair, holding out a tress at a time and then dropping it back to fall about her hips. Now she was wed, Genevra wore it confined in a caul under a veil while travelling. In the evening she hid it under a fashionable heart-shaped headdress.

But although it was seldom seen, she was still proud of her strong, straight hair, believing it to be her best feature, despite a lack of lighter glints to relieve its bark-brown glossiness. It shone best after she had washed it and so she took care to do so quite often. Meg would see to it the moment they arrived at Merlinscrag. Before tomorrow night. Before St Aubin came to her. Unavailingly, an he did.

Genevra sighed. 'I pray you are right, Meg. You must be anxious to arrive, too, for you will be able to name a day for your wedding.'

'Aye, my duck. We have talked about it, and are agreed to seek God's blessing as soon as possible. Bernard would like a son, and I might still be able to give him one.'

'Oh, Meg! But would it not be dreadfully dangerous. . .?'

'At my age?' Meg picked up on the words Genevra did not like to speak. 'Mayhap. But I am willing to risk it. Childbirth is dangerous at any age. Yet every woman longs to bear her man's children.'

Genevra gave a rueful laugh as she considered the perils facing her at some time in the future. 'Most do, anyway. And will risk anything to have a baby. Otherwise, how would the human race survive?'

On the previous day, Genevra had been disappointed to discover that her bedding had not been fruitful. She said nothing to St Aubin; she was too shy of him to bring the subject up, especially as moments alone with him were rare.

But once established in the solar at Merlinscrag, she would have to inform him. Otherwise he would come to her there only to discover her inability to receive him. Since their wedding night had not been blessed, she supposed and hoped that he would want to bed her again quickly once she had recovered.

As they approached Merlinscrag, the landscape became more windswept. All the trees leant away from the coast, their branches shaved off at the top as though cropped by shears—a strangely familiar sight that brought back memories of her mother, telling her that the gales coming in off the great ocean to the west caused it.

That same wind, which was now whipping her cloak, chilling her fingers and toes. She would be glad to arrive. Word had been sent ahead and the steward should have everything ready to receive his new lord and lady. There should be warmth and light and food aplenty.

And the prospect of a more normal sharing of her life with her husband. They would grow together, as happily wed couples should.

Her memories had been dim, fragmented. She did not really remember Merlinscrag at all. The curtain wall on the landward side, with barbican, ditch and gatehouse already fully in view, was far enough down the slope of the hill to allow a clear view of the castle as they approached from the east.

The crenellated tower could have belonged to any fortified building. The mass of buildings at its foot, dominated by the long, high roof of the Great Hall, which had a dovecote at each end and a lantern in the centre to allow the smoke to escape, had made no particular impression on her childish mind except one of looming granite, the threatening greyness of her dream. Yet much of the stonework, the tower and the Great Hall at least, had been limewashed.

As they approached, a little after noon, sun bathed the whitened walls in sunlight, banishing all sense of menace. At this point the sea was to the north and the shadow of the tower pointed toward the cliff edge like a long finger. Within a short distance, though, the cliffs turned southwards into a bay to the west.

Merlinscrag itself had not been built on the edge of the cliff but set some few hundred yards back, on a slight rise. Its position had been chosen both to deter hostile ships from sailing up the Severn estuary to Bristol and also to discourage any attempt by invaders to use the bay to come ashore from the sea.

The notes of a trumpet echoed over the intervening fields. Dwellings here were scattered, each tenant living within his own boundaries. There seemed to be innumerable sheep, far more sheep than any other living thing. Some fields were under cultivation, and each cottage had behind it a byre for the cattle and a yard where pigs and geese rooted, hens pecked, and the manure was heaped.

Not far away, a stream flowed to a distant cleft in the cliffs and ran down into the sea. A mill with a huge wheel fed by a sluice had been built beside it.

A small church, identified by its porch and the cross at the peak of the gable above, not to mention the graveyard surrounding it, stood just outside the curtain wall.

Between the mill and church a cluster of thatched buildings, where the priest, the miller, the carter, the wheelwright, other tradesmen and the bailiff lived, constituted the village.

'They have seen us,' remarked St Aubin, having reined in to one side and waited for her.

He wore a padded gambesou under a rust-coloured velvet mantle trimmed with beaver, but no mail or armour. They did not expect to be set upon by roving bands of armed robbers or by anyone else this far west. But he did carry his sword and the padding would offer some protection if they were attacked. The curled feathers in his cap were murrey and green, his livery colours, to match the plumes nodding from between his horse's ears.

She wore the new riding costume supplied by Northempston, fashioned from light blue celestrine with a dark grey velvet surcoat. It had borne the journey well, but the skirt was dusty and it exuded a distinct aroma of horse sweat. She wore her aunt's fur-lined mantle over it and the leather breech hose beneath.

The column formed by St Aubin's meinie was long, with the men-at-arms, the liveried servants, the grooms leading spare horses, the farrier, the falconer, the armourer, a train of pack-animals—mostly mules, loaded with their possessions and driven by men with long sticks and whips—and two squires and two small pages on ponies. He had been at its head, she riding as usual between the two squads of the escort for safety.

Their trumpeter answered the challenge from the castle with a blast which seemed to be carried away by the wind. She nodded. 'You sent a message. They were expecting us.'

'Will you ride to the head of the column with me? It is your castle, they are your people.'

Genevra immediately left the column to one side, as he had done, and spurred forward with him. Chloe was caparisoned in her husband's colours now. 'All I had is now yours, my lord. But I shall be honoured to approach Merlinscrag beside the lord my husband.'

They took up position just behind the Herald. Alan was at St Aubin's shoulder, flying the St Aubin banner from the tip of his lance. The men at arms carried their lances vertically, too, with the long tails of the pennons mounted on them streaming. The mass of golden eagles stamped on vert and murrey backgrounds made a brave sight.

Genevra straightened her tired back, thankful that tomorrow there would be no riding. Chloe had carried her all the way, a sturdy creature for all her nimble, aristocratic looks. The pace had been steady, the breaks frequent, for they had hunted, cooked and eaten by the roadside during the day, seeking what hospitality they could just before sundown. St Aubin knew how to conserve the energies of both men and beasts.

Trumpets sounded again, shouts were exchanged. Together, they rode through the barbican, clattered over a granite clapper bridge spanning the ditch and passed under the portcullis.

A party of men, presumably household officers, waited just inside, backed by some fifteen men-at-arms all smartly turned out, to introduce themselves and escort them up to the buildings. Most of which, Genevra was reminded, were roughly formed in the shape of a square, enclosing a courtyard, one side of which was entirely occupied by the Great Hall.

The men, except the soldiers, who stood at attention, all dropped to their knees in obeisance, their faces impassive.

'Welcome to Merlinscrag, my lord,' murmured a man of about St Aubin's age, wearing a long brown gown with a flat cap upon his dark brown head. 'My lady, we are honoured to receive you here again. I trust you will find all the arrangements to your liking.'

He was a tall man, his eyes brown and kind in a face of no particular note. Yet it was familiar. Genevra exclaimed, 'You must be Martin. I well remember being carried in your arms as a child, when you were but a squire, the son of a knight! Lord Heskith told me that you had chosen to be steward here rather than seek greater advancement elsewhere.'

A smile lit Martin's unexceptional features. 'Indeed, my lady, I remember you well. I was most grateful for the opportunity to remain here to look after your interests. I held your mother, Mistress Margaret, in great esteem. I have done my best to order the household as I believe she would have wished.'

He rose to his feet at a sign from St Aubin, as did the others. 'My lord, my lady, may I introduce Geoffrey the bailiff, who has assisted me by faithfully husbanding your lands for the past five years?'

The solid, ruddy man in fustian tunic, woollen hose and heavy leather boots, the hood of his dagged chaperon covering rough, curling hair, a peculiar shade between red and yellow, bowed his head.

Then the priest, an austere, clerkly figure in long black robes, known as Father John, was named. He was a priest rather than a clerk in lesser orders and, said Martin, a

man skilled in the arts of healing. Merlinscrag was lucky
to have his services.

Finally, the soldier was introduced.

'Captain Piero Nori,' said Martin. 'His mercenary
troop see to the defence of Merlinscrag.'

Nori acknowledged the introduction by saluting and
saying, 'At your service, *signore*,' in a strongly accented
voice. He was short and dark and wore an elaborate,
plumed helmet and a large sword with a fancy hilt to
show his importance.

'Which is your native land, Captain?' enquired
St Aubin.

'The Italian State of Florence, *signore*.'

'And the men here are all yours?'

'*Si, signore*.' Proudly. 'They are my company, and are
of many nationalities. Fine men, *signore*.'

St Aubin nodded. 'They look well disciplined. There
will be room for the men of my retinue to join yours in
your quarters?'

'Also for your horses in the stables, *signore. Il castello*,
he was built to house many more defenders.'

St Aubin nodded again. 'Very well. We will proceed.'

Led by Captain Nori at the head of his band of mercenaries and flanked by the officials, all on foot, Genevra
and her husband rode up the slope to the cluster of buildings by the tower. Heavy wooden gates guarding an
opening between the buildings stood wide to admit them
into the inner courtyard.

Here were gathered a motley crowd of people, mostly
decently if poorly clad. No one actually wore rags.
Genevra surreptitiously studied them as she dismounted.
Even at the nunnery and Ardingstone she had seen a few
ragged serfs and scullions. She did not think the relative
prosperity of the menials here was due to her uncle's

charity. Martin had contrived it somehow.

'I cannot introduce you to everyone now, my lord and my lady,' he said, 'but I should count it an honour an you would allow me to introduce my wife, Annys. She is daughter to a merchant in Barnstaple.'

The young woman, mayhap a year or so older than Genevra herself, had a child clinging to her skirts and another at her hip. Her belly was full again.

Genevra, possessed by a surge of sentimental longing, spoke for them both. 'We are glad to find you here, Mistress Annys. What beautiful children you have. What are their names?'

Annys blushed and beamed as she made an awkward curtsy. She had a fresh, open face and her hair was neatly hidden beneath a clean white kerchief. Martin had presented her with pride.

Annys put her hand on the head of the boy at her skirts, a sturdy, curly-haired child of some four or five years. 'This is Harry, my lady, named for my father. This one,' she indicated the fairer of the two children, who now stood sucking its thumb and half hiding its face in her apron, 'is named Catherine for the saint near whose day she was born two years since.'

Other children were with their parents in the yard, mostly gathered about the well, but Genevra had no time to enquire after them at that time because St Aubin turned to Martin. 'My wife is wearied by the journey. An Captain Nori will attend to the comfort of my men and see the horses stabled, mayhap you will lead us to the lord's quarters?'

Before Martin could reply, Genevra cut in eagerly. 'The solar is over the wardrobe, at the end of the Great Hall, lord. The kitchen, as I remember, is over there, away from the main buildings, where a fire can do less harm.'

'You remember well, my lady,' smiled Martin, beginning to lead them to the steps rising to the Hall door. 'Beneath the Hall you will find the wine and ale cellar and the food stores.' He swept an arm round the yard as he spoke. 'There is the dairy, there the brewery, the farrier there and the armoury under the barracks in the tower where Captain Nori will take your retinue once their mounts are stabled—'

Now St Aubin cut in. 'There will be time enough to discover the dispositions of Merlinscrag. First we must eat and rest. Pray guide us to the solar.'

The entrance to the stables, Genevra guessed, was outside the yard since the horses were being led out again. Already, the people who lived in the castle had returned to their business while casting curious, speculative looks in the direction of their new lord and lady and their squires, pages and servants, as they climbed the stairs to the Hall.

In all likelihood they were apprehensive, not knowing what changes St Aubin would decree, whether he would be a good or bad master, kind or cruel. Rather as she had been apprehensive before her betrothal. Now she knew that, although stern, St Aubin was fair in his judgements and not given to harsh punishments for disobedience or carelessness.

She herself was looking forward to renewing acquaintance with Martin. She smiled slightly at sight of his broad shoulders as he walked ahead. She well remembered being carried on the shoulder of the strong, merry lad of fifteen he had been all those years ago. He had taken the place of the older brother she did not have.

And now he was wed. She liked the look of his wife, Annys. Mayhap she would become a friend. It would not be unacceptable for her to seek Annys's company, surely.

She was not a servant, but wife of the steward, himself of knightly stock and the man who had so efficiently kept Merlinscrag solvent and in good repair. Meg would always be dearest to her, but Annys could become the friend of her own age she had hoped to find.

St Aubin was looking about him as the party passed through the Great Hall. He acknowledged the bows of those busily engaged in setting up the trestles for supper but his attention was not engaged. As he mounted the wooden stairs to the half-gallery leading to the solar door, he looked down critically on the Hall. She followed his gaze.

Fresh rushes had been strewn on the floor and it looked as though everything had been swept and scrubbed. The walls had been freshly whitened and then hung with banners between the unglazed windows set high under the eaves. Merlinscrag had been sweetened in anticipation of their arrival.

Up in the smoke-blackened rafters small birds twittered and flew beneath the thatch. An uneasy hush had fallen on the Hall as they passed through and the soft cooing of the doves in their cotes was clearly audible above their heads.

Next moment they were ushered into the solar.

Martin bowed deeply. 'I trust you will find everything here to your satisfaction and comfort, my lord. I have restored the chamber to what it was the last time the lady Margaret was here.'

Windows faced each other on either side of the chamber, one looking north and the other south. A fire burned brightly in a brazier standing on a stone slab in the centre. Genevra walked towards it and sank on a nearby stool, holding her chilly fingers to the heat.

'I remember the bed,' she murmured, eyeing with

nostalgia the heavily curtained, richly spread piece of furniture standing at the far end. When she had shared its cosy intimacy with her mother it had seemed vast. Now, she would share it with her husband, and it did not look quite so large. They would be very close.

St Aubin's boxes and packs were being carried through to a chamber beyond, known as the garderobe, although the privy itself was in a small, separate chamber off it. His squires and servants would attend him in there and Alan and St Aubin's body servant would sleep there unless dismissed below to join his other squire and pages in the Great Hall. Some of her clothes would be stored there, too, to discourage the moths, which did not like the smell from the privy.

Meg would have a bed in the curtained recess off the half-gallery she had used in the past.

It would be just possible, in the solar, to be private. But their attendants would always be within earshot.

They had eaten in the Great Hall and were ready to retire before Genevra found the privacy to tell her husband that her condition precluded lovemaking. He stood for a moment, as though irresolute, then managed a rather strained, wry smile.

'Then I will not trouble you with my presence, wife. I will find a bed with Alan in the garderobe.'

'Oh, but—'

'God give you a restful night, my lady,' he interrupted. 'You must needs be in want of it after the long journey.'

# *Chapter Six*

Why had he gone?

Genevra shivered under the covers, although she was not cold. She so longed for his human warmth, for his kindness. She would give almost anything to have his comforting presence beside her this first night in the castle their marriage had brought him. But even the hounds had gone away, had followed him into the garderobe.

Her new husband had shown no disposition to want her except for pleasant conversation, on occasion, and to use her for the necessary getting of an heir. Without that incentive, he had no desire to share her bed. He preferred to sleep in discomfort in the evil-smelling chamber adjoining. At least the moths would not bother him, she thought sourly.

She should not have built her hopes up so high. She would have to wait for her courses to finish before he would come near her again. Gentle companionship in bed had no place in his thoughts. So what would happen once she conceived? Would he abandon her for the garderobe again? Or, horror of horrors, seek some other, more exciting, woman's arms?

She sat up suddenly. She had forgotten her devotions

98

again. Mayhap God was punishing her for neglecting them. She slipped from the bed and took a guttering candle over to light the one stuck ready on a pricket on the prie-dieu.

A crucifix hung above. The flame of the candle threw grotesque shadows up the wall. But the niche designed to hold a statue was empty. Her mother had had a figure of the Holy Mother set there and Genevra wondered what had become of it. It was probably at Bloxley still. Next time she was there she would look but meanwhile she would see about obtaining a statue of her own.

She knelt, closed her eyes and lowered her lids. The reciting of the prayers, the rhythmic passing of the beads through her fingers, quietened her stretched nerves. When she returned to bed, she fell asleep quickly.


She awoke to find Meg pulling back the bed-curtains. St Aubin, fully dressed, sat at a small table by the south-facing window, writing.

He looked up but scarcely glanced at her. 'Did you sleep well, my lady wife?'

'Very, I thank you, lord. And you?'

'Well enough.' He paused to make a small correction to what he was writing. 'I suggest we explore the castle together when you are ready. Unless you do not feel well?'

'Nay, lord. I am not inconvenienced in any way save one.'

He acknowledged her rueful admission with a nod. 'I see that Meg has brought you bread and ale. I have already partaken of adequate refreshment. I will continue to deal with my correspondence until you are ready.'

Robert turned back to his writing, though he could scarcely focus on the words he was forming. She washed and dressed behind a screen, but he was acutely aware of her every move. He had kept his distance during the journey, unwilling to allow his fierce desire to master him.

But his need had not diminished with time. Rather, his frustration had grown. Last evening, telling himself that after such a lengthy denial he could at last allow himself to lie with her again, his ferment of anticipation had scarcely allowed him to contain his excitement. And she had not been available.

He prayed he had disguised his dismay when she had told him. For an agonised moment his disappointment had turned to suspicion and anger. Was she using a woman's excuse to deny him? But the doubt had lasted only for a moment. She had been too innocently apologetic, too embarrassed by her condition. The anger had remained, but anger against the fate that had denied him, rather than against his wife.

She had wanted him to share the bed, regardless.

But he could not. To do so would have been too painful, she might have discovered the depth of his need of her. So he had spent a comfortless night on a hard pallet in the garderobe, wishing he could seek some other woman to accommodate him. But he knew no one in this castle and could not ask without rousing speculation and sly looks. Besides, he had sworn before God to keep himself only unto her until his life's end. Most men took their vows lightly, but he did not.

Also, it was his wife he desired, and no other. He regretted now that he had been too agitated to question her further. He did not even know when she would be clean again.

The opportunity to ask came sooner than he had dared to hope. While Genevra consumed her freshly baked bread, Meg departed on some errand. Although Alan was in the next room he would not hear if he kept his voice low.

He looked up from the writing on which he was finding it so difficult to concentrate. 'My lady,' he began, 'may I enquire when you expect to be recovered from your woman's affliction?'

'Not tonight or tomorrow, lord,' said Genevra apologetically, blushing. 'By the next night all should be well.' She hesitated a nervous moment, breaking her bread with shaking fingers as he silently digested this unwelcome news in silence. Then she went on a trifle breathlessly, 'But would it not be possible for us to share the bed meanwhile? I would have no objection and I do not like to think of you sleeping in the garderobe.'

Robert took a firm hold on his emotions. Was he a man, or some poor creature unable to master itself, that he so feared to be near his wife because he desired her body? Of course he could sleep beside her without touching her! The experience would be a salutary exercise in self-restraint, besides proving once and for all that she held no power to enslave him. He had been close to women he wanted ere this without making a fool of himself. She was no different to the rest.

But she was. There was something about his wife that made the prospect of such close intimacy without consummation acutely painful.

He gathered his mind and spoke more sharply than he had intended. The expectation of passing two more nights like the last held little prospect of pleasure.

'The pallet in the garderobe is a luxurious bed compared to some I have slept in on campaign. I shall wait until you are recovered before I trouble you, ma'am,' he answered her.

'Very well,' acquiesced Genevra stiffly. She could not quite keep the hurt and resentment from her voice. At least, he supposed that was what it was. It could scarcely be disappointment to match his own.

Genevra was hurt, but mostly disappointed. However, she had determined to win his love and sulking would not achieve that. So she turned a bright smile on him as she finished her repast. 'When you are finished, lord, I am quite ready to accompany you on a tour of the castle.'

He had resumed his writing. As she spoke, he stopped and looked up.

He looked down again quickly. 'I have but a few lines to complete. I write to my mother, to announce our marriage. I should like to dispatch it this morning. I shall not keep you long.'

His bold strokes flowed over the page. Every now and again he paused, quill hovering, while he chose a word or phrase. Genevra watched covertly, unable to take her eyes off him.

He was dressed as a lord rather than a knight this morning, in a long furred gown of midnight blue that swept the ground about his stool. His head was covered by a small brimmed cap of the same colour, but the golden strands of his hair could not be entirely contained. The sight of him still had the power to make her catch her breath.

She hoped her attire would be adequate for the occasion. She had decided to wear the garb handed down from Hannah. It had been good enough for the joust and should serve now. The fur lining to the mantle might prove too hot indoors, but it would be chilly crossing the courtyard and she could remove the garment if needs be.

Meg had braided her hair and wound the coils over her ears, containing them in a new caul fashioned of golden threads which would shine in the sun and reflect the glow to her hair. She was, she informed herself wryly, becoming sinfully vain.

Her green eyes, lightly flecked with grey, sparkled as she gazed out of the window which overlooked the ocean. White crests topped some of the waves, while others reflected shafts of light to dazzle her. Unseen, the rollers broke against the rocks at the foot of the cliff with a sound of distant pounding, which woke memories and stirred old, childish excitements in her.

She longed to go and look down on the boiling, spuming water. But her mother would not be there to hold her safely back from the cliff edge—her mother had not been there to keep her safe for many years.

This place seemed haunted by memories of her mother. The bed, the hangings and covers, the beautifully carved stools, the clothes press and the tapestries hanging to each side of the window, which her mother had worked with her own hands, evoked longings and the feelings of desperate loss Genevra had thought long since dead. Tears sheened her eyes. How different her life might have been had her mother lived.

And yet—and yet would she now wish for anything different than to be wed to Robert St Aubin?

No. She must pull herself together. She turned resolutely from the window. 'Twas of no use mourning for what might have been when she had a new life opening up before her. But all the same, it could do no harm to look out the few small things of her own that her mother had always left here, against the next time she visited. Mayhap the statue of the Virgin was among them! She must remember to ask Martin if he knew where they might be.

She sat on a stool and watched as St Aubin finished

writing, sanded the ink and folded the parchment, sealing it with wax and his crest, cut into the surface of a ring he wore on one of his strong, sinewy fingers. Fingers which had explored her body so intimately and sensitively, despite the hard roughness of hands well used to wielding more than a pen. Genevra's pulses quickened and she blushed and looked away as he wrote the direction on the outside of the folded sheet.

He stood up, waving the missive to dry the ink, and raised his voice to call Alan, who hurried in and was given the letter to pass on for delivery. A messenger would ride to Thirkall in stages to deliver it, and return with his mother's answer.

St Aubin turned to Genevra. 'Well, wife, I am ready at last. I apologise for keeping you waiting so long.'

Genevra stood up and crossed to the window again. 'I have been watching the sea, lord. Tell me, what is it like to sail on it?'

He grimaced. 'Cold, wet and sick-making for some. I was lucky and the motion did not induce sickness in me. In many ways I enjoyed it, even when we were stuck in mid-channel for weeks because the winds were contrary. But, on the whole, I would rather remain on dry land.'

Genevra continued to gaze out of the window. 'It looks so warm, calm and peaceful, apart from the breakers.'

'The condition of the sea is always deceptive from this height and distance. Look!' he said suddenly, standing disturbingly close at her shoulder. 'See that small fishing boat, how it rocks, how the waves break over its bow? Those men with the nets will not be feeling either warm or peaceful!'

As Genevra moved away, she was intensely conscious of brushing his gown. 'I hope they make a good catch. Mayhap Martin can buy some fish for us to eat for dinner.

I remember loving the fresh sea fish when I was a child.'

St Aubin had one hand on the stonework surrounding the window. He pushed himself off. 'Mayhap.' He raised his brows as he moved forward. 'Shall I send for him?'

'No need. We shall see him somewhere about the place.' An eager smile spread across her face. 'Come, my lord! I am anxious to renew acquaintance with Merlinscrag.'

St Aubin was breathing rather fast. He moved toward the door. 'Aye. I am impatient to inspect the dowry my bride has brought me.'

Before the heavy, studded door was opened, Genevra glanced through the glazed squint, located beside it. The glass was not very clear and afforded only a hazy view of the activity in the Hall below. The instant the door was opened and they passed through, the bustle became audible.

As they descended the stairs Martin appeared at their foot as though by magic. He had been in the steward's office, which occupied more than half the space beneath the solar, the remainder being used as a store-room for things of especial value. Someone had been posted to warn him of their coming.

At his invitation, they looked briefly at his records, which appeared impeccable. The air in the store-room beside his office smelled exotically of all the expensive spices brought in from abroad, like pepper, ginger, cloves, cinnamon, galingale and mace. The sugar loaves were stored here, too.

When they entered the undercroft below the Hall, where the main stores were kept, Genevra could not help exclaiming.

'There is more than enough here to withstand a siege!' she said, eyeing the barrels of salted meat, the huge hams and bacon joints hanging from the beams, the sacks of flour and other grain, the dried peas and beans, the great slabs of salt, the strings of onions and garlic, the boxes of leeks and countless other things tucked on shelves and into corners.

At the other end, a few casks of brandy and wine and dozens of barrels of ale were stacked. Roots of fennel and bunches of dried dill, savory, rosemary, parsley, mint, thyme, hyssop and sage added a pungent aroma to the other end of the undercroft. Jars of culinary seeds, of coriander, fennel, cumin, caraway and mustard lined a shelf.

'We have many to feed here, my lady,' explained Martin. 'If necessary, we can spare supplies for any of our serfs whose family is like to starve.'

Genevra gave Martin a brilliant smile of genuine warmth. 'I am happy that you and the bailiff care for them, Martin.' The name tripped easily off her tongue. She had always called him so. 'But I am surprised that Lord Heskith did not question your generosity?'

Martin shrugged. His grin was wry. 'As long as we were able to render up the tithes he expected, his steward asked few questions, my lady. I continued in the ways your mother had approved, maintaining your inheritance for you as she would have wished. I did not think it necessary to go into the finer details of my administration unless asked.'

'But now,' remarked St Aubin, 'you must render account to me.'

His tone sounded dry. Genevra gave him a quick glance. Surely he would not decree that all charity to those who owed him allegiance must cease!

'It is only sickness or bad weather which makes such aid necessary, lord,' said Martin, now a trifle defensive.

'It is seldom needed. But the lady Margaret always left instructions for provision to be made.'

'Naturally. And no doubt Lord Heskith knew and agreed. I shall be interested to study the accounts, nevertheless.'

So he would not forbid the charity. Relieved and cheered, Genevra followed happily as Martin led the way back to the busy courtyard and across to the kitchen.

While many of the buildings lining the inner curtain wall were of timber construction, with the walls made of mud and straw and the roofs covered with thatch, the kitchen, being at hazard from fire, was built of granite with thin slabs of a softer stone covering the timbers of the roof.

Heat from three blazing hearths greeted them as they entered, the steamy atmosphere meeting them like a wall. People were working almost naked and Genevra did not blame them. A dog in a wheel turned a hog on a spit before one, and cauldrons and kettles, hung from above on hooks attached to chains and pulleys, bubbled and boiled over the flames.

Everyone stopped what they were doing to kneel when they entered. St Aubin motioned them to rise and the cooks and scullions returned to mixing, grinding, scraping, chopping, pounding, beating or whatever else they had been engaged in before. Uncomfortably warm, Genevra was glad not to linger.

They passed on to look at the other buildings in the courtyard, the dairy where milk was turned into butter and cheese, and the brewhouse where the smell of fermenting and maturing ale and mead was almost overpowering. A room set aside for the preparation of medicines and salves, which was hung with dried herbs and lined with bottles and jars, caught Genevra's

attention. A brazier and a workbench told her that someone distilled the volatile oils of herbs and flowers here.
She would return ere long.

In the place where both the armourer and the farrier
worked, mending armour and shoeing the horses, several
braziers burned brightly, most in use heating the metal.
A horse waited to have new shoes fitted.

'You have not yet inspected Captain Nori's arrangements in the tower,' Martin reminded them as they
emerged from the leather worker's shop next door. 'The
men are out exercising and training so it would be con-
venient for you to go there now, if it pleased you, my
lord. The fletcher works on the ground floor where the
weapons are stored. The barracks are above.'

'I long to go right to the top,' Genevra said, bringing
her eyes down from where the crenellations cut like teeth
into the sky to smile eagerly at Martin. 'Do you remember
carrying me up and standing me in an embrasure so that
I could see all around?'

Martin grinned. 'I do, my lady. And your lady mother
told you that one day you would be mistress of everything
you could see.'

The look of delighted intimacy they exchanged was
cut short by St Aubin. 'That day has come,' he remarked
shortly. 'Let us mount the stairs and view the extent of
your fief, my lady. You will need no shoulder to ride on
this day.'

'Nor,' rejoined Genevra, not understanding his tone
but attempting to smooth over an awkward moment,
'shall I need to stand on the wall to see!'

She led the way up the stair, lit by torches stuck in
brackets on the wall because it twisted up the centre of
the tower. The men stopped to look in at the chambers
on each level but she continued to climb. She wanted to

arrive before the others, to have a moment in which to gather her resources again.

For understanding of St Aubin's attitude had finally burst on her. He was jealous of the intimacy she had once shared with Martin the steward.

It was quite stupid of him and inexplicable too, since he did not love her. Except that, mayhap, he was a man who would jealously guard anything he possessed. She must learn to watch her intimacies with other men, however innocent they were.

She climbed the last flight and emerged on the roof to find two lookouts stationed there. They recognised her immediately and snapped to attention.

The wind blew chill at that height and Genevra, after greeting the two soldiers with a nod, clutched her mantle about her, glad after all that she had chosen to wear it. Sea surrounded her on two sides, though to the west she could see the coast turning back at the far side of the bay. A smudge in the vastness of the ocean to the north puzzled her. She pointed.

'What is that land?' she enquired of the soldiers.

'An island they call Lundy, my lady. No one lives there but a shepherd and his sheep.'

Satisfied, Genevra turned her gaze inland. The verdant landscape lay before her like crumpled, chequered green linen dotted with crumbs of bread, with larger pieces of brown crust caught in the folds and surrounded by areas of stain. There were hedges, green fields with grazing sheep and cottages set amidst ploughed fields in which the villeins grew their crops and kept their swine, geese, chickens and cows.

The lord's demesne was nearer, a large swathe of land straddling the stream and divided into several fields, some of which had been ploughed and sown and were

already showing signs of green. Day labourers had built
a huddle of huts nearby. The common grazing land on
the hillsides was dotted with animals. She heaved a sigh
of content.

St Aubin emerged on the roof, with Martin following.
She turned a glowing face upon him and swung her arm
in a wide arc.

'Merlinscrag, my lord.'

He crossed to her side and for a moment stood silently
absorbing the view.

''Twas a worthy inheritance, lady,' he murmured. 'Do
you trust me to husband it well?'

She gazed up into his face as he continued to study
the land. His expression told her little, yet she could see
the determination and power in the set of his chin, the
intentness of his concentration. He would ensure that the
land prospered.

'Aye, lord,' she murmured. 'As well as you husband
the lands that are already yours.'

He suddenly turned to her, his expression almost
angry. For a moment she thought she had said something
wrong but his words told her that the anger was directed
at himself.

'I have neglected my inheritance until now. I left it in
the hands of others while I fought for the King abroad.
They did not do well at home. You were better served
than I.'

'Yes,' murmured Genevra. 'I think I misjudged my
uncle Heskith. He left Martin in charge and did not question his administration while the revenues were good. He
was unquestionably reluctant to relinquish the income,
but I have no doubt that, had my aunt known and had
her way, she would have bled the coffers dry.'

'My lady.' St Aubin suddenly reached out and claimed

one of Genevra's hands. 'I desire to bring all the lands
under my control into prosperity and to see that the
people under my dominion are content. Will you
help me?'

Genevra returned his intent blue gaze, her own eyes,
had she but known it, almost dark with emotion. 'Aye,
husband,' she said as steadily as she could. It was the
first time she had addressed him so. 'You may command
me in any way you like. But my greatest pleasures will
be to help you to administer your estates and to bear
your children, especially an heir to inherit them.'

He caught his breath. Genevra saw something in his
eyes then which both thrilled and frightened her. He lifted
the hand he held and pressed her knuckles to his lips.

'Then I am fortunate indeed in my wife,' he murmured.

Neither of them remembered their audience of steward
and soldiers.

With a rather forced cough, Martin brought their attention back. At the same moment a bell began to toll.

'Noon!' exclaimed Martin. 'The bell sounds only three
times a day, to wake the household, to summon it to
dinner, and also to supper. Shall I lead the way down?'

'Not like the convent,' remarked Genevra as she prepared to follow. 'There they rang the canonical hours all
day and all night!'

'Disturbing,' murmured St Aubin sympathetically.

She caught the slight quirk of his lips and the glint of
a smile in his eyes. Greatly encouraged, 'It must be the
air,' she went on as she moved to the stairs, 'but I am
greatly hungered!'

Genevra truly did not understand her husband. That he
was not happy in himself was evident. He must still be
mourning his family, she supposed. But Jane and his son

had both been dead for some ten years. Grief alone could not cause his present air of disillusion with life itself.

His loyalty to the crown was not for a moment in question, but he was known to be unhappy with the way the old King and his sons were behaving. Yet surely none of this accounted for the fact that, every time she thought she was making progress in his affections, he withdrew behind a barrier of reserve. Why would he not allow their relationship to develop beyond one of polite friendship and the calculated intimacy necessary to produce an heir?

Of course, knights and courtiers were not supposed to fall in love with their wives, whom they had wed from convenience, but to cherish a courtly love for almost any other woman. She desperately wanted St Aubin to love her.

Again, she lay alone in the great bed. He had spent the afternoon in the bailey practising his fighting skills with his squires and soldiers, leaving her to acquaint herself with the running of the household.

After the encouraging intimacy up the tower before dinner, Genevra had hoped he would change his mind and share its comfort with her. But he had not. He had been as distant as he had ever been as he had bade her a polite good night and retired to the garderobe. She would have to endure this and one more night of solitude before she could expect to be quite recovered from her indisposition.

But after that. . .

She had not expected one taste of the marriage act to make her so restless, so eager to repeat it. Was she strange, unnatural? Women were supposed to endure, not enjoy. Yet Meg had enjoyed, and would again, and she was not unnatural. Genevra smiled to herself. In her present mood of anticipation she felt truly sorry for all those women destined to wed men they did not love and, worse, were forced to endure the attentions of husbands they loathed.

The following day proved to be one of undiluted pleasure as, together, they explored the terrain encompassed by the boundaries of Merlinscrag, accompanied by a small escort, the two hounds and the bailiff, Geoffrey. Wherever they rode, up hill or down dale, the people who lived on and worked the land fell to their knees as the cavalcade of their new lord and lady passed by.

'They appear content,' St Aubin remarked to Geoffrey as they turned their horses' heads toward home. 'They find little hardship in rendering up their tithes?'

Geoffrey's manner was quietly deferential without being obsequious. 'The hills give good grazing and sheep are hardy animals, though husbanding them is not easy. The wool clip is valuable, however. In addition, they manage to grow adequate crops to feed themselves and still have a small surplus to send to market.'

'You have lost none to the towns?'

'No, lord. Little has changed here, as it has in other parts. Or so I have heard.'

'The plague scarcely affected you here, I believe.'

Renewed sight of one of the derelict cottages she had already noticed on the way out sent chills down Genevra's spine. It appeared almost ghostly in its utter abandonment. Before Geoffrey could answer St Aubin, she cut in, 'What happened to the occupants of that cottage?'

'The family died of the pestilence, my lady. We were, as his lordship has just said, lucky here. Isolation has its benefits. We suffered few deaths from a plague which killed so many in the towns.'

'And in the countryside,' put in St Aubin.

'In other parts. Yet some did die here,' prompted Genevra.

'This family unwisely decided to visit friends in Barnstaple. Husband, wife and children all died there. We had another entire household succumb in their cottage here. The man went to market and no doubt brought the sickness back with him. Father John, who had himself recovered from the same pestilence in his youth, nursed and buried them without spreading the disease further. Afterwards we set fire to their cottage. All our other people escaped.'

'You were fortunate indeed,' said St Aubin grimly. 'I am pleasantly surprised to discover Merlinscrag still so prosperous. It seems that Lord Heskith was fortunate to retain the services of both steward and bailiff during his years as guardian of his niece's inheritance.'

'We have done our best, lord. We all remember the lady Margaret and her young daughter with affection. We are pleased to have you back at the castle at last, my lady.'

Genevra smiled at the man, feeling a little guilty. She did not remember Master Geoffrey as she did Martin. But then, the bailiff lived in a cottage by the church, not in the castle itself, as the steward did. In the old days, Martin had slept in the Hall with all the others in her mother's service. Now he lived with his wife and family in a small two-roomed cottage built within the inner curtain wall.

'I scarcely remember anyone,' Genevra apologised. 'I was too young. And it has been so many years since I was here.'

They paused at the top of a rise to rest the horses and admire the view. The hounds were immediately off, following some scent they had discovered.

A look of worry crossed Geoffrey's ruddy face. 'I trust they will not worry the sheep, lord?'

'I think not, they are trained to hunt deer, but it is best to be on the safe side, since there are new-born lambs about.' He put his fingers in his mouth and a shrill whistle echoed across the fields. Cain and Abel hesitated only a moment before turning and racing back to St Aubin.

'Good dogs,' he said. 'Stay.' He turned to Geoffrey. 'Is this good hawking country?'

'Aye, my lord. There are many small animals for the peregrines, and doves we can release, too, if there is a lack of wild birds for the smaller falcons to hunt. Close to the cliffs the seabirds tend to frighten off the larks and blackbirds.'

'Would you like a merlin, my lady?' St Aubin asked Genevra. He smiled. 'It would seem appropriate for you to have one at Merlinscrag. There must have been wild merlins here once.'

'Oh, yes, lord, I have always longed to fly a bird. Is there deer hunting to be had here, Master Geoffrey?'

'There are deer on Exmoor, my lady, and the lord of Merlinscrag is entitled to hunt there.'

Genevra turned a glowing face towards St Aubin. 'So Cain and Abel will be able to enjoy themselves, too!'

'We have foxhounds at the keeper's cottage, my lady. Foxes worry the sheep and have to be kept under control.'

Genevra took a deep breath of the fresh, salt-tanged air and let it out on a sigh of satisfaction. St Aubin's horse stood close to hers. She edged Chloe nearer and held out her gloved hand. Looking slightly surprised, St Aubin took it.

'I trust you are happy with the lands I brought you, my lord and husband.'

He squeezed her fingers briefly before letting them go. 'Lord Northempston did not exaggerate the attractions of either my bride or the manor she held,' he murmured.

Such a pretty speech, and before witnesses, too! Genevra coloured, then laughed. 'But you have yet to discover the joys of the sandy bay beneath our walls! Mayhap we may climb down there after dinner?'

'Climb, my lady? Do you propose an excursion on foot?'

'Indeed I do! Scrambling down to the sand and the sea is one of my dearest childhood memories.' Martin had always been at hand to help her down. Now her husband would guide her steps, should she need assistance.

The track of Genevra's dim remembrance began within the curtilage of the outer walls. A small tower stood at its head, built there to protect defenders should an enemy attempt to enter the castle that way. With her skirts kilted up rather indecorously, she descended it with little difficulty; but it was Alan's hand which offered assistance when she needed it and he who turned to help Meg.

St Aubin had bounded ahead of the others with the dogs and stood waiting at the path's foot while Cain and Abel capered and barked exuberantly and sniffed inquisitively at the strange scents.

He had withdrawn again since the morning. Genevra, hiding her disappointment, decided to ignore it. She must reconcile herself to his changeable moods.

A small hamlet nestled along the side of the cleft the stream had made and there was a wider, better-used path running up steeply beside it. The cottages she remembered had multiplied, she thought. None, at that time, had spread to nestle under the cliff-face as they did now.

'They would surely be washed away in a bad storm,' she remarked as she, with Alan and Meg just behind, emerged from among the weed and shell-encrusted rocks at the foot of the path to join St Aubin on the beach. She untucked her skirt and let it drop. 'They are new, aren't they, Meg?'

Meg was similarly occupied in making herself respectable again as she answered. 'I think so, my lady. The village has grown. There are more boats drawn up on the shingle than I remember, and—' she nodded towards a group of fishermen and their families busy dealing with the morning's catch '—more people. But it does not look as though the tide has been up that far in a long, long time.'

'True.' St Aubin considered their position. 'They are safe enough there, I think. The beach rises from here and there is no seaweed clinging to the rocks higher up.'

He looked about him, at the high cliffs with tumbled rocks and shingle at their foot, at the stretch of firm golden sand revealed by the retreating tide, with evident pleasure. His eyes followed the gulls, swooping and calling overhead, as he said, 'So, my lady of Merlinscrag, this is your beach. We should have brought the horses down. They would enjoy a canter through the waves.'

'On the morrow, lord! The moment the tide allows!'

'The sand looks dry. Let us walk along a little and then return by the path the villagers use. They, too, are your people, I assume?'

'Aye, lord, but not serfs. The fisher families are freemen who live here because they wish to. They pay us rent for their cottages, mostly in fish. We must speak with them.'

It was as they trod the path between the cottages that Genevra, looking about her and acknowledging the curtsy of a young woman nursing a baby, stumbled over a hidden rock sticking up above the surface. Her ankle twisted and she would have gone sprawling in the dirt had not St Aubin caught her. She clutched at him, steadying herself on one leg, for sharp pain shot through her ankle when she put her other foot to the ground.

The bolt of lightening which seemed to strike her as his strong arms enfolded her took all the breath she had left. Her limbs seemed to melt. She looked up and what she saw on her husband's face sent her momentarily dizzy. She closed her eyes and gulped in air.

He went on holding her. If anything his arms tightened as he supported her shaking body. 'Are you hurt?' His voice was low, little more than a growl.

As the shock waves receded she sucked in more breath. 'No, I don't think so, not badly—my ankle—'

She put her foot to the ground again and tested the ankle. The pain was less already. Meg had come bustling up, her face full of anxiety. Genevra did not notice, her attention was entirely trained on St Aubin.

She met his gaze, her eyes filled with emotion she could not hide as she clung to his shoulders. Her voice shook as she told him, 'It is nothing, husband. I can walk now.'

The breath hissed from his lungs as, instead of releasing her, he pulled her closer. Meg, seeing them absorbed in each other, pulled Alan aside and began to walk on.

'Holy saints!' murmured St Aubin. 'But how I want you, wife.'

Genera's heart gave a great bound. 'And I you, husband,' she acknowledged breathlessly. Her eyes promised all delight as she murmured, 'Tomorrow night I shall be well again.'

# *Chapter Seven*

She lay in the vast bed, waiting. Wind and rain rattled against the shutters sending draughts swirling about the room, for the weather had turned overnight and dark clouds had swept in from the sea all day with scarcely a break.

Genevra had spent the morning in conference with Martin and his wife. While she was here, she intended to supervise the domestic arrangements of the castle. There were improvements she would like made that Martin would not think it his right to instigate.

Annys, his wife, had been delighted by Genevra's invitation to join Meg as one of her attendants. Later, the children had played at their feet while the three women sat in the Hall carding and spinning wool.

'This has come from an excellent fleece,' Genevra remarked as she straightened the fibres between the wooden, nail-studded cards and then laid the wool where her companions could reach it.

'There is no shortage of such fine wool at Merlinscrag, my lady,' smiled Annys, who was expertly spinning it into thread with the aid of a wheel, 'rearing sheep being our chief concern.'

'Whose fleeces are exported through the staple at Barnstaple,' Genevra nodded with a smile. 'Except those we keep for our own use.'

Meg, spinning just as efficiently though with a distaff tucked under her arm, grunted. 'But, before we can use it to make garments, it all has to be scoured and dyed and woven.'

'There are men and women here who can do the fulling and dyeing,' Annys assured her. 'As for weaving, there is a loom in one of the outhouses which is often in use. A travelling weaver comes by to make the finer cloths.'

Engaged in such domestic activities, they had spent a quiet, companionable afternoon getting acquainted while St Aubin inspected horses, saddlery, armour and weapons.

Now, at last, the moment she had been anticipating all day had arrived. Her bleeding had stopped as expected. Meg had gone to her bed—or mayhap to meet Bernard—after bathing her all over with scented water and brushing her hair until it shone. A squire was abed in the garderobe. But as he came through St Aubin let the skin door-hanging drop behind him and they were alone in the solar, their private place.

He discarded his gown, caught up a candle and held it high as he approached the bed. His hair gleamed gold in the light from the flaring flame.

Genevra's breath caught. His expression was disguised by moving shadows but the glow burnished his splendid, muscular body, caressed the wide shoulders, the deep ribcage which tapered down to narrow hips, the smooth, strong thighs. His chest hair, soft and curling, appeared a shade darker than the straight hair on his head. There was no disguising the fact that he wanted her. Yesterday's moment of revelation had been no figment of her imagination.

The answering spear of desire shafting through her did not surprise Genevra. The sensation had become familiar since her wedding night.

'Husband,' she whispered huskily. And, greatly daring because of yesterday, she drew back the covers invitingly and added, 'You are most welcome, lord.'

'Indeed, madam, so I should hope. You are my wife,' he declared gruffly. 'Welcome or not, I have the right to bed you.'

This assertion of his rights was not the response Genevra had hoped for. Her daring had not paid. Her colour flared, not entirely with embarrassment. There was a sharp edge to her voice as she retorted, 'Mayhap you would prefer me reluctant, lord? Mayhap 'twould give you more satisfaction were I to resist you?'

For a moment he looked down at her without answering, his expression inscrutable. He moved the candle to aid his inspection. It flared again and left a trail of smoke which danced before her eyes. Then he reached down with his free hand to untie the ribbons of her night smock.

'Nay, madam.' His voice sounded terse. 'I need no added titillation to enable me to serve my wife.'

Still blushing furiously and despite her growing anger, Genevra made no resistance as he removed the garment and retrieved the light, which he had set aside. He held it over her again to study the lines of her naked body, gleaming like alabaster in the candle glow.

Genevra clenched her fists at her sides, resisting the urge to curl up into a ball to hide herself. She would show no shame before her husband, would have flowered under his scrutiny had he only approached her with understanding. But although possessive desire was evident in him, more tender emotions were not.

His gaze lingered on the swell of her generous breasts, the curve of hips designed for child-bearing, the lithe perfection of her slender thighs. She flinched slightly as he touched her cheek, but the hand he ran down her neck and shoulder to linger in the cleft between her breasts was gentle. Genevra could not disguise the tremor that ran through her body at his touch or prevent the small gasp of pleasure as his palm cupped her breast.

A smile—of what? Satisfaction, admiration, antici-pation, amusement?—touched his lips. He turned to replace the pricket and douse the flame. 'You are quite beautiful, my wife,' he murmured as he returned to the bedside. 'It will be my pleasure to get you with child.' So saying, he swept the curtains about the bed and joined her in the warm, secret, scented darkness.

His arm beneath her shoulders drew her to him. Despite his possessive attitude and evident need, he did not hurry her but took care to give her pleasure: all without uttering one single word of tenderness or affec-tion. Yet, under the persuasive movements of his hands and lips, Genevra relaxed and forgave him his uncompro-mising approach. He was doing what he always did, attempting to prove to himself and to her that although he had taken her to wife he felt no more for her than for any other woman he had known or with whom he had enjoyed bedsport.

His exploration of her body not only excited her, but gave her the confidence to respond. Much as he might wish otherwise, this would be no arbitrary, soulless pos-session. His touch was urgent yet caring. He could not entirely suppress his more tender emotions.

At length Genevra abandoned the last of her hurt and

her pride and let her immoderate desire speak. 'Please!' she whispered.

His hand and lips stilled. 'Aye, my wife,' he murmured, and turned her under him.

This time there was no pain, simply a glorious, exquisite sensation of mounting bliss. Genevra clutched him closer, wound her legs about him, gasped her pleasure and then, as her whole body seemed to tingle and quiver, unknowingly shouted his name. All reality was distilled into one, overwhelming experience of soaring fulfilment.

She came to herself again to find her husband's weight still heavy on her. He seemed to be holding his breath. She tightened her arms about him and he expelled it with a great shudder. Momentarily he lay still, his face buried in the pillow beside her head. Then he lifted his weight from her and rolled aside.

Genevra felt his going as a deprivation. If only he had remained longer, sheathed inside her! But his immediate withdrawal could not shake the sense of completion she had experienced. She knew now what she had missed on her wedding night. He had remedied the matter tonight, waiting for her so that her passion could peak before he allowed his own to explode.

He must feel something for her or he would not have bothered. He must know that she had been transported by his possession. Yet he did not gather her in his arms again, as she longed to be gathered. But neither did he turn away. He lay on his back, his flesh still touching hers.

Nervously, she sought his hand. 'I thank you for the pleasure you gave me, lord.' She swallowed and added huskily, 'I pray I did not disappoint you.'

He stirred, withdrew his fingers from her tentative hold. 'We both found pleasure, wife. I had little doubt that I should be pleased, as you must know. The ability to find enjoyment together, however, is something for which we should thank God.'

'I asked the Holy Mother to guide me, lord. I shall thank her, too.'

He gave a grunt, shifting again, leaning over her. For a moment she thought he might kiss her, but he did not.

'Sleep now, wife.' He touched her cheek, a fleeting caress, involuntary, she thought, because after that he said, 'God's blessings be on you, wife,' in a curt tone and turned away.

Genevra suppressed a sigh and shifted to face the curtains. Like a snail retreating into its shell, he had withdrawn into himself again. He might possess her, body, mind and soul, but would she ever possess him in any true sense at all, except as his legal wife? His body, mayhap, during brief episodes like tonight. He could not disguise his desire and he had, she knew, lost himself in her in the end. But the wealth of his mind and his soul might always elude her.

Robert, astonished, pleased and yet dismayed by the passion with which his wife had met and satisfied his need, lay fighting a craving to take her again. Dismayed because his first wife, Jane, who had never shown such an astonishing response, had allowed another man to lie with her. Genevra, possessed of such a deep well of passion, must surely feel a greater temptation to bed with other men.

There was one way to ensure that the temptation would be minimised: if he took care to keep her sated himself.

It was a persuasive argument, and an entirely pragmatic solution to his immediate problem. She was not yet asleep. He turned back and allowed his passion its freedom.

His hands on her body woke her again at cock-crow. She responded to him instinctively, delighting in meeting his desire with passion of her own, cherishing the knowledge that she could rouse such frequent need in him.

During the nights that followed, St Aubin seemed insatiable and Genevra gloried in his ardour. It must surely mean that he felt something for her, that he had begun to care.

By day she was a little weary, but not enough to dim her enthusiasm for riding out with him to explore or to hunt or to take lessons in how to fly her merlin, at every possible opportunity. Her skin glowed, she looked radiant—to all appearances a woman loving and loved. Only she knew of the reserve St Aubin still maintained between them. It saddened her, but she hid her disappointment deep, where it scarcely marred her happiness at all, and lived in hope.

For in the evenings, sometimes, their minds met in discussion of some ancient philosopher's thoughts, and once or twice they had tuned their instruments and made music together. It was not enough, yet. But it was a beginning.

Meg wed Bernard on a wet and windy day two weeks after their arrival at Merlinscrag. That evening, the castle rang with the noise of its first celebration in years, a feast in honour of the newlyweds. Not a feast fit for a king, but one which pleased the people gathered in the Great Hall, for Meg had found favour with the women of the household and Bernard had made himself popular in the stables.

Meg and Bernard were elevated to the High Table for the occasion and a new cask of ale had been tapped, as well as a small barrel of mead. As they watched the tumblers Martin had managed to engage for the occasion, Genevra motioned for Alan to refill their mazer with mead. She took a drink and offered St Aubin the bowl.

'Martin tells me this was made with honey from our own hives,' she said. 'I think it is very good.'

He lifted the mazer and gazed into the clear golden liquid critically before tasting it.

'You agree?'

'Aye.' He drank again, rolling the liquid round his mouth before swallowing. ''Tis an excellent wine. It should be enjoyable mulled and spiced in the winter. The local red wine we had earlier is good to drink, too. It is almost as fine as that I enjoyed in Aquitaine, made from the grapes grown near Bordeaux. It has a great advantage in that it does not need to be kept so long in the barrel before it is fit to be drunk.'

Genevra smiled. 'And it is much cheaper than bringing wine across from Bordeaux by ship. I always knew living at Merlinscrag had much to recommend it!'

'So does residence at Thirkall and my other manors, madam!'

His tone teased and Genevra's smile widened. 'But I have yet to discover their delights, lord.'

His expression darkened immediately yet when he spoke his voice did not reflect a change of mood. 'All in good time, wife. I am happy to postpone resuming the responsibilities of administration for a little longer. Since my return I have arranged my affairs differently. I left the manors in excellent hands. We have no need to leave here yet. I should like to continue to enjoy the hills, the wildness of the moors, the rugged coast.'

His tone took on a teasing note. 'I even appreciate our proximity to the Western Ocean, despite the fierceness of the wind and the frequency of the rain.'

'The horses and the dogs will miss sporting on the shore, lord! Cantering through the surf strengthens the horses' legs.'

The messenger had yet to return with a reply to the letter sent to his mother. It was too soon. Although Genevra was curious to meet Lady St Aubin, she was apprehensive, too. The dowager might disapprove of her son's marrying a woman of base birth. She did not, therefore, object in the least to postponing her husband's return to Thirkall. And, although he still maintained a distant reserve for much of the time, his defences were crumbling. Sometimes he looked youthful and happy. Sometimes, like tonight, he smiled.

A month passed. A warm, mainly dry May turned into a hot June. To Genevra's acute disappointment, her courses reappeared.

That night, full of apprehension, she told St Aubin, choosing a moment when they were virtually alone.

A slight frown crossed his brow. 'I am disappointed,' he admitted. 'We have coupled often enough. I should have thought. . .' He did not voice the fear gripping Genevra, the fear that she might prove barren. 'But no matter,' he went on, 'there is plenty of time for you to conceive.' He noticed her anxious face and sought to reassure her. 'Do not fret, Genevra.' He smiled. 'I will join you as usual when I am ready for bed. I shall teach you how to pleasure me, my dear.'

Genevra's eyes widened at sight of the intimacy, the meaning he infused into that smile. This was a St Aubin she did not yet know. And he had, for the first time as far as she could remember, called her by her name.

'Robert? Husband?' She responded by using his name, her tone questioning, for she did not understand what he meant.

He ran his roughened thumb across her lips, making her gasp. 'There is much a man and a woman may do together without coupling,' he explained. His eyes burnt with a fire she recognised. 'You are no longer an innocent virgin, my wife. You are ready to learn more of the arts of love.'

She was not. She was. He sent her senses spinning and her body limp with aching sweetness while she helped him to find his release. Afterwards, she laid her cheek on the rough hair on his chest and dampened it with tears.

His muscles tensed as he felt the moisture on his skin. 'You are crying? We did nothing to cause you distress,' he protested sharply.

Genevra swallowed convulsively and tightened the hold of her arm about him. 'My husband, forgive me but they are tears of gratitude for a joy I did not expect,' she said, the catch in her voice plain for him to hear.

The steady beat of his heart beneath her cheek quickened. She felt the touch of his hand on her tangled hair. When he replied his voice sounded somewhat strangled and his chest heaved with suppressed laughter. His arm drew her closer. 'Then all is well, my little nun.'

He was laughing at her, but in her euphoria Genevra did not care. 'I was never a nun!' she protested with mock indignation, then chuckled, matching his light-hearted banter with her own. Her breath warm on the damp, matted hair of his chest, 'I never did feel called to the celibate life,' she divulged.

\*     \*     \*

Two days later the messenger returned from Thirkall. He
had been gone a month and a day. They were all in the
Hall after dinner when he arrived to drop to his knees to
deliver the missive into Robert's own hand. Robert did
not break the seal at once, but mounted the stairs to the
privacy of the solar.

Genevra watched him go, a slight frown between her
grey-green eyes. She wondered whether to follow, but
decided that it would be wiser to allow him to peruse
the contents alone, as appeared to be his intention. He
would tell her his mother's response when it suited him.
Meanwhile, she and Meg had an old tapestry to mend.
A quietly blooming, contented Meg, enjoying her new
status as Bernard's wife.

The hounds had remained in the Hall with her, too
sated with food to bother to follow their master. She
hoped that Robert did not mind that they had transferred
some of their affection to her. He had told them early
on that she was their mistress and they were to guard
her when he was not there.

She thought they had understood because, when he
was absent, they attached themselves to her and growled
when anyone they did not recognise came near, which
was often at first, because they did not know the castle
servants or the mercenaries who comprised the garrison.
She had become stupidly fond of both animals.

When Robert returned to the Hall, she glanced up from
her work. It was often difficult to gauge his reaction from
his expression but, normally austere, it was now lightened
by a slight smile. She hadn't realised how tense she had
been until she felt her nerves relax.

He seemed in no hurry. He delayed to answer questions
and direct several of the servants working about the place
before he came over to her.

'The news is good, lord?'

He sat on a stool at her side and passed the letter to her. 'My mother is overjoyed that I have wed again at last. She and my sister, Alida, send their congratulations and wish us every happiness.' His hand fondled Abel's ears as the dog put its nose on his knee. 'Read it, my lady. They look forward to meeting you when we return to Thirkall. They particularly wish to welcome the new Lady St Aubin into the family.'

He still tended to be very formal with her before others. Only occasionally did he forget himself and make some personal remark or address her by her given name. But Genevra could now hug to herself the knowledge of the intimacy they shared in the seclusion of their bed.

'I am glad,' she responded quietly, reading the letter. The tone, to her, lacked warmth but Robert appeared satisfied. She looked up. 'Should I write to them? To thank them for their wishes?'

'Aye, do so. There are a couple of business matters I must deal with. The letters may go together. I shall send my master of the horse back with them. He will be of more use in the stables there, and I now have Bernard here to take his place. You will have no objection to my promoting your groom to be in charge of the stables while we remain here?'

'Nay, lord! Meg will be delighted.'

'Good. The other man will be happy to rejoin his family at Thirkall.'

Genevra nodded affably. 'I shall write to your mother and sister in the morning,' she promised.

Meg was predictably delighted with Bernard's preferment, and told Robert so.

\*     \*     \*

The letters were dispatched the next day and the easy, pleasant life at Merlinscrag continued to keep Genevra amused by day. Only sometimes did Robert's reserve, verging on indifference, pique her. Especially on those occasions when he chose to go off hunting on Exmoor with only his squires and a few men-at-arms for company. She swallowed her disappointment at being excluded from his more physically demanding pleasures, believing patience to be her best ally.

The nights, however, made up for all else. Robert's ardour did not diminish. Her own ability to respond, encouraged and fed, amazed her. She looked upon the curtained bed as a place of contentment and joy. Most often, now, they fell asleep in each other's arms.

Two further weeks passed. They were standing in the bustling yard, preparing to mount, taking the hounds and falcons hunting with them, when the horn blew from the gatehouse, announcing the imminent arrival of a messenger. He wore the St Aubin badge on his arm.

He brought his pouch across the instant he had dismounted from his lathered horse and dropped to one knee in the mire.

'Ask in the Hall for a mug of ale,' Robert said, taking the pouch and dismissing the man. 'See that the horse is fed and watered,' he reminded Bernard.

Only then did he open the bag, take out the parchment and break the seal. Horses stamped and shook their harnesses, pigs grunted, chickens clucked. As he read, a deep frown of concern drew his fair brows together.

''Tis from my sister,' he said at last. 'Written by a clerk, of course, because she cannot see, but signed by her. She learned to write before her accident and can still form her name if her hand is guided to the right spot.'

All disturbing sounds had faded to nothing, for Genevra had no attention to give to anything or anyone but him. She had no real need to ask. His expression said it all. Nevertheless, 'It is bad news? she enquired.

He crumpled the parchment in his hand. 'Not good. My mother has been taken ill and is asking for me. I must needs go.'

'Of course,' said Genevra. 'Shall I accompany you?'

'Nay, wife, I shall travel hard. When I take you to Thirkall, we shall enjoy a leisurely journey there.'

He turned to his men to issue orders, sharp and fast as a flight of arrows. An escort to prepare and be provisioned, the fastest horses to be saddled, no sumpter animals, everything to be carried in their saddlebags. Then, with Genevra following, running, behind, he strode to the steps and up them to the Hall, where he sought out the exhausted messenger.

'The lady Alida informs me that the Lady our mother has been taken ill, although she gives no details. You were told to make all speed?'

The man had risen to his feet from the bench where he sat and now dropped to his knees, his eyes on Robert's cordwain boots. 'I was told to hurry, lord, by the sergeant-at-arms. I know nothing of the Lady. I am just an archer, lord. You must know that neither the Lady nor the lady Alida take their meals in the Hall. I have not set eyes on either lady recently, lord.'

'But there were no rumours of Lady St Aubin's sudden sickness running through the castle?'

'Not that I heard, lord.'

'Sir Drogo is at Thirkall?'

'Aye, lord, some of the time. He takes your place at the High Table when he is there.'

Robert grunted. He would. And haunt Thirkall rather

than reside at his knight's fief three leagues thence. 'Very
well. Bide here to rest for a day and then make your way
back at normal speed. There is no need for undue haste
on your part.'

When the man raised his weatherbeaten face, his eyes
held relief. The messenger was not to be beaten for bringing bad news. 'It shall be as you command, my lord.'

Robert took the stairs to the solar two at a time, followed by Alan and the lad Robin. Genevra trailed behind
more slowly. By the time she arrived, all three had disappeared into the garderobe. There, she discovered,
Robert was changing into serviceable riding wear which
included his padded gambeson. He did not intend to don
his mail.

'Armour would slow me down. I shall have an
adequate escort, my lady. Do not concern yourself over
my safety. I cannot say when I shall be free to return. It
must depend upon the state of my mother's health.' He
frowned again. 'It puzzles me that word of the Lady's
sickness had not spread to the barracks. By the way, you
have probably realised that my mother is always referred
to simply as "the Lady",' he said as an aside. 'However,
the mystery will not be solved unless I go and unravel it.'

'Of course, lord. How long will the journey take?'

'I shall not ride Prince, for I shall hope to find frequent
changes of horses. That way it will take ten days, mayhap.
The messenger did the journey in that time, travelling
some seventeen leagues on most days. If we cannot
change the horses it will take almost twice as long, unless
I wish to kill the beasts. Alida's summons was made on
behalf of my lady mother.'

He frowned slightly. 'It is odd that she did not write
herself. She cannot be that ill. However, mayhap she did

not wish to trouble me. But it seems that she would appreciate my presence.'

'Then of course you must go to her.' Genevra hesitated. 'It is possible that you will be away for two months.' She hid her dismay at this conclusion under a show of practicality. 'With the help of those in charge of the household, the domain and the garrison, I shall prove to you, my lord, that I can run and defend this castle in your absence just as you would wish.'

With a hand in the small of her back, he hurried her through to the solar and let the skin covering the doorway drop behind him, isolating them from his attendants. As though he could not help himself, he took both her hands in his.

'I do not wish to leave, wife, especially as you are not yet fruitful, but I must.'

'It is possible that I have already conceived, Robert. I shall know before you return.'

He rewarded her optimism with a wry smile. 'I pray that it is so. As for the rest, I have no doubt of your ability to manage and to hold this place even without the help of officials who have undoubtedly already proved themselves both competent and trustworthy. I have no qualms about leaving on that score.'

He lifted her hands and kissed the knuckles of both, in turn. 'Wife, I am leaving Alan here as captain of half of the men of my personal escort. They will accompany you wherever you wish to go. I charge you not to venture out without them.'

Genevra frowned. The precaution seemed overprotective. 'You think that necessary, Robert?'

'I shall feel happier knowing it to be so. Robin comes with me. I believe both squires will be happy with the arrangement.'

'Oh, Robert! I shall miss you so!' Genevra could not stop the cry of distress which escaped her at the thought of losing him for so long. Her grey-green eyes swam with tears she refused to shed.

Robert drew a sharp breath. The vivid blue of his gaze darkened. He dropped her hands and took her by the shoulders instead, drawing her close, his fingers gripping painfully tight. 'I shall miss you, too, Genevra,' he admitted gruffly, reluctantly. 'Have no doubt that I shall return as swiftly as possible.'

His kiss was hard, possessive, but his lips did not linger. 'I must be gone,' he said, releasing her so suddenly that she almost fell. 'God's blessings be with you, my wife.'

Genevra, recovering a precarious balance, whispered, 'And with you, my dear husband.'

Then it was time to join the hurriedly assembled escort, make their public farewells and speed St Aubin on his way with a hurriedly prepared stirrup cup.

She climbed to the top of the Hall steps to watch the party gallop off, following the cloud of yellow dust, raised by flying hoofs from clay hardened by sun and recent lack of rain, for as long as it remained in view. She wished he had not had to go away. Particularly as she could not know for another week or so whether she was breeding or not.

With a deep sigh, she turned to re-enter the Hall. Alan and the dogs, also left behind, trudged after her. She turned to the squire with a rueful smile.

'I am sorry, Alan. Remaining to look after me must be a sore trial to you.'

His youthful, honest face crumpled into a wry grimace. 'Well, my lady, I cannot deny that I would rather ride with my lord. But I have been given command of half the men-at-arms of the escort, in their captain's absence, so I have some compensation. Besides,' he added with belated but genuine courtesy, 'how could I regret being responsible for your safety, my lady? You must know how much I admire you and long to serve you.'

That night, lonely in the huge bed, Genevra slept fitfully. In her dream, she thought she had lost Robert. She searched the castle, struggled up steep stairs, penetrated unknown, dark and forbidding passages, became caught in the heat of hellish furnaces over which the cook presided with a huge trident, stumbled among horses with stamping hooves and gleaming teeth—but he was nowhere to be found.

In desperation, she ran to seek the postern in the inner wall, which led to the cliff. It looked strange and refused to open. She struggled. Then, somehow, she was outside and running for the edge of the cliff. She stood there, as she had once before in her dreams, watching the foam boiling around the rocks below. And, as once before, when she turned she saw the Golden Eagle watching her.

'Robert!'

Whether she cried his name aloud or not she did not know. But as his image dissolved she woke, sweating.

Two days later the gate-ward's horn warned of the approach of a group of horsemen. Their horses' liveries suggested a man of some consequence was about to demand entry to Merlinscrag.

Genevra watched from the solar window as the party trotted up. She did not recognise the livery colours or the badge on the flying pennon, but the knight being escorted, even though by only four men-at-arms, a servant and the Herald, rode a lavishly caparisoned horse of some value and was himself clothed in a brilliant scarlet tunic beneath a short white mantle. A scarlet cap sat on his head, covering his hair. When the sun showed itself between the scudding clouds, he positively blazed with costly splendour.

They stopped before the barbican. The Herald announced his master and the gate-ward answered. Genevra had no way of knowing what was said. But Captain Nori, escorted by several men of his garrison on foot running behind, rode out to greet the travellers.

After a short exchange he, personally, escorted the knight across the moat and through the gatehouse. So the knight had been allowed entry. Nori was already leading him up the hill toward the inner bailey and the Hall. He must consider him a friend, and no threat.

She would have to go down and greet the man, whose gorgeous apparel made her feel like a drab sparrow in her old grey gown.

'Meg! We have a visitor! Find me something more suitable to wear.'

Meg was mending a rent in her riding gown. She put aside the work and rose, giving Genevra a questioning look. 'Who is it, my duck?'

'I have no idea, but Captain Nori has admitted him and his men so it must be all right. I cannot go down to offer him hospitality dressed for the nunnery.'

'Indeed not, and you Lady St Aubin now!' Meg brought out one of the new gowns she had sewn for Genevra since their arrival at Merlinscrag. His lordship had sent to Barnstaple for the lengths of silk. 'Will this do?'

The kirtle was of thin sarcenet, its colour that of primroses. A sideless surcoat of amber samite had been fashioned to go over it, with jewelled buttons to fasten it down the front.

'Yes. Quickly, Meg. I am anxious to discover who it is. A young man, I think. A knight.'

Meg helped her to change and then replaced her simple veil with a wired head-dress fashioned from gauze. It hid her hair completely and showed off the smoothness of her high brow. Excited colour glowed in her cheeks. He was their first guest and she must welcome him alone.

'You'll do, my love.'

As Meg spoke one of Robert's pages tapped on the door and entered at her word.

'Sir Steward sends his compliments, my lady. He wishes to know whether you will receive Sir Drogo St Aubin.'

'Sir Drogo?' murmured Genevra faintly. 'His lordship's brother?'

'Aye, my lady.'

She could not expect the boy to know what Robert's brother was doing here. She must discover that for herself.

'I will come down,' she told the page. She would rather receive him in the Hall than in her private solar. Brother-in-law or not, he was a stranger to her.

There was, she thought, something odd about this sudden, unannounced visit.

# *Chapter Eight*

$\mathcal{G}$

Drogo St Aubin, judging by his neatly trimmed beard, was fair like his brother, with the same blue eyes but lighter, tending to grey. His hair, revealed when he doffed his cap to her, proved to be of a similar shade to Robert's, but wavy whereas Robert's was straight. He had missed his brother's beak of a nose and Genevra supposed that many would think the younger man—he must be some five years Robert's junior—more handsome, especially as his features lacked the hard definition, the stamp of authority, Robert's had gained over his years of campaigning.

The knight's greeting was impeccable in its courtliness. But his eyes held a questing look bordering on insolence when they met hers, and quickly slid away from her own frank gaze. She much preferred the lines of character written on Robert's face to the soft fleshiness which characterised his brother's, the line of whose jaw was obscured by his beard; but the growth could not disguise the pouch of an incipient double chin. As for Sir Drogo's mouth, it was bowed and vividly pink. Robert's was wide, well-shaped and firm. When Robert smiled her insides melted. Drogo's smile made her stomach muscles clench. She did not trust it.

The two, she had already discovered, were as unlike in character as possible. Drogo paid scutage rather than endure the discomforts demanded of a knight rendering his sworn service on campaign, whereas Robert had spent long years abroad, living and fighting hard. Yet it was easy to see that they were brothers. The differences in appearance were subtle, but to her they cried aloud.

He might be Robert's brother, but she did not like him.

It was pure instinct. Robert had never spoken a word against his brother although his reserve had deepened at mention of Sir Drogo's name. Cain and Abel did not like him, either. They bristled and growled at his approach and she had to quiet them.

'Stupid animals,' Drogo drawled carelessly, aiming a vicious kick in Abel's direction which mercifully did not land. 'I do so dislike dogs.'

'Mayhap, sir, they sense it,' replied Genevra, stroking Abel's head to soothe and reassure him.

As for Genevra, although she entertained him with all the ceremony and courtesy demanded, she sensed in her bones that Sir Drogo's visit boded ill.

When Sir Drogo was seated with a flagon of ale and a mug before him, Genevra picked up her needlework. It was something to occupy her hands and an excuse to avoid his gaze.

'I regret that my husband was not here to greet you. You bring news of your mother, mayhap?' she enquired.

'Lady St Aubin? No, why do you ask?'

'The lady Alida, your sister, sent a message to say that your lady mother was ill and wishing to see Lord St Aubin. You knew nothing of this?'

Her eyes still ostensibly lowered to her work, she watched his face from beneath her lashes. Just the merset flicker of a satisfied smile touched his mouth.

'No, nothing, sister. I was hoping to be welcomed by my brother and formally introduced to his charming wife. Since he chose not to inform his family of his nuptials I, like my mother and sister, was unable to attend the ceremony. I made haste to come to offer my felicitations on the happy event.'

'The messenger,' said Genevra carefully, 'mentioned that you spent much time at Thirkall during his lordship's absence. It seems strange that you heard nothing of your mother's sickness.'

Drogo waved a careless hand, long-fingered like his brother's but free of the calluses and scarring caused by active soldiering. 'It was probably a ruse, my dear lady, a ruse to bring her son to her side. My mother was upset not to be informed of St Aubin's marriage before it happened.'

Genevra could understand that, but the message of congratulation her mother-in-law had sent, though somewhat formal, had set her fears at rest. No, Sir Drogo's explanation did not ring true. The lady Alida had signed the letter. Robert had not questioned it for one moment. And, she knew, he loved and trusted his sister implicitly.

'When were you last at Thirkall?' she asked.

'Oh,' he said airily, 'a month since, I believe. I have made several visits to friends on the way here. This castle is, after all, at the very edge of civilization.'

'Prince Edward holds several castles in Cornwall,' pointed out Genevra mildly. 'They are even further west.'

'But he takes little interest in them. He takes little interest in anything these days.' He could not quite hide the satisfaction in his voice. 'I hear he is sick unto death. And the King is senile, pandering to that whore Alice Perrers.'

He smoothed the scarlet silk of his short tunic over his thigh in an affected gesture which irritated Genevra. The white brocade mantle in which he'd arrived was carefully hung on an empty perch. 'Small wonder that my dull but esteemed brother decided to retire from the lists, so to speak. There is no longer a cause even he could consider it worth fighting for.'

Genevra did not intend to defend Robert to his clearly critical brother. She thought it wiser to say nothing.

'More ale, Sir Drogo? she asked instead.

At his nod, she motioned a servant to fill his cup. His man had already been taken to the guest house, a long, low building near Martin's house, nestling under the inner curtain wall next the postern her dream had taken her through again last night, she remembered, and shivered.

Drogo drained his cup. 'When did my esteemed brother depart for Thirkall?' he asked.

Genevra stood up. She had no wish to prolong the interview with her brother-in-law. She needed time to adjust to his presence, to rationalise the feeling of disquiet his arrival had roused in her. The hounds rose too, to station themselves at her heels.

'Two days since.' She forced a hospitable smile. 'The evening meal will be served in an hour, Sir Drogo. Mayhap you would like to retire to your chamber, meanwhile? Your manservant and baggage are already there.'

With studied elegance, Drogo rose to his feet, jangling his golden spurs as he did so. Robert's spurs rang when he wore them, but Drogo's reminder of his achievement in being dubbed knight had been deliberate.

He addressed the groom of the bedchambers deputed to escort him. 'Bring my cloak.'

The man obeyed the imperious command with an expressionless face.

Genevra, full of grave misgivings, watched Drogo leave the Hall. She wondered how long he intended to stay. With Robert absent, there was surely no need for him to lie at Merlinscrag for more than one night.

Genevra's hope that Drogo would soon depart was doomed to disappointment. She could not, without appearing rude and inhospitable, ask him to leave. And as day succeeded day, she began to think that he intended to await his brother's return.

'Twould not have been so bad had he not set himself to charm her. He sought her company at the slightest excuse and invited her to ride and hunt with him, though she always refused, riding, if she wanted, while he was away.

He asked innumerable questions about herself and Merlinscrag, which she answered as briefly as possible, challenged her to games of chess, which she took care to lose, subjected her to a barrage of sentimental songs sung in a light tenor voice accompanied by a lute fashioned from ebony and ivory, and allowed her to deduce that he found her attractions overwhelming. And that, if he could, he would seduce her.

'What can I do, Meg?' she asked in exasperation after a week of this treatment. 'I dislike him intensely, yet I cannot be rude to him, for Lord St Aubin's sake.'

'He is maybe jealous of his brother, my duck. My Bernard has been talking to some of the men-at-arms. There's rivalry there, your lord's men think Sir Drogo resents being the youngest son. Wants the barony for himself.'

'So he is trying to ingratiate himself with me to

annoy his brother? But Robert is not here!'

'True, my duck, but he'll know, the servants will talk. Not that ours like his. Young Alan has a task on his hands keeping the men of the two escorts from coming to blows. And his are making a nuisance of themselves, riding all over the manor without regard to the welfare of animals or people.'

'Really? Oh, Meg, I didn't know!'

'Don't go anywhere without your escort, my duck. I wouldn't trust that other lot as far as I could throw them. Neither does Alan, and Lord Robert left your safety in his hands. You know he sleeps outside your door at night and has men stationed at the top of the stairs?'

'No.' Genevra frowned. She did not much like the look of Drogo's men, either. For Drogo to attempt to seduce her himself was one thing. But she could not believe that he would allow his men to harm her.

'We are probably imagining things, Meg. But I will be careful. Mayhap it is as well the dogs follow me about and share the bed with me while Lord Robert is absent! And you have moved your truckle in here. Poor Alan!' She sighed, not for the first time recently. 'If only Robert had not had to go!'

'Alan is a capable lad and would guard you with his life. He bids fair to make you the object of his unrequited, courtly love! But he knows more about that Sir Drogo than we do and he is concerned. Pray that your lord returns quickly!'

'He can scarce be back under three weeks,' lamented Genevra. 'Longer an he wishes to spend time with his mother.'

Her tone sounded so dispirited that Meg sought to cheer her up. 'Time will soon pass, my duck. And Sir Drogo does exert himself to entertain you!'

'But I have no wish to play chess with him or to listen to his songs, let alone sing duets with him! And I know he carouses with his men after I have retired.'

'If they all become incapable, they cannot do much harm.'

Meg's shrewdness always astonished Genevra. 'True.' She grinned. 'I shall not begrudge them the ale in future, an it renders them harmless!'

But not so harmless that Alan felt he could sleep easy in his bed.

Somehow the time passed, a succession of hot, airless days punctuated by storms when the sky blackened, the lightening flashed and the thunder cracked and rumbled, frightening the animals so that even Cain and Abel cowered beneath a table.

But, since the first week in July, Genevra had gone about her busy days hugging a new secret to her bosom. Only Meg shared it with her. She had missed her flux and must be breeding at last.

Drogo had been at Merlinscrag now for three endless weeks. Alan was out in the bailey with his men practising archery at the butts. Drogo had gone hunting with his escort; she had seen the party leave. Meg had gone, with Genevra's permission, to seek her husband. Everyone else was occupied about the place, including Annys, who was near her time and needed to rest.

Genevra was glad to snatch a few moments alone. Life generally was lived in such a close communal fashion that most people felt lost without company, but Genevra had learned the joys of solitude and silence in the nunnery and valued the moments she could spend by herself.

Especially today, when she intended to investigate the

contents of her mother's box. Martin had found it for
her, hidden in the loft above the solar, which had a
boarded ceiling closing off the space below the rafters,
except for a trap which could be opened to allow smoke
from the brazier to escape.

'The lady Margaret had the ceiling put in, my lady, to
stop some of the draughts,' Martin had explained. 'I do
not know what is up there, if anything. The trap door is
reached with a ladder. I will fetch one and see what I
can find.'

He had discovered cobwebs and the dusty coffer,
exquisitely carved, in which Genevra had already found
the missing statue of the Virgin. She had placed it in its
niche above the prie-dieu and had just begun to look at
the rest of the contents, when her chamber door was
unceremoniously opened.

A low growl from Abel, lying with Cain in a pool of
shadow behind a large chest, warned her. Instinctively,
she closed the lid of the coffer as she turned to see who
had come. Her heart leapt into her throat.

'Sir Drogo!' She lowered the tone of her voice with
a conscious effort. 'What are you thinking of, to enter
my solar without invitation?'

His smile sent shivers down her spine. He stepped
closer. He wasn't drunk but he had been drinking, despite
the early hour. Genevra retreated and found herself
stopped by the raised platform surrounding the bed. She
put out a hand to support herself on the post. Her legs
were trembling so much she thought she might fall.

'But you would not have invited me, would you, my
dear sister? You have been treating me as an interloper
ever since my arrival. Do not think I have not noticed
your attitude. Your ill-concealed distaste for my company
has made me very angry. What has my dear brother

told you to make you so wary of me, eh?'

Genevra tried to answer firmly. 'Nothing,' she asserted truthfully. 'He has said nothing to make me distrust you, sir.'

'More fool he!'

'He did not have to, sir! Your own attitude and actions have been cause enough!'

'I doubt my brother is worthy of such praiseworthy fidelity, my lady. He will not be so abstemious, take my word. He will think nothing of entertaining some tavern wench in his bed at night.' He grinned maliciously at her look of shock and took another step towards her.

Then, suddenly, his expression changed. Genevra gasped at the menace she saw in his face. 'You will dismiss your bodyguard tonight, my fine lady, and allow me to pleasure you in ways of which your husband is incapable.'

Genevra felt sick. 'No,' she said.

'Why not, my dear?' He had become ingratiating again. 'His first wife, the unfortunate Jane, preferred me to him. Did he not tell you?'

'No,' said Genevra again. She was trembling in every limb, but pushed herself from the bedpost, refusing to be intimidated. What was he implying?

Drogo's feverish eyes dismissed her defiance as of no account. 'You have played the cool temptress for too long, my lady. Why should I wait to make you melt in my heat? An you will not come to me willingly I must force you. I shall take you now, while we are alone.'

He had never intended to wait. She knew it with sick certainty. And he had chosen his moment well. She must do something! But he was on her before she could move, had forced her up the step and toppled her back over the bed, his hand scrabbling at her skirt.

'No!' This time she shrieked.

The dogs, used to her tolerance of Drogo's presence, had remained passive but alert. The panic in her voice, the waves of fear emanating from her body, roused them instantly to her defence. They leapt at Drogo as one, snapping and snarling, teeth bared. Their jaws snapped shut on the cloth of his cotte-hardie and between them dragged him off her. He rolled on the floor, desperately seeking to throw off the grip of the sharp fangs, cursing foully, struggling to reach his knife, the only weapon he carried. Cain had hold of the arm he had used to defend his throat, Abel's teeth were sunk into the padded shoulder of his cotte-hardie, but his right arm was free.

Genevra, coming out of her trance of fear, saw what he intended. With the knife in his hand he could kill the dogs. She leapt forward, avoiding his kicking legs, and reached between the heaving, furry bodies and snatched the knife from its sheath.

She held it like a dagger and stood over him. 'Let go,' she ordered the dogs. 'On guard!'

They crouched, one each side of him, panting and growling.

'Remain exactly where you are, *brother*,' instructed Genevra, breathless but grimly triumphant, and reinforced her order to the snarling dogs. 'Cain, Abel, on guard!'

She backed away to the table where Robert worked, under the window. He kept a hunting horn there. She picked it up, her eyes never leaving Drogo. He was nursing the arm Cain had sunk his teeth into. The hound had drawn blood but he was not badly hurt, though his clothes were torn and dishevelled. His face radiated frustration, anger, hate.

'A murrain on you and your filthy animals,' he snarled.

'You must know that they are Robert's hounds,' Genevra said. 'He left them to guard me.'

'Like that lapdog, Alan of Harden! He could not have stopped me had I chosen to challenge him. I could deal with that whelp with one hand tied behind my back!'

'Mayhap I should let you try it!' retorted Genevra grimly.

He made a move to get to his feet. The dogs snarled and snapped at him, making little threatening movements.

'Do you wish me to set them on you again?' demanded Genevra. He subsided back to the rushes.

'Stay!' she ordered the dogs.

Then she turned to glance out of the window. Alan and the escort, together with Captain Nori and the men of the garrison, had gathered by the entrance to the inner ward, mustering for some exercise. Breathing a silent prayer of thanks, she sounded several urgent blasts of the horn out of the open window.

That should bring help.


Captain Nori placed Drogo under guard in the barracks, where the punctures in his arm made by Cain's fangs were treated and bandaged. The wound was trifling.

The moment Drogo's men returned from their diversionary hunt, he and they would be ejected from the castle. His servant, they discovered, had left the castle on Drogo's horse and wearing his cap and white mantle. The ruse had worked well. Believing him out hunting, they had all lowered their guards.

'My poor duck!' cried Meg when told the story.

Alan, already pale with shock, turned shades whiter and fell to his knees.

'How can you ever forgive me, my lady? I failed in my duty to protect you!'

'None of us expected Sir Drogo to resort to such a trick,' said Genevra soothingly. Her hands still shook as she raised him to his feet. 'We all thought him out with the hunting party. I feared one of his men might attack me, but not my brother-in-law!'

'I should have been warned.' Alan shook his head. 'I knew there was bad blood between my lord and Sir Drogo, but I did not know why. If what Sir Drogo claimed is true, 'tis no wonder my poor lord holds him in such aversion and has been so wary of committing himself to another marriage—until he met you, my lady. But it all happened before I came into Lord Robert's service and I never discovered the details.'

'It may not be true,' said Genevra. 'Drogo may simply have been boasting.'

But if it were, it did explain so much about her husband that had puzzled her.

'He will trouble you no more, my lady,' promised Alan. 'Captain Nori and his men-at-arms are prepared to expel Sir Drogo's men by force if necessary. But if we hold Sir Drogo until they are outside the castle walls before we allow him to join them, they will not dare to oppose Nori.'

'I hope they will not wreak vengeance on the villagers as they depart,' Genevra worried.

'We shall be prepared,' was all that Alan grimly replied.

'And we shall not leave you alone again until they are well gone!' cried Annys, who felt as shocked and guilty as the others.

'You must rest, Annys,' said Meg severely. 'You may lie on my truckle while you are here in the solar.'

Soon afterwards, the bell sounded to call everyone to dinner. Genevra knew she would be unable to eat, but it was her duty to show herself at the High Table, calm and unharmed. A watch was being kept for the returning hunters but, since they had taken bread and wineskins with them, they were not expected to return for the meal.

In the event it was mid-afternoon before the deep note of the tocsin rang the alarm. Drogo's men appeared bemused to approach a barbican bristling with arrows and to be admitted only to recover their possessions before leaving again.

'You wish *il signore* to live?' enquired Nori in his most chilling voice. 'Then leave your horses and weapons here, pack your saddlebags and return immediately. You understand?'

His Italian accent and fierce black beard added to his deliberate air of menace. Despite the odd curse and a few defiant gestures, Drogo's men obeyed. After all, they were greatly outnumbered.

Some time later they returned sullenly, under guard, to await Drogo's arrival. They would leave first. When they were safely outside the castle, he would be allowed to follow.

It was while Drogo and his servant were being mounted in the inner courtyard that the horn sounded from the gatehouse. Genevra, watching the departure from the steps of the Hall, strained her eyes to see who was approaching. At first she could not make out who the newcomers might be, only that they were much nearer than she would have expected and approaching at a gallop, as though the furies were after them.

Then she caught a flash of green and mulberry red amongst the glint of steel helmets.

'Robert!' she whispered.

Joy and relief surged up in her and then fear washed

over her as though someone had doused her in a bucket of cold water.

The brothers would meet, probably by the gatehouse, for Alan would not allow Drogo to leave now. She picked up her skirts and began to run.

The soldier leading Drogo hesitated as the distinctive sound of St Aubin's Herald's horn answered the watchman's. Drogo, wearing a fresh tunic under his mantle and showing no sign of discomfort from his wound, wrenched the horse's head round, snatching the headstall from the man's grip. His spurs dug savagely into his mount's flanks, drawing blood, sending the tired beast— the servant impersonating Drogo had ridden it quite hard—bounding forward.

Robert St Aubin, arriving at full speed at a castle in turmoil, was hurriedly appraised of the situation. He sat like a rock in his brother's path, mounted on a foam-flecked horse steaming with sweat. His men, on equally exhausted horses, formed a phalanx at his back.

Drogo's few men, menaced by archers with drawn bows, stood to one side with their mounts, waiting uneasily for their knight. The only sound came from the drumming of hooves as Drogo cantered down to confront his brother.

Genevra was still a hundred yards away when the two men met. Drogo drew his horse to a showy standstill, sitting easily in the saddle as the horse reared and neighed its protest.

Then Drogo laughed. It was not a pleasant sound, even from a distance. Genevra sped on, ignoring the stitch in her side, her gaze fixed on her husband's features. She had to admire Drogo's reckless courage in the face of Robert's grim, ferocious glare.

'What,' demanded Robert in a moderate roar, 'are you doing here, sir?'

Drogo doffed his hat and made a mocking bow. 'Why, my lord, entertaining your exquisite lady, what else? 'Tis simple to cuckold a man who so regularly absents himself from his wives' sides.'

Genevra was still yards away but Drogo's words fell on her ears like blows. She stopped, her chest heaving, and cried, 'No!' But barely a sound escaped.

Drogo wanted to taunt his brother, that much was clear. He sat now, apparently quite at ease, a malicious smile twisting his woman's mouth. 'I had thought to be gone before your return, brother,' he went on, since Robert appeared rendered speechless at his effrontery. 'It seems you found our mother in good health?'

Robert drew a deep breath. He glanced briefly in her direction, his eyes chips of blue ice that held no recognition. He had allowed his beard to grow while he'd been travelling. Like his eyebrows, it was lighter than his hair, she noticed inconsequentially. It changed his appearance. He had come back a stranger.

He spoke. 'As you well knew, Drogo, since you contrived the false message that drew me to her side. I expected to find you here.'

'And Alida?' queried Drogo smoothly. 'She, of course, will never be whole now, but I trust she is well despite her lack of sight?'

'You used her blindness,' accused Robert savagely. 'She did not know what she was signing. Another deceit I can never forgive, *brother*.'

Neither man wore mail and Drogo's scabbard was empty. Robert's sword scraped noisily as he drew it. His eyes fixed with murderous intensity on Drogo's, 'Give him his sword,' he ordered Alan, who hovered anxiously nearby holding the weapon, which he had intended to restore to its owner as he left Merlinscrag.

'You wish to fight? Gladly. On horseback or on foot?' drawled Drogo, eyeing Robert's blown horse with simulated amusement.

Robert slipped easily from his saddle, threw off his short cloak and stood, legs astride, sword in hand. 'On foot.'

Drogo dismounted, handed his exquisite mantle to his servant, who had ridden down the slope behind him at a more sedate pace, and exchanged his horse for his sword.

Did he really believe that he could fight Robert and win? wondered Genevra. He appeared tauntingly confident. She had never seen him indulge in swordplay, had no idea of the extent of his skill. And then she glimpsed the venom which was driving him to taunt and challenge a man he must know was his master with the sword.

Men tried to still their mounts, which moved restlessly on the edge of the arena they formed. Sounds of pecking hooves and jangling harnesses, the occasional word of command, a guffaw, quickly silenced, added to the tension. Genevra closed her eyes and prayed. She heard Robert's ringing challenge, answered by Drogo's reckless laugh. Then, at the first ring of steel on steel, she forced herself to look.

Meg had caught her up. She felt the supporting arm about her and gratefully leaned her weight on her panting friend.

'Robert is exhausted,' she whispered.

'But his brother is ill-conditioned.'

'He is strong.' Genevra remembered the muscle hidden beneath Drogo's flabbiness, the swordsman's strength she had surprised in his grasping fingers.

For a while Drogo seemed still to be taunting Robert,

dancing in circles around him, feinting and suddenly thrusting, only for his sword to be met by Robert's blocking steel. For Robert had a longer reach and, Genevra realised, a longer, heavier sword, well-used in battle, not one worn for show and self-defence, a sword of damascened steel.

Unlike Drogo's, which flashed with a brilliant, showy brightness, a brightness that could dazzle his opponent were it to flash in his eyes. But, gradually, inevitably, Robert was drawing Drogo into the shadow of the towering wall. He had been aware of the danger.

Genevra began to relax a little, for she realised that, although Drogo had acquired all the skills of a trained knight, he had allowed them, unlike his sword, to rust.

Then Robert was retreating further into the shadows under a sudden, frenzied attack by his opponent. Genevra gasped and crossed her arms before her, hugging herself for comfort against what she saw.

Alan had come to stand at her back. 'Do not worry,' came his calm voice in her ear. 'My lord is allowing Sir Drogo to tire himself out. See, he is breathless already. Lord Robert defends himself easily. When he is ready, he will attack and win. 'Tis how he fights in practice.'

It seemed to be so. Robert, calm and unflurried, continued to present an unbreakable defence, while Drogo's attack became ever more desperate. The smile had left his face, the bravado had gone from his manner. His lips were drawn back over his teeth. The venom which had lured him into the confrontation showed clearly as he began to realise that he could not prevail.

Yet he could not admit defeat.

'You will never kill me, brother!' he panted.

'You think not?' enquired Robert coolly. 'Think you that I will spare you again?'

His anger had been condensed into a practised, cool efficiency. Sweat ran down his face in rivulets, as it had done ever since he had charged furiously into the castle's bailey. But his breathing was even, his arm apparently tireless.

'Must Drogo die?' wondered Genevra. She could not believe that Robert would kill his own brother.

Alan confirmed her belief. 'Nay, lady. 'Twould cause their lady mother too much grief. Sir Drogo knows this. 'Tis why he felt able to risk provoking Lord Robert. Doubtless he fancied himself able to defeat him, since my lord is plainly exhausted.'

'He must be mad,' whispered Genevra. 'Would he have killed Robert an he could?'

'Oh, aye,' Alan spoke in a tone of deep disgust. 'He has no scruples, that one.'

Even as he spoke, it was over. No one, least of all Drogo, saw the final thrust coming. Drogo screamed and the sword dropped from his nerveless hand. Blood spread rapidly from a deep cut on his upper arm, soaking his sleeve.

Robert rested his weight on his sword, its point on the ground at his feet. He was breathing heavily now but the murderous look had long gone, to be replaced by tired contempt.

'You are a disgrace to the order of knighthood, Drogo. You deserve to die,' he told his brother wearily. Drogo was standing, clasping his arm in an attempt to stop the flow of blood, but it seeped through his fingers and dripped to the ground. His servant moved forward to support him.

'However, you are my brother,' Robert went on. 'I have no wish to distress our mother further. But be warned. Twice I have spared your worthless life. I shall

not do so again. Now.' His stance stiffened, his voice
rose. 'Leave Merlinscrag and never seek to return. You
will not be admitted. Any authority you may have
enjoyed at Thirkall has been cancelled. You will be
admitted only to visit our mother and sister.

'Neither will you be allowed to enter any of the other
castles and manors whose owners owe allegiance to the
St Aubin barony. Orders to that effect were dispatched
before I left Thirkall, for the clerk confessed to the trick
you bribed him to play on our sister. He is no longer at
Thirkall,' he observed grimly. He paused. A horse's bit
jangled in the silence that ensued. 'I believe that is all.'

Drogo made no answer. Defeat had momentarily subdued him, but the look in his eyes as he returned his
brother's glare was one of pure hatred.

'My lord!' exclaimed his servant. 'Sir Drogo cannot
ride. His arm must be attended to.'

'Then take him outside these walls and see to it. There
is a priest in the village who is skilled in healing. And
I doubt he has lost so much blood that he cannot sit a
horse. I care not where you rest this night, so long as it
is outside these walls.' His chilling gaze returned to
Drogo. 'By noon on the morrow you will have left these
lands, or you will be driven off. You hear me?'

Drogo raised a slight smile and spoke at last. 'I hear,
brother. But my memory will linger on here, will it not?
Your wife has been so very hospitable.' He turned a
mockingly intimate smile on a horrified Genevra, a smile
belied by the inimical stare of the pale blue eyes. 'Mayhap you should consult her wishes before you ban me
from her domain.'

Robert had only glanced at her the once. He did not
look now. Genevra made to move forward, to protest
that she wished never to set eyes on Drogo again,

but Robert spoke before she had the chance.

'My wife's opinion is irrelevant. Farewell, brother. I pray it may never be necessary for us to meet again.'

He wiped his sword on a tuft of grass to cleanse it of blood before sheathing it. His horse still stood nearby. Alan rushed forward to make a cradle of his hands to help him to mount. No question of his springing lightly into his saddle now. Exhaustion could be seen not only in his face but in his every move.

Drogo was lifted into his saddle. His silent retinue preceded him through the gatehouse, across the drawbridge and through the barbican. Someone had tied a scarf about his bleeding arm. He held the pommel with his good hand while his servant led the animal to follow them. He made no attempt at bravado now. Only when the barbican gate had been shut and barred behind him did Robert move.

He wheeled his horse and cantered it up the slope towards the Hall. Genevra, with Meg beside her, walked slowly behind.

He had not looked at her.

# *Chapter Nine*

Her stomach ached. Sickness threatened to engulf her. Genevra entered the solar, sank down on a cushioned chest and buried her face in shaking hands.

She had sent Meg away. She had to face Robert alone. At present he was still in the garderobe, changing, so she had a few moments more to gather her strength.

She could not *know* why he had refused to look at or greet her, but had an agonising suspicion that he had believed Drogo's insinuations.

Yet he had arrived at a time when Drogo was being ejected from Merlinscrag under guard! Was that not evidence enough that he lied?

In any case, Robert should not need proof of her innocence. How could he believe such a thing of her?

Dear Lord! The reason hit her suddenly. It must be because, according to Drogo himself, he had suffered such a betrayal by his first wife. With calculated cruelty, Drogo had opened an old and only partially healed wound.

The task of healing it seemed immense. She had to reassure Robert, to make him cast off, once and for all, the shadow of a past which had haunted their marriage from the first. Robert had never trusted her—was unable to trust her. She could see it now.

Alan and Robin came through first, Alan with an anxious and unhappy expression on his face. He murmured something inarticulate as he passed on his way to the Hall, compassion in his eyes, but he did not linger. She had heard the abrupt tones in which Robert had dismissed his squires. His servant scuttled through on their heels.

She felt a little less sick now that she had begun to understand the ghosts that haunted Robert's life, and the pain in her stomach had eased. But her muscles tensed and her heart pounded as she waited for her husband. So much depended on what she said and how she said it.

She had never seen his face so grim, so lined with weariness and disillusion. Her heart cried out with pity for, just before leaving for Thirkall, his demeanour had lightened, he had shown signs of regaining the carefree happiness he must have enjoyed in his youth. She had hoped he was beginning to trust and love her.

Drogo had destroyed all that.

'Well, wife,' he said, his voice flat.

Genevra struggled to her feet. It was difficult to find words, but she must. She clasped her hands together hard and swallowed.

'My lord, you cannot know how very glad I am to welcome you back to Merlinscrag.' His brows lifted as though in incredulity and she hurried on. Now she had started, the words flowed. 'Sir Drogo arrived with his retinue but two days after you left and oh! Robert, despite his being your brother, I disliked and mistrusted him from the first. He tried to flirt with me and I could not be discourteous to a guest, but I had no idea what his object was. Until this morning.'

Robert still did not speak. He stood, his arms folded across his chest, eyeing her coldly. Unbelievingly.

'His men caused trouble,' she went on quickly. 'Alan must have told you how he set a guard on the gallery outside this door?' He acknowledged this with a nod. 'And how I refused to ride out with Sir Drogo?'

This time he frowned as well as giving an abrupt nod. 'Aye.'

'Even so, I did not expect to be assaulted in broad daylight and it never occurred to me that Sir Drogo himself would. . .'

Her voice failed and she closed her eyes for a moment. Still Robert did not help her, still he said nothing.

She gathered her wits again and went on. 'But today, by a trick, he caught me alone and unguarded in here, and he did attack me. Luckily, Cain and Abel were in here with me. They were more than a match for him! They held him off until help arrived. Robert, they were so good!' She heaved a fresh breath. 'The rest you know. He was being ejected from Merlinscrag when you returned.'

His narrowed gaze pierced into her. 'He did not lie with you?'

'No, my lord husband. How could I voluntarily lie with him when it is you I love?'

Her declaration did not seem to penetrate the dark blanket of suspicion which enveloped him. He made a dismissive gesture. 'Mayhap he forced you.'

She shook her head and tried again to reach him.

'My lord, I had hoped the good news I have for you would please you. I believe I am with child.'

This struck home. He spun abruptly to turn his back.

'How can I be sure it is mine?'

Genevra's cry of horror brought him swinging back again.

His voice was harsh. 'You can prove to me that there was no moment during the first days when you could not have succumbed to my brother's undoubted charms?' he challenged. 'When his seed, not mine, could have quickened your womb? I have no doubt 'twas his aim in coming here.'

'An it was, he did not succeed, my lord!' Genevra choked back a sob. How could she convince him? Of course she had been alone on several occasions in the week before her courses were due. No one but she could swear that Drogo had not lain with her either here in the solar or in some other secret corner of the castle.

'You must believe me, husband,' she insisted, 'for your own sake as well as for mine and that of our unborn child. I would not lie to you. Sir Drogo repelled me.'

At Robert's look of disbelief she exclaimed, 'Oh, yes, he did! He tried to seduce me with languishing glances and pretty words, even with suggestive touches—' she closed her eyes as a shudder coursed through her at the memory '—but he failed!' she cried and flung her hands wide in a gesture of helpless appeal. 'Why else should he try to force me?'

'An he did.'

She tossed her head angrily. 'He did.' She drew a calming breath. 'But your hounds saved me. You should be thanking God, not accusing me of lying to you! You might well have had something to worry about had the dogs not been in the room. But even had Drogo succeeded in forcing me, although he could not know it, by that time I already knew I carried your child. The baby cannot possibly be any other man's but yours, Robert.'

She reached her hands out in appeal but he did not

take them. He said, 'Jane's child was his.' The words
sounded torn from his throat. 'I was out of the country
when my supposed heir was got.'

Genevra gasped. This was worse than she had believed
possible. How he must have been hurt! The instant compassion she felt must have shown on her face.

He moved impatiently, rejecting it. 'I do not desire
your pity, my lady. Only your fidelity.'

Now she glared at him again. 'Yet you refuse to believe
me when I tell you that you have it!'

'I know my brother,' he said bitterly. 'I know how
easily he can seduce women. I know how vindictive he
is. He would not easily be deflected from his purpose.'

Breathing as though she had been running, Genevra
walked up to him and put her hands against his chest.
'He did not seduce me, Robert. I swear it by the Holy
Virgin and will do so on the Holy Bible an you wish.
And even if he had succeeded in raping me this morning,
he would have failed in his intent to cheat you of your
rightful heir.'

With great deliberation, she repeated what she had
already told him, for he seemed unable to understand
what he heard. 'Your child was already growing in
my womb.'

She lifted her arms higher and clasped them about his
neck, pressing her body against the arms he still held
crossed over his chest. He had had no chance to bathe
properly, so the sweat was still on his body, and the odour
of horse—the smells she associated with her husband, her
beloved.

She closed her eyes as the wave of passion flowed
through her body, making it tremble. He was back. She
wanted to lie in his arms, to have him make love to her,
not stand there accusing her of unspeakable things.

'Robert!' she whispered, and drew his head down. His beard, a three-week growth, she presumed, was long enough for the hairs to have softened. They brushed seductively against her skin as her seeking lips touched his.

For a moment he resisted. Then, with a stifled curse that sounded almost like a groan, he gathered her into an iron-band embrace and kissed her. A punishing kiss that spent his frustration, anger and desire in an assault upon her mouth.

Genevra did not quail, although his teeth hurt and she tasted blood from a split lip. It did not matter. She met his passion with her own, fuelled by her desperation to convince him of her love and loyalty. Before the kiss ended, he had lifted her and carried her to the bed, which was just as well, because she had lost all use of her limbs.

His hands were rough, demanding, as he flung her skirts up. And then, without further preparation except to fumble with his own clothes, his weight descended on her and he was inside her.

The lack of his usual care and consideration roused a fierce, answering response from Genevra. It was a coupling that lacked tenderness, that feasted on unbridled passion and demanded more. The climax, when it came, took them both by storm.

Genevra came to herself and found she was crying. She was a little worried about the new life she was nurturing, for some held that coupling could harm the child, could cause a miscarriage, and on top of the traumas of earlier in the day she could not help but fear.

But her tears were not for that. Her tears were of happiness, for Robert had been unable to deny his need, had so completely surrendered to passion that she could no longer doubt that he desired her almost beyond reason.

And, despite everything, his possession had in no way been cruel. He had not beaten her or made her suffer the kind of indignities or depravities about which she had heard other women whisper.

The man she loved was a normal man, capable of great anger and passion, but free of vice. And so she wept.

Robert, coming to himself, wrung out physically and emotionally with all he had experienced and suffered over the last weeks, saw the tears.

An oath escaped his lips as he rolled aside. He had not meant to inflict physical pain. He believed her assertion of fidelity. How could he do otherwise, when she was such a transparently honest woman?

And yet, buried deep in his mind, there lingered a doubt.

He knew from experience how women would lie and cheat to escape the results of their own perfidy. Jane had tried, although her guilt was evidenced by time and by the witness of others.

Time. Had his unrestrained conduct harmed the child his wife claimed was in her belly? If 'twere indeed his, he could work out the latest it should be born.

But he would still not be certain, for Drogo had arrived at Merlinscrag a mere eight and forty hours after his own departure. Drogo had had time and opportunity to take his revenge for a former defeat at arms and for all the other jealousies and grievances stored up against him from the moment Drogo had realised that, being the younger son, he would inherit nothing of his father's holdings except a minor fief, that he would not become the baron.

Robert moved impatiently. A murrain on Drogo, who had soured his life for the past twenty years! It seemed that he would never be immune to his younger brother's vicious jealousy. He had thought he could never be hurt so deeply again as he had been by Jane's betrayal, but he had been wrong. If Genevra had betrayed him, his suffering would be beyond bearing.

Jane's death and that of her son had come as a relief. The choice between disowning the child or allowing his brother's bastard to inherit the barony had been a hard one. At a stroke, his problem had been solved. But, despite the distance he had so studiously kept between them, despite his determination to avoid emotional involvement, he would never recover from the loss of Genevra.

He did not seek to ask himself why.

For a moment, Robert almost hoped the child would miscarry. Drogo had foiled his attempt to ensure that any heir born would assuredly be his, by luring him from his wife's side. That would not happen again. Next time, come what may, he would watch over her until he knew his seed was safely planted in her belly.

Genevra's tears angered him. After all, she had provoked the storm of feeling which had resulted in that unbridled possession. She had brought any hurt upon herself.

He leaned over her. Her hair was still in its fret, but the net had become somewhat dislodged. He imagined the pleasure of running his fingers through the luxurious brown strands were he to release them. His anger increased. She held too much power over him. 'Dry your tears,' he rasped. 'Be thankful that I did not beat you.'

Genevra answered his harsh words with a wavering smile of such sweetness that his breath caught. His anger stood no chance against it.

'My tears are of happiness, husband.' Her voice was

as uncertain as her smile. 'Sir Drogo is gone, you are back with me again and we have renewed the intimacies of the marriage bed.'

His anger died; but she must not discover the power she had to move him. 'You are my wife. Whatever I may think of you, I have the right—'

Genevra reached up and touched his lips, silencing him, her eyes shimmering with love and tears. 'And the desire, lord. Do not deny the joy we give each to the other.'

He suddenly slumped, lowered his head and buried his face in her neck. 'I do not,' he groaned. 'I pray I have not harmed the baby.'

She stroked his golden hair, darkened at the roots with sweat. 'Nay, my husband. How could your possession harm me? But Meg, who is wise in these things, tells me that I should take care when riding, at least until the fifth month. 'Tis blows and twists and falls that might dislodge the baby. Unless, of course, 'tis not destined to live, and the Lord God wills a miscarriage.'

He lifted his head and gazed searchingly into her brilliant green eyes. 'You wish to bear this child, Genevra?'

'Oh, yes, Robert! Believe me, it is yours, it could not possibly be anyone else's, and I long to give you an heir. But most of all I long to hold your child in my arms.'

She did not repeat that she loved him and he did not remember her previous declaration. But he did believe her to be sincere.

Even so, he kept his voice steady and cool as he said, 'Then we shall do our utmost to see that it is safely born.'

It was still daylight. There was supper to face. The castle's inhabitants must be reassured. He rolled from the bed and began to straighten his clothes.

'Shall I call Meg for you?' he asked Genevra, who had made no effort to get up.

She pushed her skirts down, sat up, put her hands to her hair. And grimaced.

'Mayhap 'twould be wise.'

Robert forced one of his rare smiles. 'We must appear for supper to show that all is well. And I must confess that I am starving. I will send someone to find her.'

But even before he had left the solar, a tall, outwardly confident, golden knight, the doubts had returned.

He had lived with disillusion and distrust for too many years to slough them off so easily.

Genevra was sitting on the chest staring down absently at her still-trembling fingers when Meg entered the solar. She looked up as Meg gave an exclamation of dismay.

'My poor duck! What has he done to you?'

Although her lip was stiff and painful, the smile that illuminated Genevra's face instantly reassured her tiring-woman.

'Naught but what a man normally does to a woman.' She stood up to reach for her mirror. ''Tis only my hair, it needs tidying. And I need water and towel to wash.'

'Your lip is bleeding. If you go down to the Great Hall in that state, they'll think he's hit you. Or maybe forced you.'

There was enough of a question in Meg's voice to make Genevra shake her head. 'I was not forced, Meg. Rather the other way round.' She gave a secret smile as she touched her sore lip, inspecting the damage in the polished metal. 'I rather think I seduced him. Yet I do not think I quite managed to convince him that Drogo failed to have his way with me. Their enmity is longstanding and goes deep.'

She sighed, replacing the mirror on the table and frowning. 'Had he warned me, I should never have allowed Drogo within the walls. Meg, Drogo is truly evil. He cuckolded him with his first wife, gave him a bastard for an heir, and did his best to do the same with me.'

Meg gasped. 'And that is why they fought before?'

'It must be. So how can I blame my lord for suspecting the worst now? I did my best to convince him of my innocence, but I am not entirely sure I succeeded. He gave me one of those smiles of his, which do not reach his eyes.'

'My poor duck!' Meg put a comforting arm about her. 'I shall tell him he has nought to fear!'

'Nay, Meg, 'twould serve no purpose. You were not at my side every moment of every day. No one was. And if he cannot believe my word, then I must resign myself to his mistrust. 'Twill be hard to bear, but not impossible. And one day he must discover the truth.'

''Tis a mortal shame,' said Meg, bringing out a fresh gown for Genevra to change into. 'You were made for each other, my duck. That Drogo!'

If looks could have killed, Drogo would have dropped down dead wherever he was. Genevra shook her head as she smiled and stepped out of her crumpled gown.

'At least I do not think the lord Robert will treat me badly, Meg. Neither do I believe he will reject my presence at his side. He will, I think, ignore the incident. At least on the surface.'

'Wait until you give birth, my duck. That will cure him of his doubts!'

'I pray you may be right, Meg. But nine months is a long time to wait.'

''Twill soon pass, you'll see. And I have something to confess to you, my lady.' Meg had coloured and looked unusually nervous. 'I think I may be breeding, too.'

'Meg! But are you not too old?'

Meg laughed, albeit rather ruefully. 'I am not quite in my dotage yet, Mistress Genny!'

Genevra smiled guiltily. 'I'm sorry, Meg! But you've always been grown up to me!'

'All the same, you are right. I am old to have my first child. But Bernard is so delighted that I cannot regret taking the risk. We shall be delivered within days of each other, I shouldn't be surprised. My only regret is that I shall be in no condition to wait on you.'

Genevra donned her fresh gown and Meg began to lace her up at the back. 'Annys will be able to help and she will know of other women here who are experienced.'

'The old woman who brings herbs to the castle tells me she has successfully brought more babies into the world than she can count. She has delivered all of Annys's brood so far and will be present at the new baby's birth. I should like her to attend me.'

'I must meet her,' said Genevra thoughtfully. 'Mayhap she will help me, too.'

'An your lord will allow it. Some say she is a witch.'

Genevra twisted to eye Meg questioningly. 'But you do not think so?'

'Nay, lady, she has the gift of sight, or so she claims, and heals with her herbs. But there is nought of the devil about Old Mariel. But Lord St Aubin may wish to have a physician to attend you.'

'Where from?' asked Genevra with a shrug. 'I dare swear the nearest physician will be in Barnstaple, or even further afield. I shall be content to put myself in Old Mariel's hands, since she comes so well recommended.'

'There is one other thing, my duck. If you wished it, I may be able to wet nurse your baby as well as my own.'

Genevra had finished dressing and Meg was twisting her hair back into the caul. She put her hand on her breast. 'I had been thinking about that, Meg. I know ladies are not supposed to, but I should so like to give suck myself.'

She had no way of knowing whether a baby feeding from her breast would arouse similar sensations to those excited by Robert when he suckled her dry nipples. But she had watched many women feeding babies; the love and pleasure on their faces was unmistakable. She wanted to be close to her children, to love and succour them. What better way to begin than by supplying their milk herself?

'Well, my lady,' said Meg in a doubtful voice, for she was more jealous of her mistress's new dignity than Genevra herself, 'there will be those who will disapprove and say that only the lower orders suckle their own babies. Your breasts should be bound so that the milk will dry up.'

'What a waste, Meg! God must have intended all women to feed their own babies, otherwise he would not have provided them with the means!'

'True, my lady. But man does not always do what the Lord intended. And 'tis not the fashion for a lady like you to give suck.'

'Even so,' said Genevra with sudden resolution, 'I am determined to do so if I possibly can.'

'You'll have to see,' said Meg.

'Aye. I've time enough to make up my mind!'

'True, my duck. There—' giving Genevra's hair a final tweak '—you'll do now. I'll just put some salve on your lip.'

'It has stopped bleeding. I hope no one will notice.'

'You have no need to worry. You look well kissed,

and that's the truth, but maybe 'tis a good thing. An you both look cheerful at supper, harmful gossip will be stopped.'

'Aye,' agreed Genevra thoughtfully. The bell had rung to call the castle to supper a few moments earlier. Robert would be waiting for her at the foot of the stairs with his Herald to announce them and a page with water ready for the ceremonial washing of hands. Ceremony at Merlinscrag was slight, but some had to be observed for appearances' sake. From Martin down to the lowliest scullion, everyone expected it.

Her main emotion as she left the solar and trod down the stairs was one of immense relief that Drogo and his retinue had gone. She had hated sitting beside him at table and watching his men carouse down in the body of the Great Hall.

But the moment Robert extended his hand to take hers and escort her to her seat, all other considerations fled.

He was home and she was carrying his child. Happiness flooded through her as their hands met.

It was the next day before Genevra remembered the box Martin had brought down from the loft. Robert had not noticed it.

He'd shared the bed last night, coming up to join her when she was almost asleep, but had not made love to her again. This had disappointed her, but not as much as if he had decided to return to his pallet in the garderobe. At least she had had him beside her, even if he had been in uncommunicative mood.

He had gone out early, anxious to inspect the garrison and to check on how the steward and the bailiff had exercised their responsibilities in his absence. He would, she supposed, soon discover that she had ordered some changes in the running of the household.

She was alone. Even the dogs, her faithful friends over the last weeks, had deserted her to follow their master.

Now was therefore a good time to investigate the contents of the coffer further. The statue of the Virgin looked so at home in its niche. She had made her devotions before it last night and felt closer to her mother than she had for many years.

The coffer did not lock, but the domed lid fitted tightly. She prized it open with the small blunt knife Robert kept on the table for opening seals. She had not given its presence a thought when Drogo had attacked yesterday. His own knife had offered a far more accessible and effective weapon.

She thrust the unpleasant memory of Drogo aside as she removed the contents of the coffer and spread the papers on the table. Only then did she see the black velvet pouch that had been hidden beneath them.

She brought it out and weighed it in her hand. 'Twas not heavy but neither was it light. Her fingers fumbling in her eagerness, she drew the strings apart and emptied the contents on the table.

The glitter of gold and gemstones, in themselves, did not surprise her. Nor the presence of five golden coins, which she recognised as some of the first nobles struck, in the twenty-fourth year of the King's reign, the year 1351, when Margaret Heskith had left Court pregnant and she had been born.

She scrutinised the design, which incorporated a warship commemorating the victory at Sluys, and Edward's arms, which quartered the leopards of England with the lilies of France. The coins glinted up at Margaret's daughter, new and shining as brightly as that daughter's husband's hair.

Her mother's private hoard, secreted away in case of need.

If the presence of the jewellery did not surprise her, its quality did. The largest piece was a pendant, a locket on a chain, the gold elaborately chased and set as a flower, with a large rose diamond representing the bloom and small emeralds the leaves. Genevra gazed at it for a long time and then examined the gold rings, one a seal ring and the other set around with small diamonds flashing fire, both of which had also fallen from the bag. Excitement welled up in her.

A wedding band? Whose seal? And what would the fabulous locket reveal? She pressed the clasp and the two sides sprang apart.

It held a lock of hair. Dark hair, brown much like her own. Her mother's had been lighter, with chestnut glints, so it was not hers.

Her father's, then?

These were the first things Genevra had ever seen that might have belonged to or been handled by her father. The finger she touched to the lock of hair trembled. The strands were wiry, more likely a man's than a woman's.

She snapped the locket closed and studied it anew. It had been expensive. The donor had been rich, or been able to command credit from his goldsmith! The same with the diamond ring—a ring she had never seen her mother wear, but mayhap she had been too young to notice.

Genevra slipped it on a finger on her right hand. It almost fitted; it was only a shade too large. It felt much lighter than the heavy gold wedding band Robert had placed on her finger.

She regarded both rings and then lifted her own wedding ring to her lips and kissed it. She did not mind its weight—it served as a constant reminder that she was indeed wedded to the man she loved with an ever-deepening understanding and with an abiding passion. For that she should be eternally grateful.

She picked up the locket and fastened the chain round her neck. The stones flashed in the sunlight as she breathed and her breast rose and fell, but the surface of her copper mirror, although highly polished, dimmed the effect. She touched the pendant with her right hand and her mother's ring blazed fire.

She examined the heavy seal on the other ring. It was not a device she recognised, but it matched a small decoration on the reverse of the locket. She hadn't realised what that was at first, but now, with the help of the larger engraving on the seal ring, she saw that it was a spiked wheel, the rowel of a spur. A man's ring, then, a fact confirmed when she tried it on. It dropped off her forefinger.

She took the pendant and diamond ring off and replaced everything in the velvet pouch. Then she began to search through the papers.

Letters, mostly. Letters her mother had received at Court from family and friends. A copy of her letter of resignation. And one from the Queen, dated two years before that, appointing her as a demoiselle-in-waiting. She found an account from a costumier, another from a shoemaker. Her mother had purchased gloves, veils, frets woven of gold and silver and matching circlets for her hair. Perfumes, too. All while she had been at Court.

So far she had found no official document recording any marriage. The only place left to look was among the bundle of letters she had not yet read. She untied the pink ribbon holding the sheets of parchment together, and caught her breath as they scattered.

Every letter bore the rowel seal. Letters from her father!

Her excitement as she opened the first grew as she scanned it. The hand was educated, firm. They were love letters, letters written by a young man to the one he adored. At first he had simply signed himself 'A'. His later letters, written after Margaret had left Court and the lovers had parted for ever, though they were not to know that then, were signed, 'Your devoted husband, A.'

She read on. He had failed to persuade his father to allow them to marry and had been sent abroad. He railed against the fate that placed him in his father's power. His sire could take from him the fortune he would inherit at the age of one-and-twenty if he defied him now. He promised that, if he could not persuade his father to relent before then, he would come for her and their daughter as soon as he was in possession of his fortune.

But after a year or so the letters from abroad stopped. He had never come.

What had happened? Had the ardent lover changed his mind? Had he fallen in love with another? Been forced to wed a bride of his father's choice? He could not do that if he had, indeed, been through a marriage ceremony with her mother. Even were they simply hand-fasted, he would not be free to wed any other woman.

But if the marriage were as close a secret as it seemed, then he would be safe enough in breaking his vows, except that he would be sinning in the eyes of Holy Church.

She did not believe he had done that. She read the letters through twice and began to picture a thoughtful, earnest young knight desperately in love, but prevented by circumstances from simply defying his father and doing what he wanted.

She wished she could read her mother's replies. As the months went by and she had been forced to endure the ignominy of apparently giving birth to a bastard, she must have despaired. It seemed she could not have proclaimed herself wed for fear of prejudicing her lover and his fortune. She must have loved him very much to have remained so loyal.

But Genevra was, now, convinced that she was not base-born. She believed that her parents had been married. The only thing was, she still had no idea who her father had been, or whether he was alive or dead. And had no proof.

She had a few clues. He came of a family of some consequence. He had been at Court while her mother was there. He had been sent abroad. And his badge had been the rowel of a spur.

In the years ahead, she should find plenty of opportunity to discover his identity.

# Chapter Ten

M eg had come back to tidy her mistress in readiness for the meal and Annys was brushing the mud from the hem of a gown, when Robert returned to the solar just before dinner, carrying a bundle in his arms. Alan and Robin entered at Robert's heels but passed straight through to the garderobe, unlike Cain and Abel, who flopped down just inside the solar door.

Genevra turned her head to smile a greeting, a guilty flush staining her cheeks, for she now had a secret to hide. Her precious letters were back in the coffer, which in turn was stored in the bottom of one of her chests. She was reluctant to share her new knowledge. She wanted to surprise Robert with the truth, once she had discovered and proved it. If she failed to do so, then there would be little point in involving him in the shadowy events surrounding her birth.

A squeaky yelp brought her attention to the small animal wriggling to escape her husband's grasp.

'My lord!' she exclaimed. 'You have brought a puppy!' while excited cries of pleasure came from both Meg and Annys.

'Aye, my lady. Despite my haste to leave Thirkall, I

took time to choose a whelp for you, as I had promised. It is a bitch.'

'Oh! Let me have her!' The squirming pup changed hands. Genevra held it up to study the small, long-nosed features, exposing its pink stomach, and the long tongue leapt out to smother her flushed face in licks. She laughed delightedly and hugged the small body closer. 'Oh, thank you! I love her already! How old is she? What is she called?'

Robert's smile was surprisingly indulgent, considering all that had passed between them. 'It is ten weeks old and as yet has received little training and has no name. You may call it what you will.'

'She is daughter to Abel and sister to Cain,' mused Genevra, trying desperately to gather her wits, seeking some neutral subject to discuss while she did so. 'We must take care not to allow her to whelp from either of them when she comes into season.'

'Agreed. The bitch will have to be watched carefully and mated with some other, more suitable dog.'

As they spoke impersonally about the puppy's future, Genevra played with its ears. Meg and Annys both gave it an approving tickle and pat. Genevra found it difficult to think with Robert so close by. She did her best. Its coat was an even grey with no trace of brindle, light at the moment but the colour would probably darken. At length she smiled. 'It was my whim to have a hound, and yours to grant me my wish. I shall call her Whimsy.'

He laughed. He appeared remarkably relaxed. 'Well, Whimsy,' he addressed the pup, 'you must learn to answer to the name your mistress has given you.' He chucked it under the chin, demonstrating that he already had an affection for the animal. 'And do not tease your elders.'

'What do Cain and Abel think of her?' wondered Genevra, releasing the pup to explore. The hounds had been watching jealously as the pup drew all the attention. 'Where was she yesterday?'

Oh, dear. She blushed self-consciously. She should not have mentioned yesterday. But Robert showed no sign of embarrassment.

'In the stables,' he told her smoothly. 'My groom carried her here in a basket and, since I was occupied with more weighty matters and had forgotten the whelp, he did not bother me with it until this morning.'

To Genevra's silent relief, the bell rang for dinner. She would be glad to escape an exchange made the more embarrassing because of their audience.

The pup, busy sniffing around her father, had she but known it, looked up and yapped, disturbed by the unexpected sound. Cain rose sedately to his feet, regarded his offspring with patient disdain, and prepared to precede his master to the food. Abel, slightly less tolerant of the competition presented by his sister, snapped at the troublesome youngster in passing.

Whimsy took not the slightest notice of the implied threat, but scuttled after the huge hounds. At the top of the stairs she stopped, defeated. As Genevra caught up, she gave a little, pleading whine and looked up expectantly.

'All right, Whimsy,' chuckled Genevra, and bent down to pick up her pet. 'You'll have to grow quickly, won't you?'

As she descended the stairs to the Hall, she felt a new though wary hope, and rejoiced inwardly as she kissed the pup's head. Robert had remembered her and his promise even in the grip of a frenzy of anxiety over

Drogo's intentions. She was much comforted by the knowledge.

On the surface, relations between them reverted to what they had been before Robert's departure for Thirkall. There were, however, several differences.

He shared the bed at night, but sought to make love less often. When he did, he kept his desire well under control. There was never any suggestion of a repeat of the explosion of passion that had burst upon them on the afternoon of his return.

Whether it was because he was afraid of harming the baby or for some other reason, Genevra could not tell. But their unions, to her, seemed mechanical. Robert exhibited few tender feelings and sought only the minimum arousal necessary for him to find release. Her response suffered as a consequence.

He watched over her comfort and health and saw that she did no strenuous riding. But often he galloped off, followed by his string of retainers, as though the very devil himself were after him, and remained away from the castle all day, occasionally all night, too, hunting. She discovered that the party found shelter in shepherds' huts at the extremities of their land.

And he not only watched over her, but watched her, too, as though, by doing so, he hoped to discover her innermost thoughts.

He still did not fully trust her. She accepted that. But on the other hand they made music, played chess and talked together in the evenings, often in the comparative privacy of the solar. They were, imperceptibly, becoming friends.

Meanwhile, both Genevra's and Meg's pregnancies had been confirmed. Meg suffered more with morning

sickness than Genevra. Annys was nearing her time. All
three women spent a large part of their days sewing baby
clothes and spinning and weaving fine shawls to keep
the new infants warm.

During September, once her condition was well established, Robert announced that he must visit his mother
and some of his other holdings, all to the south of
Thirkall, before winter set in and travelling became difficult. His progress would not be leisurely; he would see
to his business as quickly as possibly. But it would not
be rushed, either.

He intended to ride Prince, but the horses would not
be changed on the way, so the distance they could cover
each day would be limited. He expected to be back at
Merlinscrag before November was more than a few
days old.

'I shall be delivered at the beginning of March,'
Genevra reminded him. Both had counted up the weeks
with some care. 'Do you intend that I should remain here
at Merlinscrag for the birth?'

'Yes.' His tone was suddenly abrupt. 'Do you object?'

'No. I had already planned on it. This may not be your
chief hold, but it was my mother's and will be my dower
should I outlive you. I am pleased to give birth to our
first child here.'

Our child, he noted. She never forgot to press that
point home. Was it from guilt? Or simply because she
knew he still doubted her?

He could not explain, even to himself, the need he felt
to see this child born in a place remote from both his
family and the Earl of Northempston. In the darker
recesses of his mind, he harboured the unreasonable fear
that he would not be able to recognise the whelp as his.

And he wanted as few witnesses as possible to this reaction if it came.

He nodded. 'We both find it agreeable here, I believe.'

He did. There was something clean and revitalising about the air, the hills, the quietly grazing sheep. And he had come to enjoy, even to crave, his wife's company. But he could not admit to that. He had learned the hard way how unwise it was to fall in love with one's wife. To offer courtly love to someone else's was the fashion, though he had never felt inclined to indulge in such dalliance.

'I have certainly come to appreciate both the sea and the countryside hereabouts,' he told her as a compromise. 'I shall return as speedily as I am able.'

So, leaving Alan and a number of men behind to watch over his wife as before, he and his retinue, which included Bernard this time, departed one golden September day, leaving Genevra and Meg to keep lonely vigil while they awaited the birth of their babies.

Annys went into labour in the first week of October. She retired to her own home as the contractions grew stronger and more frequent and both Genevra and Meg went with her.

Old Mariel was fetched from the village. The birthing stool was brought out, its shape designed to enable the mother to sit while the baby emerged. Genevra watched in fascination and some anxiety as she and Meg assisted Old Mariel, who at first sight appeared to be a bundle of skin and bones wrapped in rags. But, for all her frail appearance, she was strong and her rags were respectably clean.

The pain of childbirth was clearly intense. Annys screamed in agony, the sweat pouring down her face.

And yet, the moment the baby emerged from between her legs, Annys seemed only concerned to hear the infant cry.

''Tis another bonny boy-child,' announced Mariel in her gruff West-Country brogue as she wiped his nose and mouth and slapped the small bottom.

At the first sound of a loud wail, a look of such love and happiness flooded Annys's face that tears sprang to Genevra's eyes. All the labour and pain must have been worth it.

'He has a strong pair of lungs,' smiled Meg.

'What shall you call him?' asked Genevra.

Annys smiled, shy but proud. 'Martin and I hoped you would not mind an we named him for the lord Robert.'

'Another Robin?' said Genevra with a smile, watching as Mariel dextrously cut and tied the cord with bent and bony fingers, wiped the baby clean with a wet cloth, dried him carefully and began to bind him with swaddling bands. 'Of course we shall not mind. I am certain his lordship will be flattered.'

'You will not wish to call your own son Robert?'

'Possibly.' They had not discussed the question yet. Genevra did not know what she wanted and even less what Robert wished. 'But if so, we would probably call him Rob, at least while Robin is still with Lord Robert as his squire.'

'Here, mistress, take thy babe.' Mariel thrust the tightly bound, squalling infant into its mother's arms. 'Put he to thy breast. Thou hast to pass the afterbirth afore 'ee can rest.'

Genevra and Meg did not leave until Annys was lying in her bed and baby Robin slept in his cradle.

'I'll come to see you on the morrow,' promised Genevra.

The two women walked back to the Great Hall in

sombre silence. 'Well,' said Genevra at last, 'I now know why birthing a child is called labour.'

'You will bear the pain bravely, my duck. And you are young.'

'And so will you, Meg. I will pray every day that you may be granted an easy birth, for 'tis no fault of yours that you have waited so long to be wed.'

'Have you spoken to Old Mariel about attending you, my duck?'

'Not yet. But watching her at work today has given me great confidence in her ability. I shall be glad to have her tend me. I will speak with her soon.'

Genevra often went to the hut where the herbs were pounded, distilled, infused or brewed, formed into pills and made into creams and ointments. These were used by herself, Father John and anyone else who tended the sick and injured.

Having assisted the sister apothecary and the sister infirmarian in the Convent, the preparation and use of medicines had become a particular interest of hers and she knew herself to be reasonably able in caring for the sick and injured. Her expertise was often called upon within the castle.

She had, however, never until now run across Old Mariel, who visited the castle only rarely, to deliver herbs she had gathered or to attend a birth. For anything else, people visited Old Mariel in her hut on the outskirts of the village.

She was considered to be the local wise woman, though some folks tended to be frightened of her because of the rumours of witchcraft that surrounded her. She must be a witch, they whispered. How else was she able to see into the future and to effect such miraculous cures?

But the priest tolerated her presence, used her skills on occasion, and she was received by those within the castle, so no one dared to harm the old woman.

Having been witness to Old Mariel's extraordinary skill in delivering Annys's Robin, Genevra determined to visit her hut herself. It was within sight of the castle gates and there was little to fear in so remote a spot.

Drogo's advent had been both unusual and unwelcome. Anything similar was most unlikely to occur again. Even Alan agreed that she might venture so short a distance by herself. Genevra wanted to go alone, for Old Mariel might say things that she did not wish even Meg to hear.

She chose a bright autumnal day when a fresh breeze ensured that the coast was free of the sea mists that often shrouded it in the autumn. She took with her as an offering an old but warm fur-lined cloak and a woollen kirtle to help keep the winter chills at bay.

Genevra knocked at the sagging timber door and accepted the old woman's invitation to enter. Old Mariel had a cauldron heating over a brazier and a wonderful aroma filled the hut.

Genevra pulled the door shut behind her and coughed. Slivers of light filtered through the gaps between the door's planks. Other than that, the only illumination came from a small window set under the thatch of the eaves and covered by a thin, translucent skin, and the small opening in the roof that allowed some of the smoke from the brazier to escape.

Once Genevra's eyes had adjusted to the dim light, augmented only by the glow of the brazier, she saw that the place was furnished with two stools, a smallish, roughly made chest and a pile of blankets, presumably the bed.

In the smoke haze drifting beneath the turf roof, she could see the beams festooned with bunches of dry and drying herbs, amongst which hung a few utensils. Bottles and jars, flagons and small boxes lined two rough shelves fixed to the long side of the room. The floor was of mud, strewn with fresh straw and herbs.

'Well,' said the old woman, 'so 'ee came.'

Genevra dabbed at her smarting eyes. 'You were expecting me?' she asked uncertainly.

'Aye, my lady. You'm expecting. You wants Old Mariel to tend 'ee and 'ee've something to ask her. When's the babe due?'

'Early in March, I think.'

The old head nodded. 'That be about right. That be a couple of weeks afore thy woman be due, eh?'

'Yes. We will both be in childbed together.' Meg, thought Genevra, would have to lie in a guest chamber. Though mayhap she should consider asking Martin to oversee the building of a small dwelling for Meg and Bernard. Meg was, after all, an important member of her household. The granting of such a favour would be justified. The baby had probably been conceived in the stables, but it should be given the chance to live in better surroundings. 'Will you be able to attend us both?'

'Aye, never fret. There be plenty of women to help. Mistress Annys will be fit by then.'

'Unless she is breeding again.'

'Nay. She has enough childer. Her knows how to prevent another coming.'

Genevra did not question this. Since time began women had been finding ways to prevent or abort a pregnancy—not always successfully, of course, for the methods were unreliable. Annys had done her duty and dearly loved the children she had borne Martin. But more would become a burden. She could see that, although Holy Church taught that God would provide.

So, 'I see,' was all Genevra said.

Old Mariel stirred her simmering pot. 'So what did 'ee want to know, my lady?'

'Who my father was.'

There, she'd blurted it out.

Old Mariel's aged eyes were sharp enough as she stared through the haze into the anxious green ones facing her over the brazier. Such poor light as there was flickered. Yet she seemed satisfied with what she read there.

She transferred her gaze to the gently-moving surface of the liquid in the cauldron. For long moments she stared into its depths, as though she could see something Genevra could not, for all *she* could see was the slow movement of a dark liquid shot with faint glimmers of light.

'Aye,' pronounced Old Mariel at last. 'You'll find out who he be.'

She did not seem anxious to say more.

'How? When?' demanded Genevra.

Mariel's thoughts seemed to go off at a tangent. 'There be distrust atween 'ee and thy man. 'Twill all be resolved when 'ee meets with the darkness. From darkness will come thy light.'

Her voice had become sing-song, as though she spoke without conscious thought.

'What do you mean?'

Genevra's anxious question seemed to bring Old Mariel back from wherever she had been. She blinked and lifted her eyes. They appeared almost blank.

'I saw nought but darkness and death. But 'twas not

a threatening darkness or a sorrowful death. They spoke of hope. I cannot tell 'ee more.'

Genevra could make nothing of the old woman's words. Disappointment made her tone sharper than she intended. 'That tells me nothing!'

Old Mariel moved abruptly, took up her stick and began to stir the pot again. 'It tells 'ee all thee needs to know. You'll discover thy father's identity, be accepted by his family. And gain the trust of thy husband. What more can 'ee wish to know?'

'When?' whispered Genevra.

'That I cannot say. But I can tell 'ee that thy babe be a boy.'

Genevra gazed at Mariel in astonishment. 'You can see that?'

'Aye. I have that gift.' Her gaze went blank again. She looked down into the bubbling liquid. ''Ee may tell Mistress Meg that she bears a daughter and a son.'

A gasp escaped Genevra. 'Twins?'

'Aye. And her'll be safely delivered. She'll bear no more after that. But I see thee with a clutch of little ones about 'ee, my lady. Three sons and two daughters. 'Ee'll find true happiness, my lady.'

Genevra drew in a deep breath and rose to her feet. 'Thank you, Mariel. I am deeply grateful to you.'

The old woman's eyes were sharp again as she, too, stood. ''Twas a pleasure, my lady.'

Genevra pushed the bundle of clothes into Mariel's arms. 'To keep you warm this winter, mistress.' She pressed a gold noble into the claw-like hand. 'And please take this for your trouble.'

'Thank'ee, my lady.' Mariel tucked the coin into some pocket beneath her ragged garment. 'You'm welcome to come to see me at any time.'

'An I have other problems, I will.' She held out her fingers to the warmth of the brazier. Somehow her hands had become chilled. She noted the small pile of logs and kindling stacked in a corner of the hut. Did the old woman collect her own fuel, or did the villagers bring it to her from the woods and common land where they were entitled to forage?

She would ask Master Geoffrey, the bailiff, to see that Mariel was kept supplied. But even that might not be enough. 'Mistress Mariel,' she went on, 'should the weather become too cold and this brazier prove insufficient to keep you warm, please feel welcome to sit by the fire in the Great Hall.'

'I'll remember thy kindness, my lady.' The old woman's voice trembled. 'I'll pray the Lord to look after 'ee.'

With these words she nodded, sat down and began to stir the cauldron again. Genevra had been dismissed.

Genevra pondered long and hard over what Mariel had prophesied, by turns fearful and elated. She could not imagine what the prediction of darkness and death could foretell, but it seemed that they would help rather than hinder her search for happiness.

She told Meg nothing of that part of her visit but, alone in the solar with her friend, did confess to consulting Mariel about the birth and to being told that she bore a son.

'The lord Robert will be delighted to have a son and heir,' murmured Meg, looking up from her needlework to beam at Genevra.

'Aye, an he can bring himself to believe 'tis his.' Genevra sighed as she regarded her own work critically. The smocking on the tiny garment was coming along well. 'If only he would trust me! But his first wife's infidelity has soured his nature and he would mistrust any woman, I vow.'

'I could curse that brother of his,' declared Meg fiercely. 'By what I hear, he has managed to blight his brother's entire life.'

'Aye. He has blighted his own, as well. What can it serve anyone to allow envy to turn into an obsession? He seeks to repay his brother for doing him an imagined wrong. The lord Robert could not help being born first. It makes no sense. Sir Drogo could have made his own way, earned a title, wed an heiress—'

'He lacks the character of your lord, my duck. He finds too much satisfaction in the pleasures of the flesh and in idle pursuits. You do know that he sought out a succession of wenches to take his pleasure with while he was here?'

'No.' Genevra frowned. 'I trust they were willing and that he left none of them in trouble. We do not want his visit to result in a crop of bastards.'

'We shall discover in due time.'

'The wenches must be looked after, of course. They were not responsible for bringing that libertine here to seduce them.'

'Neither were you or his lordship. He descended on us like a plague sent by the Devil.'

The Devil equated to darkness. Genevra thrust the thought aside. Deliverance from her troubles was unlikely to come from Drogo.

'Can you picture him fighting a real enemy, or administering his estates, like the lord Robert?' Meg went on, not waiting for Genevra to comment.

''Tis difficult,' Genevra conceded. 'He only dares to rouse my lord's anger because he knows that the lord

Robert would never kill him. To be injured and beaten in a duel with my lord only serves to fuel his hatred.'

'It seems to me that he has tried to do his worst and failed. You carry your husband's heir. The succession is secured.'

'I hope so, Meg.' Genevra stopped sewing again. 'But babies so often die. I am glad Old Mariel predicted that I shall have other sons. Surely one of them will survive to inherit the St Aubin barony.'

Meg rested her needle, too. 'She did, did she?'

'Aye. And I have not told you what she said about you, Meg. You are to give birth to twins, a girl and a boy. They will live, and so will you.'

Meg's face had lost all its normal colour and her fingers had clenched on her work. 'Twins?' she echoed. 'At my age?'

''Twill be hard, doubtless, but you will not be troubled again. You will have no further children. Or so Old Mariel says. Do you believe her?'

Slowly, Meg relaxed her fingers and lifted her sewing again. Her hands were shaking but she tried to form a stitch. 'Aye, my duck. I must make two sets of baby clothes. Do you believe her?'

'I want to, Meg.'

She badly wanted to believe that, somehow, she would struggle through to true happiness.


Robert returned as promised in November, but a week later than predicted, since heavy rain had made most of the roads almost impassable. The entourage arrived, weary and covered in mud.

Bernard, of course, had to tend the horses in the stables. Genevra sent Meg after him.

'You may tell him that your cottage has already been

started,' she grinned. 'And that he is to be the father of twins!'

Both women had begun to think that Mariel's prediction was true because, although she was at least two weeks behind Genevra, Meg's stomach was more swollen.

Genevra's pregnancy had only just begun to show when Robert left. Now it was obvious the moment her surcoat was removed. Her kirtle, although full, could not hide the bump.

Robert went straight through to the garderobe to bathe and change, attended by Alan and Robin. Genevra awaited his reappearance with eagerness. He had looked tired, but not unhappy on arrival. And he had put his hand on her stomach and given her the most generous smile she could remember.

In fact the progress had been good for Robert. Riding free, journeying from hold to hold, he had been able to relax. The affairs of his estates had occupied much of his mind, but they were in good hands and prospered.

He had seen his mother and sister but not, thankfully, Drogo, and visited Northempston at Ardingstone, where he had been reminded of Genevra's background and excellent reputation. His suspicions had been made to seem foolish, and so he had arrived back at Merlinscrag in high good humour.

Genevra had looked well and had greeted him with decorous warmth. He intended to couple with her come the night. He had managed to banish his demons, at least for the moment, and he looked forward to the quiet months of companionship while they awaited the birth of Genevra's child.

He still could not quite bring himself to think of it as his.

# *Chapter Eleven*

~~~~~~~~

Robert's relaxed mood continued and they spent much time together over the next weeks. It was as though he had put aside his suspicions, since he began to treat his wife as the friend and helpmeet she should be.

Once the critical fifth month of her pregnancy had passed, Genevra felt able to ride more often. She greatly enjoyed the mild exercise and benefited from the fresh air despite the cold and damp and high winds which seemed to prevail. Robert showed great patience in riding slowly with her, reserving his hard riding for the days he spent hunting with his men.

In this harmonious manner, they visited most of the villeins and cottars spread about their lands, became acquainted with the families and discovered their problems and needs. After such an excursion she returned to the castle glowing with health and, if they had been able to advise or to promise help, with satisfaction, too.

Robert's lovemaking, though carefully controlled, had regained much of the warmth it had lacked before his last absence. Genevra, basking in the aura of his new, more cheerful persona, watched with approval as he set about guiding Martin and Geoffrey into new paths which would ensure greater profitability for Merlinscrag.

''Tis fortunate that your father can sell the fleeces for us, Annys,' Genevra remarked one day, watching Robert and Martin conferring with the factor in another part of the Hall.

Annys glanced across at her father with affection. 'He is honoured to be entrusted with the business, my lady.'

At that moment a number of boys raced out of a side chamber shouting, pushing and shoving as boys will. Behind them, tut-tutting and frowning over his pupils' rowdy behaviour, came Father John, the priest, who, at Genevra's request, had taken on the task of educating Martin's and Geoffrey's eldest sons, together with the two pages Robert had brought with him and any boy whose parent could spare him for the time needed to come to the castle to learn.

Genevra herself taught a few of the older girls serving in the castle or living in the village. When she had done they would be able to sign their names, to read and write simple words and to sew. When she was not there, Annys would take over the task, for she had learned to read and write as a youngster.

Mayhap, later, Annys's daughter would study with Father John. She showed every sign of being a bright child. Genevra, knowing how much an education had enriched her life, could see no reason why other girls should not benefit, too. In truth, any parent who wished to see their children bettered in life would find no difficulty, except that of expediency, in achieving this aim at Merlinscrag.

Annys made an exasperated noise. 'Harry!' she called. 'Come here, child! Behave yourself!'

Reluctantly, Harry obeyed his mother, stood before her and made a bow. His eyes lingered enviously on the two pages, separated now from the other boys and rolling on the rushes in a mock fight.

He was too young as yet, but Genevra, seeing that look, took pity on the child.

'One day, Harry, an your mother and father agree, you could become a page.'

The boy's eyes lit up. 'Now, my lady?' he demanded. 'I would serve you well!'

'Not quite yet, Harry. You should wait until you have passed the seventh anniversary of your birth.'

'But I am not yet six!'

'Harry,' admonished Annys, 'You should be thanking the lady Genevra, not bemoaning your age! Indeed, my lady,' she said, turning to Genevra, 'although he did not choose to go on to become a knight himself, I am certain my husband would welcome such an opportunity for his son.'

'Who could also choose to seek his fortune in other ways. It is the education which is important. So learn diligently, Harry, and we shall see.'

Harry, with the eagerness of a child and all the courtliness of a knight in the making, grasped Genevra's hand and kissed it. 'Thank you, my lady!'

Annys smiled fondly at her first-born as she began to suckle her new son.


Christmas came. It was no great surprise, after all their travels about their domain, to find their vassals eager to accept an invitation to come, with those of their families who could be spared from husbanding the livestock, to stay at the castle for the seasonal festivities that would follow the moot court, held on the eve of Christ's birth.

They arrived washed and dressed in their best tunics and kirtles, those worn by the better-off made of coarse broella, kersey, falding or homespun stuff, and those of the poor cottars, who held barely enough land to keep themselves fed and had to work as day labourers to make ends meet, in homespun made from unwashed wool which gave off an unpleasant odour, particularly when wet.

Genevra and Robert sat in state on the dais to receive the tithes and homage due to them as overlords, and administered justice as necessary. Martin the steward, Geoffrey the bailiff and Father John between them kept the records and gave advice on the local manorial laws. The disputes, fortunately considering the festival about to be observed, were not serious and easily settled.

At first the children sat quietly on the rushes, overawed by the splendour of the Great Hall. But they soon lost their shyness and before long had crowded round to listen to Martin, who had a gift for story-telling. And then there was dinner, a splendid meal, more sumptuous than any they had previously eaten. Some had to be persuaded that the food on the table was edible, for they had never seen anything like it before.

Supper was served to the children later, while the adults fasted. Just before midnight, as Father John prepared to celebrate mass in the Hall, for the church would not hold so large a congregation, the huge Yule log was carried in and one end thrust firmly into the fire. Holly and ivy had already been gathered and brought in to decorate the pillars and rafters and the place blazed with light from a multitude of candles and torches. Few of the children had fallen asleep. They were too wide-eyed with wonder.

Genevra knew that this would be the happiest Christmas she could remember.

And so it proved. The company might not scintillate

with the cloth of gold and flashing jewels of a more lordly court, but the West-Country people proved warm-hearted and anxious to please, as well as to enjoy themselves. Alan had been appointed Master of the Revels and Lord of Misrule and, with the lively assistance of Robin, always up to any mischief, had devised a programme of amusements which kept them all playing games, watching travelling acrobats and jongleurs, singing, dancing and laughing. During this time Robert showed a side of his character that gave Genevra a glimpse of the happy, lively young man he must have been before marriage, betrayal, war and the state of the monarchy had turned him into the sadly disillusioned man she had wed.

The villeins showed no desire to leave the good food, warmth and amusements provided in the castle, despite the sparse comforts offered by the necessity of sleeping huddled together in the Hall. However, once the New Year, in the form of Father Time (Martin in a false white beard and wig), had been greeted with great ceremony, they returned to their farms to prepare for the spring sewing of crops.

Annys's family had travelled from Barnstaple to celebrate with them. They and the more prosperous villeins occupied the guest chambers. Meg and Bernard were already installed in their new cottage, next to Martin and Annys.

Altogether, thought Genevra, she would be sorry to leave Merlinscrag when the time came. But come it must, for Robert had other, greater responsibilities he must attend to and she had no wish to be always left behind. Once the baby was born, she would enjoy to go on progress with him.

Annys, of course, would not leave her husband and children to travel with her, but her younger sister, Sigrid, was to join Genevra as one of her ladies. Meg would probably leave her twins in Annys's care and accompany Bernard. Genevra sincerely hoped so. And Sigrid expressed herself eager to travel with her, so she would be adequately served.

And the baby would have his own nurse—she already had a young woman from the village in mind. A wet nurse would not be necessary because she had decided to suckle the baby herself.

As the weeks went by and her belly swelled, Genevra gave up riding. Her back ached and she found it difficult to be comfortable in bed. Her restlessness disturbed Robert and it was at her suggestion that he began to spend his nights in the garderobe. It would not be for long, she consoled herself and him.

Meg was huge. There could be no doubt now that Old Mariel's prophecy would prove correct, for Genevra had put her ear to Meg's belly and, listening carefully, had heard the faint beating of two tiny hearts.

Genevra had worked out that her baby should be born early in March. The time came and nothing happened.

'Oh, Meg!' she lamented, clasping her swollen stomach. 'I cannot bear this much longer! He is so heavy! He must come soon!'

'He will,' consoled Meg, who was in a worse state than Genevra, though both women had kept remarkably well during their pregnancies, apart from swollen feet. And, as it happened, Meg went into labour a week early, so her twins were born before Genevra began to feel her pains.

Birthing was women's business and both Bernard and, later, Robert made themselves scarce while Old Mariel dealt with their wives. She had plenty of women to assist her and Meg was comfortably installed in her own bed with the twins in cradles by her side, exhausted, weak, but happy, when Genevra insisted on waddling to the cottage to see her. It was while she was exclaiming over the babies, small because they were twins and born a little early, that her own labour began.

The birth was painful, as she had expected, but not too difficult. Twelve hours later, Genevra was safely in bed with her son mouthing her breast.

This was the moment she had been anticipating with eager joy. The moment when she could show Robert their son.

The bed-curtains were not closed. As he entered the solar, Annys and Sigrid left. He stood for a moment, studying the picture of maternal pride and happiness made by his wife and baby before he moved forward. The expression on his face sent a shaft of fear through Genevra. All the recent ease and felicity had left it. He stood looking down at her with much the same expression on his face as that he had worn when first they met.

Genevra did not allow her dismay to show. She shifted the swaddled baby in her arms to show him to Robert.

'See, husband, your son and heir. What shall we call him?'

He did not move. He stared down, inspecting the crumpled red face minutely. 'What colour is his hair?' he demanded. He could not see it for the swaddling bands.

Genevra swallowed. As she had begun to fear, the old mistrust had returned. 'Fair.' She tried to keep her voice steady. 'Old Mariel says the colour may change, at least a little.'

The baby was not asleep but stared up blankly with the large, unfocussed eyes of the newborn.

'He takes after you,' ventured Genevra, though it was

difficult to tell in a baby so young.

'Does he? His nose does not appear aquiline to me. How can I be certain that he is mine?'

Distress and weakness brought tears to Genevra's eyes. How could Robert change so? He had been all solicitude until she went into labour.

'He is yours,' she affirmed as firmly as her shaking voice would allow. 'I have lain with no other man. He must be yours.'

'He is as much like Drogo as me. More. He lacks my nose.'

'But he is only a few hours old! Babies grow and change. Their features develop. And if he does not grow up to have your nose, mayhap he will have mine! Oh, Robert!' she held the baby close, cuddling it defensively. 'Accept and love your son! 'Tis not his fault that Drogo has planted this unwarranted seed of doubt in your mind!'

Robert gazed down at his exhausted and distressed wife and wished fervently that he could shake off the suspicion Drogo had sown by his cynical intrusions into both his marriages. He wanted to believe—he did believe—that Genevra was not like Jane, that, because she was convent bred, she must be true and honest. But against that he knew that a woman, forced to dwell in a convent against her will, could react by behaving rebelliously once she were freed.

But Genevra was not like that. He had detected no trace of rebellion or deceit in his wife's manner during the pregnancy. She had used her time in the convent to develop her fine mind. They had shared a happy and rewarding companionship once he had thrust his doubts aside—he'd thought forever.

But they had returned. And the bastard carried by the kitchen wench who claimed Drogo as its sire had yet to be born, so he could make no comparison between the babies. This child in his wife's arms could be Drogo's. But, deep down, despite everything, he knew it was not. It was his.

He longed to take them into his arms and to allow the pride and joy bubbling beneath the surface of his emotions to take over. But he feared to believe in his happiness for it could spring from a falsehood.

He compromised. He leaned over the bed and kissed Genevra's forehead. She lowered her lids to receive his peace offering. The dark lashes fanned against her pale skin, emphasising the shadows beneath her eyes, the lines of tiredness radiating from them.

'Let me take him.'

Genevra, looking into the troubled eyes of her husband, gladly released her precious son into his arms. Robert stood for a long time, holding the baby awkwardly, looking down, bouncing it a little when it made a faint protest at having been passed to someone else.

'What name would you chose?' he asked.

'Robert. But that might prove a little confusing.'

'We could call him something else. Lord Northempston brought us together. His name is William. Robert William, known as Will?'

Genevra nodded, smiling. 'I like that.'

'I'll ask Father John to arrange the baptism.'

'He will be conducting another soon. Meg and Bernard are calling their twins Edana and Wystan.'

Robert looked slightly doubtful. ''Tis their own business what they call them. I prefer simple names.'

'What would you have suggested for a girl?' asked Genevra, intrigued.

'Alida,' he replied without hesitation. Then added, as

though slightly embarrassed, 'After my sister and grand-mother.'

Genevra smiled. 'Very well, husband, our first daughter shall be called Alida.'

'You speak of it already, while you are weary from delivering Will?'

'My lord and husband, I wish to give you many children, an the Lord so wills.'

She did not mention Old Mariel's prophecy. But she knew now that true happiness still eluded them. She could only trust that that part of the prophecy would be fulfilled, too.

Although summer came in early that year and the baby throve, Genevra could not shake off the depression which had followed her realisation that Robert still did not fully trust her. It must be that causing it, she considered, since there could be no other reason for her black, dejected mood.

Robert was not being unkind. He had returned to her bed and, once she had been churched, resumed marital relations. She did not mention her troubles, even to Meg, but none of her companions could fail to know that she found it difficult to rise in the morning, hard to concentrate enough to teach the girls, almost impossible to smile.

''Tis maybe because you are feeding the baby,' Annys suggested doubtfully.

Genevra stabbed listlessly at her needlework. 'You fed yours and Meg is feeding two. It cannot be that.'

'But you are a high-born lady. We are not.'

'I am still a woman, made the same way as you are.'

'But your feelings are finer—'

'Nonsense.' For a moment Genevra was stirred from her apathy. 'Mayhap they are finer than those of the serfs in the kitchens but finer than yours or Meg's? I think not.'

'Well, then, why should you feel so dismal?'

Genevra sighed. She sighed often these days. 'I do not know. There seems to be a black cloud hovering over my head, pressing down on me, and whatever I do I cannot shift it. It is bearing me down.'

They were sitting in the pleasaunce her mother had designed and Genevra had seen restored to order. This summer its cherry, plum, pear and apple trees would provide shade and the plants colour. Already the gilly-flowers were scenting the welcome breeze.

The garden lay outside the inner walls and commanded a view over the ocean. It was the most agreeable place to be, for the early heatwave was not helping Genevra. Her skin was always damp, great circles of the cloth beneath her arms were wet. Her thighs stuck together. The others suffered the same discomforts, but they did not appear so bothered by them.

Her despair knew no bounds. She had become lifeless in bed. She could not respond to Robert as she should. Neither could she sleep. Even feeding Will had lost its initial pleasure and her milk was beginning to dry up so that the baby was being weaned on slops. She could scarcely be bothered to eat herself.

She did not know what was happening to her. She, who had been so full of life and hope, who had fallen so deeply and irrevocably in love with Robert St Aubin, no longer cared whether she lived or died.

He had noticed, too. How could he fail? He looked at her strangely these days and watched her. The wariness had re-entered his eyes, though she knew its cause was probably different. He did not know what to make of her or how to treat her.

Old Mariel had mixed her a tonic and told her that

she had known other women who suffered in the same way after giving birth.

'It cannot be that,' protested Genevra. 'I wanted the baby. And the birth was not difficult.'

'I don't know why,' said the old woman, 'but it happens. You'll feel better soon.'

Genevra had doubted it. She could see absolutely no sign of light at the end of her dark tunnel. Meg still had plentiful supplies of milk and was helping to feed Will. Genevra's sense of frustration and failure grew daily.

Sigrid came from the Hall, bringing Will and his nurse, a buxom youngster of some sixteen years, with her. Soon Meg and her thriving twins joined them. Robin brought his flute. The sweet notes drifted on the air, backed by the idle crash and hiss of the waves breaking gently on the rocks below and the cries of the gulls wheeling overhead.

The only discordant note was the sound of clashing arms coming from the landward side of the castle and, in quiet moments, the hiss of arrows being loosed in the butts. Even in this heat the men-at-arms must keep in training. Robert was out hunting. A year ago she would have been with him.

As the sun began to go down, they retired to prepare for a late supper. Robert and the huntsmen had returned a turn of the glass earlier. As Genevra finished her toilet, he came through to the solar, followed by Alan and Robin, who bowed to her as they passed on their way to the Great Hall.

'You have had a good day, my lady?' he asked.

'Aye, I thank you, my lord.'

With a wave of his hand he dismissed Sigrid, who had been attending her. Sigrid dipped a curtsy and left.

Genevra glanced over her shoulder at her husband.

'You wished to speak with me alone, Robert?'

'Aye, wife. I found a letter awaiting me on my return. An invitation to attend my lord of Northempston at Ardingstone next month, to help him to entertain the Duke of Lancaster and his new wife, Constance of Castile.'

'John of Gaunt?' mused Genevra, her heart sinking. She did not feel up to making the journey to Ardingstone and yet did not wish Robert to go without her.

'Aye, John of Gaunt. King of Castile as he now styles himself. He wed Constanza in the hope of gaining the throne of Castile, of course.'

'Will he?'

'I doubt it. Do you wish to travel with me, wife? The invitation is addressed to us both.'

'Then I had best prepare for the journey. I have no wish to inconvenience the Earl. Or you, husband,' she added, for 'twas love of him that would make her stir herself. 'I know I have disappointed you recently. I will try to throw off this dreadful fit of melancholy that assails me.'

Robert came up behind her, gripped her shoulder hard and squeezed it. 'You must, my dear, for Will's sake as much as for mine.' He hesitated. 'If my doubting of your faithfulness has caused your distress, I can only say that I do not mean to cause you pain. I can no more help that than you, I infer, can overcome your present low spirits.'

'Your distrust grieves me sadly, Robert, although I do understand its cause, but I do not think that to be the root of my listlessness.' She asserted, with a momentary return of spirit, 'It simply makes me angry, for I am innocent—there is no reason for your suspicions. And I'm sad, of course, that you should judge me so harshly,

when you must know by now that I am not a faithless
or dishonest woman.'

'I do know it, Genevra, and by my troth, I shall try to
cast my burden aside an you will do the same!'

Genevra, who had been sitting on her stool, rose to
her feet and turned to face him. Tears streamed down
her cheeks. 'Oh Robert,' she murmured, and flung her
arms about him.

His came about her and tightened. 'Genevra,' he murmured. She felt the sudden surge of desire that overcame
him and, for the first time since Will's birth, a flicker of
response stirred in her.

The bell clanged, calling them to supper.

Robert drew a deep breath. 'We must go down,' he
declared, releasing her.

Genevra drew back, found a kerchief and dried her
tears. Given a few more moments of privacy, the dam
holding her emotions in check might have burst. As it
was, only the merest trickle of feeling had escaped. But
the dam had shown its first cracks.

That night, when Robert approached her, Genevra managed a semblance of response. But the obstruction was
still there. It seemed unbreachable.

Two days later, despair took her through the postern to
the cliff edge. She loved watching the breakers foaming
beneath her; somehow, the sound and the sight of the
fury of the sea calmed her. She was, for once, alone apart
from Whimsy, who had become her shadow. She had
dismissed Sigrid, and both Annys and Meg were
attending to their own domestic duties.

And, since storm clouds had gathered and it might rain
at any moment, no one else had ventured out apart from

the servants and men of the garrison, who were all within the inner curtain wall and on the other side of the buildings going about their business.

She wanted to be alone. . .alone to brood on her inability to return to normal. Alone to seek God under his heavens, even if He did show His wrath by rolling His thunder around, sending lightning flashes to simulate hellfire and pouring down the rain to soak her. Whimsy whimpered and cowered in the inadequate shelter of a rock.

God appeared to think mere rain inadequate, though, for huge hailstones began to fall, to bounce off her and to lie, small lumps of ice, on the turf all around. She threw back her head, welcoming the sting of ice on her face, the swirl of the wind as it drove the particles slanting across her vision.

The wildness of the storm seemed to be effecting some sort of healing, to be bringing peace, its antithesis. Elation took hold of her. She laughed aloud and bent over to watch the storm-whipped spumes, the crashing, swirling and sucking of the sea below.

An alarmed bellow made her straighten, to step back from the brink.

She looked round. A figure was flying towards her, shouting.

Robert. In a flood of memory her dream came back to her. Here she stood, in shadow, on the edge of the cliff. And behind her, though not in sunlight, was the Golden Eagle, not in all the splendour of his shining helmet and heraldic colours but in his everyday outfit of padded jupon, breech hose and boots, an arming cap upon his head. And he did not turn his back but continued to race toward her, calling her name.

She waited.

He stopped some three yards away, as though afraid to come closer, and held out his hands beseechingly.

'Genevra,' he pleaded, 'don't do it.'

'Do what?' asked Genevra, exhilarated but bemused.

'Jump off, of course! Genevra, wife, you must not kill yourself! Sweeting, Will and I need you!'

His words, his look of anguish, demolished the dam in an instant. But Genevra did not cry this time. The hail still fell, belabouring them both with its force, though neither was aware of it. Genevra smiled, the kind of joyous smile that had been absent from her face for almost five long months.

'I was not going to jump, Robert. I was asking God to heal me. And He has answered my prayer! Oh, Robert!'

And she ran straight into his waiting arms.

Then the tears came, healing tears that dampened Robert's jupon more than the hail, which was easing off.

'Sweeting,' he said again, his cheek resting on her kerchief, 'thank God. I thought I had driven you to commit the deadly sin of suicide.'

'Nay, Robert. But the storm suited my mood. I found it soothing, and I have always loved watching the sea break over the rocks. I was in despair, but did not quite wish to die. I love Will too much to abandon him.'

She did not mention her love for Robert again, for what purpose would be served? He had no use for it. But it seemed that he did need her. That, for the moment, must suffice.

'Thank God,' he repeated. 'But you are soaking wet. Come.'

He did not wait for more, but picked her up in his arms and began to stride towards the Hall, followed by a dejected, shivering Whimsy. It was a longish way and

Genevra feared he would find her weight too great, but he did not falter.

She put one arm about his neck and pressed her other hand against his chest. The thump of his heart was reassuringly steady. He mounted the steps with easy strides and swept through a suddenly hushed Great Hall to carry her up to the solar.

Sigrid's fresh young face turned to the door as they entered and her eyes opened wide in astonishment.

She had been sewing. She jumped to her feet. 'My lady! You are wet. Allow me—'

'You may leave us,' said Robert shortly. He had begun to breathe heavily at last. 'Take the dog with you and dry her off.'

Sigrid bobbed, dipping her head. 'Yes, lord.' She left, her eyes still wide, hustling a reluctant Whimsy before her.

Genevra wondered what story she would tell in the Hall. She did not care, for Robert laid her on the bed and began to take off her damp clothes himself.

An exultant, feverish passion had taken hold of them both. Genevra made no protest but aided him as he stripped off her clothes. He made no demur when her fingers tore clumsily at the fastenings of his gambeson, the ties on his shirt, the points of his hose. It took them only moments before they lay naked together on the bed.

But Robert did not rush to completion, as his passion demanded. Genevra did not urge him to. The acts of tenderness and arousal, the latter not strictly necessary, became precious moments of deepening understanding, of mutual delight, leading to an eventual coming together that healed the divisions of the last months, even if it could not entirely eradicate Genevra's insecurities in the face of Robert's lack of love for her and his hidden doubts.

The final release, when it came, was mutual and jointly satisfying. Genevra seemed to float above her body for a while, seeing it spread, lax and satisfied, beneath the harder, muscular form of her husband. His face was buried in her hair which he had released from its kerchief and net. And then, as he raised his head, she returned to her body to gaze up at him with all the love she felt clearly visible in her eyes.

But he did not see it. He murmured, 'Sweet heart,' and kissed her, gently this time, before he rolled to one side and gathered her into his arms, nestling her head into his shoulder.

'I wish we did not have to go to Ardingstone,' he murmured, kissing her hair. 'I would much prefer to remain here. But we should go to Thirkall soon. So I suggest that we travel there after our stay with Northempston.'

'And after that?' asked Genevra drowsily.

'Twill be too late in the season to return here. We shall celebrate Christmas at Thirkall and return here, via my other manors, in the spring. This shall be our summer residence, Genevra. An you agree?'

Genevra knew he had already decided, but it was nice to be asked. 'I am your wife,' she murmured contentedly. 'Your wish is my command, my lord.'

He gave a chuckle. 'An I did not know you better, I should almost believe you.'

'But it is,' protested Genevra. Then she chuckled. 'Unless, of course, you demand of me something I do not wish to do.'

'Hussy!' he teased. And began to stroke her again, his purpose abundantly clear.

# *Chapter Twelve*

Preparations for the journey were put in train immediately. Robert intended to arrive at Ardingstone in a style worthy of a baron, so his entire retinue and many of the household—including Father John, who was to travel as their personal priest—made ready to take to the road. This meant much polishing of weapons and armour, removal of rust from chain mail, mending and cleaning of saddles, harnesses, caparisons, pennons and banners.

The journey would take at least two weeks, possibly more, for they had Will's welfare to consider. Whimsy had grown to full size over the summer and would run beside the horses with Cain and Abel, but the young bitch's stamina might not be great. As a puppy, she had learned to ride crouched in front of Genevra and so could, at a pinch, be taken up by one of the retinue, as long as the horse would accept its unusual burden.

Meg, discovering the length of their intended absence from Merlinscrag, had asked permission to bring Edana and Wystan with her. Bernard was travelling as head groom of the horses, so the family would be together. And Robert, since Father John was to travel with them, had agreed to allow Annys's Harry to join the pages so that he would not miss his lessons. Harry, needless to say, was ecstatic, Annys less so.

Genevra was sad to leave Martin and Annys behind. Even Captain Nori had become a friend. But the parting, they were promised, would be for no more than half a year.

The day came and they set out, a colourful train of mounted horsemen, sumpter animals and followers on foot. They could scarcely make more than four miles an hour, or cover more than seven leagues in a day and, even so, some of those walking straggled. The days were, in any case, beginning to shorten.

Genevra, renewed and eager after sloughing off her low spirits, basking in her improved relationship with Robert, enjoyed the days in the saddle, the nights spent under strange roofs, although mostly she was not able to lie with him. Now, though, she knew it was from necessity rather than from his choice.

Unfortunately, at one period, it rained for several miserable days on end. When the sun finally came out again in equinoctial brilliance to dry them off, no one greeted it with more relief than Genevra.

Will travelled tucked up in a small crib that she carried strapped on behind her saddle. His young nursemaid did not ride well enough to take the responsibility. The fighting men, who included Robert, Alan and Father John—the priest carried a large sword that he was well able to use—would not welcome a burden that would prevent their responding if attacked.

Genevra could not bring herself to trust the baby with any of the other, more menial servants, or even with Meg or Sigrid, so she carried him herself.

Will remained dry beneath the sheepskin covering the crib but somehow, during those wet days, he seemed to sense the others' misery and tended to grizzle. Besides, he was sitting up now, a sturdy, active child who, travelling in bad weather, was forced to lie still. Another reason for him to protest.

Bernard rode with a basket pannier slung on each side of his horse, a child in each. Meg, sitting a horse lumpily just behind Genevra and beside Sigrid, also no horsewoman, kept peering back anxiously to where Bernard had charge of her precious twins.

'They are quite safe,' Sigrid kept telling her. 'Bernard is an able horseman and quite capable of looking after the twins! They will come to no harm in his care.'

'I know,' Meg confessed. 'It just seems strange to be so far from them.'

Genevra, overhearing, smiled to herself and glanced over her shoulder to where her baby, safely tucked into his crib, was asleep.

With the sun out again, Genevra decided to give him a change, took him from the cradle and propped him up before her in the saddle.

'Do not drop him!' said Robert, anxiously eyeing his son and heir, who smiled widely and blew him a bubble.

'No, lord. Chloe is good-tempered and must get used to carrying him.'

As must Prince, Robert decided as he acknowledged Genevra's reassurance. Watching the pleasure on the child's face, he could scarcely wait for the proper opportunity to take his son and heir up before him.

His son and heir. He must be. Yet there was, as yet, no discernible feature to clinch the question of Robert William's paternity. Mayhap there never would be. After all, many children did not resemble their parents in any way. At least Will was fair of hair and blue of eye.

So was Drogo.

Robert thrust the treacherous thought aside. He had vowed to overcome his distrust and he would, but he had not quite succeeded yet. That kitchen wench who had lain with Drogo had been delivered of a dark child with brown eyes.

Castle gossip said she was more likely to be the bastard daughter of one of the stable hands than Drogo's. But no one, possibly even the wench herself, who was middling fair, could be certain, and so the girl would be taken care of, her child brought up within the castle's walls.

Drogo. His troubles always originated with his young brother. Guilt, jealousy, mistrust, disillusion, all had been born of Drogo's vindictive, unreasonable envy. Drogo had unquestionably cast a deep shadow over his entire life. The cursed knave had much for which to answer.

But so had he, Robert realised for the first time, for allowing the emotions evoked by Drogo to take root.

An uncomfortable conclusion he was not yet ready to face.


The St Aubin train did make an impressive sight and the inhabitants of every town or village through which it passed turned out to watch. Most faces wore expressions of interest and due deference, though some scowled, even spat, while a few merchants hastily put the shutters up over their wares, anticipating trouble.

But Robert's men were well disciplined, at least while under his eye. On only one occasion, when the night's rest was taken near a town, did a band of his men descend on the local tavern, quaff too much ale, cause trouble and end up being flogged.

'They will not be so foolish again,' Robert told Genevra grimly, joining her after supervising the punishment.

'No,' agreed Genevra. 'Twas the first time she had known Robert to order a flogging, but it had been deserved and necessary. He wanted no ill-repute attached to his name as he toured the countryside.

Before approaching Ardingstone Robert ordered a day's halt, during which everyone refreshed themselves, groomed their horses and smartened up their equipment.

Before they set out on the final two leagues, Robert inspected his men, their horses and trappings, to ensure that all traces of the long journey had been eradicated. He wanted everyone, including himself and his wife, to arrive immaculately turned-out, with banners and pennons flying. For the occasion, he had donned his coat of mail and over it wore his heraldic jupon.

And so Genevra entered the castle gates, riding at the side of the Golden Eagle, though he had merely a shining steel bascinet on his head, from which depended the chain mail which protected his throat. Golden heaumes with impressive crests were reserved for jousting at tournaments and for other ceremonial occasions.

Genevra almost burst with pride as the long, brilliantly appointed train followed them into the bailey. Accommodating the entire company inside manors, castles and religious establishments on the journey had been difficult. Many of the retinue had been forced to sleep in tents, the grooms in stables with the horses.

Here, she thought, looking round, it would be the same. Silken pavilions housing knights, and skin tents for men-at-arms and tradesmen, were already scattered about the outer bailey.

No doubt the train of the Duke and Duchess of Lancaster, the self-styled King and Queen of Castile, had been far larger and more splendid than theirs. Prince John would have brought several of his more important vassals with him, including a number of knights.

He was not often in England and was unpopular with the people, who thought him stern and greedy for power, but Robert did not share this view. He approved of him; and anyone Robert liked, Genevra was willing to like, too.

They had been allocated a largish chamber furnished with a velvet-draped bed, its headboard and posts decorated with golden scrolls. Truckle beds for their personal servants, with whom they must share the room, were stored beneath, to be pulled out at night. But their own privacy would be assured by the thick red curtains enclosing them.

Northempston greeted them warmly when they entered the ante-room in response to the summons to the banquet. He wanted to know whether they had found Merlinscrag a worthy inheritance, asked after their health and congratulated them on the birth of their son.

'You must come to me in my private apartments,' he said. 'I shall send for you—say on the morrow, before supper? What say you, Robert?' At Robert's nod of agreement, he chuckled. 'Bring the child. I long to meet my namesake.'

He then presented them to the Duke and Duchess and to other important guests. John of Gaunt, Genevra noted, remembered Robert as a brother-in-arms. They had fought together on several occasions, most recently at Najera in Castile, when the seeds of John's later ambition to become its king had been planted.

Like everyone else present on this glittering occasion, Genevra wore all her jewels: those she had inherited, including the ones from her mother's coffer, and those Robert had given into her keeping—family heirlooms

which were passed from eldest son to eldest son and
worn, mostly, by their ladies. For the occasion, Robert
had ordered the most costly materials, which had been
fashioned into a new gown before they left Merlinscrag.

Genevra loved the soft, clinging green silk of the low-
necked kirtle and the stiffer bronze samite, woven with
threads of gold, from which her highly decorated sideless
surcoat was made. A golden eagle spread its wings across
her breast and decorated the long train that swept the
rushes as she moved.

She had to lift her skirts to walk and the jewels in
her slippers flashed with every step she took. Her
wired, heart-shaped headdress was of gold tissue, with
more jewels nestling on her forehead between the
swelling lobes.

Following his more sober inclinations, Robert confined
his display of jewellery to a minimum, wearing merely
a brooch in his pleated cap, several rings and his jewelled
knightly belt, which rested on his hips over a costly
cotte-hardie of black brocade shot with gold thread and
decorated with clusters of pearls.

But even he wore embroidered slippers set with
precious stones and the hilt of his knife was richly
wrought and encrusted with cabochon gemstones that
flashed as he used it. In this company, some heed must
be paid to appearances. There was a need to display one's
wealth, for it tended to establish one's position of power.

However, with a duke and several earls present, a
baron was of minor consequence. They were not, therefore, placed at the High Table but at one nearby, with
other guests of similar rank. Her uncle and aunt, Genevra
was relieved to discover, were not present; whether from
choice or because they had not been invited, she did
not know.

From where she was seated, Genevra could watch the Earl of Northempston and his distinguished guests. The Duke and Duchess were ensconced in the chairs of state. The lord William was engaged in a discussion with Lancaster for much of the time; she could not help but admire the assured way in which he addressed his exalted guest, who was, of course, the younger man.

But she thought that, even in the seventeen months since she had last seen him, the lord William had aged. It must have been a severe blow to him to have lost his remaining heirs to the pestilence and, although his energy seemed undiminished and his figure was still stalwart, his tendency to melancholy had grown.

Quite often, when she looked in his direction, she caught him studying her even while speaking to Lancaster. It made her self-conscious. Mayhap he was wondering whether his matchmaking had been successful, whether she had turned out to be worthy of her position as a baron's wife.

She thought that, considering the matter objectively, theirs was a better match than most, particularly remembering Robert's past experiences and her own background, both of which cast shadows that made their relationship difficult. Although she tried to ignore it, from the first she had feared that her base birth would affect her husband's attitude towards her, and she was becoming more and more certain that it did.

Like mother, like daughter. How often had she heard that said? Had she been the legitimate daughter of a nobleman of repute, he would surely not have doubted her integrity. But she was not, and he did. And so, at the moment, theirs was not the perfect union she had once thought to make it. It seemed unlikely that Robert would ever come to truly love and trust her.

The hours passed as the banquet ground on its inexorable way. The atmosphere became more heated and hazy with smoke, the laughter louder, the behaviour more lax. Robert had imbibed a good deal, but he was not drunk.

She again gave thanks that her husband never degraded himself by his behaviour or by ending the evening in a drunken stupor. But, having exhaustively discussed the present dire state of the monarchy with his neighbour, he had become engaged in a deep discussion of how the perfect tournament should be organised. He scarcely noticed when she decided to retire.

True to his promise, Northempston sent a page to fetch them the next afternoon. The nursemaid carried Will into his presence but, once the elderly nobleman had the child safely in his arms, was summarily told by the Earl to wait outside.

Will immediately protested at being removed from the comfort of familiar arms to others that smelled and felt strange. Genevra, agitated, moved to take him herself, but the Earl merely chuckled as he waved her away and sat in his carved oak chair.

Genevra, thus silently instructed to sit on a nearby stool, had never seen Northempston so relaxed, not even on his visits to the convent. Here, in his private chamber in his own castle, he seemed prepared to drop the last vestiges of the dignity required by his rank.

'Go on, my lad,' he urged. 'Show us what strong lungs you have. Lungs worthy of your inheritance. Your voice will surely carry across any battlefield!'

'Should I not take him, lord?' asked Genevra, afraid that, for all his present benevolence, the Earl might become irritated by the red-faced, bellowing infant he held. After all, he had the reputation of having been a stern and unyielding parent.

But Northempston merely shook his head. He bounced the baby and murmured reassuring words and, miraculously, Will's cries turned first to hiccoughs and then ceased. To Genevra's relief the child seemed to be reassured, even to have taken to the Earl. He gave a wide, gummy smile and clutched at the glittering brooch fastening his lordship's gown.

It was then that Genevra caught sight of the regret, the longing, in the Earl's expression. He had no sons, no grandchildren, let alone great-grandchildren, no one to inherit his title. His possessions would go to remote kin, she supposed. Death, largely in the guise of the plague, had deprived him of his true heirs. Only last evening Robert had remarked on the softening in the Earl's manner over the last years.

'Grief has not hardened him,' he had said when he came to their room and joined her in the bed, 'but made him more compassionate. He did not treat his sons well, even I could see that. They could not help being what they were. No doubt he thought it necessary to be harsh in order to mould them to his will, but it did not serve in the end. His sons dared not cross him in life, but now they are dead and he is left bereft of children and grandchildren.

'Mayhap,' he had mused, 'it is because of this that he chose to become patron of your convent. As an atonement to a God who has seen fit to punish him by depriving him of all his heirs.'

'But many men in his position think it their duty to be harsh with their children and they are not made to pay,' Genevra had said.

'Are they not? Think you the lord William is the only

nobleman left without progeny to perpetuate his name? Many think that the visitations of the pestilence were punishments for mankind's sins.'

'Mayhap they were,' Genevra said. 'But if so, then the punishment fell most unfairly, on the good and the bad alike.'

Robert had leaned over to kiss her. 'Be careful, sweeting, or you will be named a heretic.'

'You do not think me so?' she had asked.

'Nay, wife. I know 'tis but your questing mind that asks these questions. And if you are a heretic, then so am I.'

He had kissed her again before turning over to sleep. But now, studying the man who held her son in his arms, she could feel nothing but sadness for a father who, however misguided, had sought to do his best for his sons and been, in her view, unfairly punished.

'Well, Robert,' the Earl said when he had done with jollying the child, who now seemed quite happy to remain where he was, 'you have a fine son and heir. I congratulate you again.'

'I thank you, lord. I am indeed proud.'

Genevra watched Robert's face as he made the affirmation and saw his clouded blue eyes evade the Earl's gaze. He shifted uneasily on the seat he had chosen, the stone sill of the window embrasure. He was not comfortable with his mentor's congratulations. She found it in her heart to curse Drogo.

Northempston, noticing nothing, went on, 'So your squire, Alan of Harden, is to be knighted by His Grace the Duke, eh? You are satisfied with his worthiness to receive the honour?'

Now Robert relaxed, smiled even. 'Aye, lord. Alan has served me well and faithfully and excels in all arms.

He will make a comely, gallant knight.'

'He has had an excellent tutor, Robert.' The Earl sighed. 'If only you were my son!'

'I have always regretted that I am not, my lord. Yet I believe you could not have been kinder to me an I were.'

Northempston gave a brief and rather bitter laugh. 'Say truth, Robert! I was too harsh with my sons. I treated you with more tolerance and understanding, mayhap because I had grown older; they were men or almost men when you joined me. But they lacked your spirit, boy. I had only to shout and they quaked, even then!'

He paused, bumping Will on his knee and scrutinising the child with assessing eyes. 'But mayhap there is yet time to remedy some of my mistakes. Have your nurse take the child away.'

Robert called the girl, who relieved Northempston of a crowing Will and carried him from the chamber.

Northempston turned to Genevra, indicating the rose-decorated locket resting on her breast. 'That is an unusual jewel you wear, my lady. May I ask where it came from?'

Genevra's fingers touched the pendant as she answered, 'From my mother, my lord.'

'The lady Margaret Heskith. Aye. Do you have other mementoes of her, my dear?'

Genevra hesitated. She had brought the small coffer with her because she would not be returning to Merlinscrag in the immediate future and she wanted it with her. She had hoped to pursue enquiries into her father's identity while staying nearer London and meeting a wider circle of acquaintances. But she had not yet shared the knowledge of her find with Robert.

The jewellery she had worn because the locket and ring might have been among the things her uncle, Lord Heskith, had passed on to her before her wedding. But were she to admit having found the letters without telling him, would he be hurt? There was something in Northempston's eyes, however, that almost compelled her to confess.

'Other jewellery, my lord, including this ring.' She held out her right hand, where her mother's ring, possibly her wedding ring, snugly encircled her finger. 'And letters.' She glanced quickly at Robert, who stilled and looked at her in surprise.

'Letters?' he asked.

'Aye, Robert. They were with some things she left stored at Merlinscrag. Love letters. I found them in a small coffer in the attic above the solar. The contents were too painful to me to share at the time. You see, they were from my father. But they were unsigned, except for the letter "A".' She swallowed, then said almost inaudibly, 'In them, he called himself husband.'

Robert stood up, moved to rest a hand on her shoulder. 'And that gave you pain, my wife? To think that mayhap you were born legitimate but could not prove it?'

Genevra gave him a quick smile. She should have had more faith in Robert's understanding. 'Aye, Robert. I have always wished I might have brought you an untarnished birthright. I thought I had overcome my dismay at discovering myself born a bastard, but—' her voice shook '—I have not.'

'My dear—' it was Northempston who spoke '—never think yourself unworthy because of your birth. May I see your locket?'

'Gladly, lord.'

Robert undid the clasp for her and handed the chain and its pendant to the Earl. Northempston turned it about, examining the chasing and the jewels with minute interest.

His eyes, quite green in colour as they regarded her, were bright. 'May I open it?'

'Of course. It contains a lock of my father's hair.'

'Ah! Not a miniature?'

Genevra smiled. 'No, lord. I doubt he could afford to commission the painting of a miniature!'

'Yet he could afford this exquisite piece.'

The comment, made in a musing tone, did not require an answer. Genevra waited, wondering what his interest was.

He snapped the locket closed at last, leaned forward and held it out to Genevra. 'May I see the ring?'

She slipped the ring from her finger and, without rising, exchanged it for the locket. Robert moved back to the window.

Northempston examined the ring. 'Good stones,' he remarked, handing it back. 'Both pieces come from the same goldsmith, in London.' He smiled wryly. 'I wonder whether he ever got paid! An he did not, he never complained.'

The last sentence was spoken softly. Robert stirred again. Genevra wondered whether she had heard correctly.

'My lord?' she ventured.

He eyed her thoughtfully. 'Did you never wonder whose badge is on the locket?'

'The rowel? Aye, lord. I possess a seal ring inscribed with the same device. I intend to try to find out.'

The Earl seemed to come to a decision. 'Come here, Genevra,' he commanded.

Genevra rose and took the step necessary to stand in front of Northempston. He took both her hands in his. He smiled. Genevra began to tremble.

'My dear,' said the Earl of Northempston, 'that badge

was adopted by my second son, Arthur. You are my granddaughter.'

The room swum. As she swayed before him, Northempston sprang to his feet to support her. Robert strode from the window to put an arm about her. It was he who spoke.

'Your granddaughter, my lord?'

'Aye, Robert. Now you know why I was so insistent that you wed the wench. I'm only too happy that the match seems to be to your liking.'

Genevra extricated herself from their supporting arms and sat down on her stool. 'But—' she began.

'How did I know? Arthur told me whom he wished to wed, of course. I forbade it, for I had an earl's daughter in mind for him.' He hesitated, then shrugged. 'I sent him to Aquitaine. He died there of wounds received in a skirmish. I was well repaid.' He could not keep the bitterness from his voice.

'That was why my mother waited in vain for him to come for us,' whispered Genevra.

'I fear so. But I had other sons, even a grandson by that time, so Arthur's loss did not appear to be such a tragedy. He had threatened to defy me and, at the time, his death seemed a just punishment for his unfilial behaviour.'

He saw the anguish on Genevra's face and his own softened again. 'I pray you can forgive me, as I believe God has done. You, my dear, are now the only direct descendent left to me.'

'Oh, my lord!'

He grimaced rather than smiled. 'I knew of your existence, for I kept myself informed of Margaret Heskith's activities. You, of course, were why I interested myself in the Convent of the Blessed Virgin in Derbyshire.

Arthur was dead. You were kin, I had to suppose, since my son had been so concerned for your welfare, even if illegitimate. Now, bastard or not, you are the only direct heir I have. I choose, therefore, to leave most of my possessions to you.'

Stunned, Genevra merely gasped.

Northempston waved a hand. 'Something to my sister, of course, but she does not want. I arranged for you to wed a man I trust to administer the estates, and now you have a son to inherit.

'The earldom, Ardingstone and everything else which goes with the honour of Northempston are not included, naturally. But nevertheless it will make a fine inheritance, joined to the barony of St Aubin. To that end, I shall recognise you as my granddaughter and heir. God, in His goodness, has been kind to me at last.'

'My mother,' whispered Genevra, 'told Meg, who is my maid and companion now but was then her tiring-woman and my nurse, that she had wed my father in secret because my father, who had no means of his own, was fearful of being disinherited should he admit to defying his sire.'

Watching the Earl's face she saw him frown, but since he said nothing she went on. 'He intended to seek to change his sire's mind before admitting to his disobedience,' she continued bravely, and saw him wince. 'For that reason, my mother persisted in refusing to name her lover or proclaim herself wed, and died with the secret locked in her heart. Meg, sworn to secrecy, did not tell me all this until my own wedding day.'

Northempston was searching her face intently. 'This Meg believed her?'

'Oh, yes, my lord. And the letters seem to confirm the story.'

'Then she was a loyal and brave wife to my son and we must make inquiries. Others must have known of any marriage which took place. A priest, most certainly.'

''Twas over twenty years since, my lord. The priest may well be dead.'

'True. But I will try. Meanwhile, we must spend time together, my child. And I shall arrange a private audience for you both with the Duke of Lancaster. You already know him, Robert. I have a request to put to him in your presence.'

'A request, lord?' wondered Robert.

'Aye. I shall not tell you what it is. Do you hunt with us on the morrow?'

The subject had been changed. Robert nodded, as did Genevra who, although still slightly dizzy from the news so recently imparted to her, felt that a good gallop across country was just what she needed to clear her head.

That Northempston should be her grandfather seemed incredible. She had believed her father to have been the son of a powerful baron, but not of a magnate as important as Northempston. And to think that all her grandfather's possessions, apart from Ardingstone and other properties which were attached to the earldom, would be hers and Robert's one day!

Robert's, she amended in her mind. She would make it all over to him, then Will would inherit on his death rather than hers. That must be right. It was already agreed that she would have Merlinscrag as part of her dower. Mayhap she could bequeath that to her eldest daughter.

Northempston embraced her and kissed her forehead as they took their leave. Genevra had the strange experience of being made to feel as though she belonged. Not since her mother's death had she known it so strongly.

She had tears in her eyes and her head was still whirling when they left the Earl's apartments to return to their chamber. As they traversed the long, stony galleries and corridors, her hand resting on his as he escorted her to their wing of the massive pile, they scarcely spoke.

'Are you not happy, my husband?' asked Genevra at length.

'Of course. Delighted for you, sweeting. And most grateful to his lordship for bestowing his granddaughter's hand upon me.'

It was a cool speech. Mayhap he was as confused as she. 'And conferring on Will a splendid inheritance,' she reminded him.

'Aye. There is that, too.'

And therein, thought Genevra sadly, lay the root of his colourless response. Illogical though it was, he still could not entirely convince himself that Will was his son and worthy to inherit the St Aubin barony.

The hunt next morning refreshed Genevra much as she had hoped. Added to the excitement of the chase was the knowledge that they were riding over land that was her grandfather's, that she belonged here at Ardingstone. They returned with a couple of wild boar to add to the table and with appetites that could have consumed the animals there and then.

Alan was engaged in his preparations for the ceremony of knighthood. He must bathe and keep vigil all night before the altar of the church.

Harry and the pages had quickly been absorbed into the company of others of their age and status, though Father John kept a careful eye on them to see that they came to no harm and did not fall into bad company. Harry was ecstatically happy.

'I shall be a knight one day,' he vowed, helping Alan

don the accoutrements with which a knight must be equipped.

He must have a shirt of mail, a helmet, shield and lance. These Alan had been collecting in anticipation of the day he became a knight. He already owned a decent sword and Robert presented him with a fine chestnut destrier and the golden spurs which only a knight was entitled to wear.

Six squires were to be dubbed next day and afterwards they would try their skills against each other in a small tournament watched by their assembled lords.

The ceremony went without a hitch. Alan was by far the most handsome of the aspirants, considered Genevra, as each one in turn went forward to make their vows and be struck on the shoulder by the Duke. Afterwards, watching the jousting, she thought nostalgically of the tournament from which the Golden Eagle had emerged the victor. She remembered how Robert St Aubin had seemed to her to embody the very concept of chivalry, to be her perfect knight.

Of course, he was not perfect. He was simply a man with all a man's mixture of strengths and weaknesses. Hers had been a girlish dream of a love that overcame every difficulty and ensured everlasting happiness. Life was not like that. Perverse emotions got in the way, causing reactions to events that one seemed powerless to overcome. But that did not mean that her love had died. She loved Robert now, knowing his faults and sympathising with his doubts, more deeply than ever.

She believed that, despite everything, he had grown fond of her. One great service her grandfather had undoubtedly done her was in not telling Robert of their relationship, confining himself to urging the match.

Compared to the inheritance that was now to be hers, Merlinscrag was almost inconsiderable.

But he had not known of her prospects. He had wished to please Northempston, and had not expected much profit to himself to result. So—had he not been able to face taking her as his wife, he must surely have refused. And her grandfather would have found some other worthy lord to espouse her.

That Robert found her desirable was proved night after night. She knew he enjoyed her company. That, too, was evident. Without Drogo's shadow constantly darkening his mind, Robert might have learned to love her as much as she loved him.

Alan distinguished himself in running his courses on the lists. Others continued to demonstrate their skills as a page came to call them to the loge where Northempston entertained his distinguished guests. And it was there, while the tournament carried on and the cheers rang out, that he presented them again to the Duke of Lancaster.

'Your grace,' he said, 'I asked for this opportunity to present Lord St Aubin once more because I have a favour to ask of you on his behalf.'

John, who had greeted them with engaging warmth, lifted his fair brows. They could have been brothers, Genevra thought, her husband and Prince John, although Lancaster wore a beard and Robert remained clean-shaven. They shared the same colouring.

'A favour, Northempston?' the Duke asked, his manner immediately tending towards the imperious.

'Aye, your grace. You have known St Aubin these many years, though mayhap not intimately. What you have not known until now is that his wife, formerly Mistress Genevra Heskith, is my granddaughter.'

John of Gaunt glanced from Northempston to Genevra

and back again. 'Granddaughter, William? I did not know you had issue still living?'

'I lack legitimate issue, your grace. But Genevra Heskith's mother and my son Arthur were lovers. We believe they may have been secretly wed, though that is yet to be proven. However, I should like to think that my great-grandson, her son Robert William, shall one day inherit Ardingstone and all else so graciously bestowed upon my ancestors by yours. For that to happen, the title I hold must be his, too.

'I therefore pray your grace to use your influence with the King your sire to grant the earldom to Genevra's husband, Robert St Aubin, on my death. My grandson would then, in due course, inherit the title.'

Genevra held her breath. She heard Robert catch his. The request was unexpected but not so strange. And it was one with which John of Lancaster, surely, could sympathise. He had been granted the earldom of Lancaster as the husband of the eldest of the two daughters who, on the old Earl's death, had inherited his possessions. Only later had the honour of Lancaster been elevated to a royal dukedom.

Slowly, Lancaster nodded. ''Tis a reasonable request. I will approach the King and further the matter to the best of my ability. But my powers and influence are not great, as you must be aware.'

'I can ask no more, your grace, but for your sympathetic backing. I shall send to my sovereign lord the King immediately with my request.'

Genevra could see the sudden, flaring joy on her husband's face and knew supreme happiness. She would be the instrument through which his promised good fortune would come. 'Twas every man of rank's ambition to rise higher, to enrich his family, to wield a wider influence.

He bowed his knee before Lancaster. 'My lord of Northempston has been as a father to me these many years, your grace. I have him to thank for my present happiness. Should I be fortunate enough to be granted the honour of Northempston, I shall do my utmost to uphold its dignity with my heart and with my sword.'

Genevra's heart swelled as she watched Robert kiss the Duke's hand. Then, having made their parting obeisance, they were escorted back to their own places.

'Well, wife,' murmured Robert when they were more or less alone again—at least, no one could hear what they said, 'I had not thought this visit could hold so many surprises. We leave for Thirkall on the morrow. I wonder what awaits us there?'

Drogo, thought Genevra, and shivered.

# *Chapter Thirteen*

❧❧❧❧❧

Thirkall was not what Genevra had expected. She had never questioned Robert about his chief residence, the home where he had been born and spent his early childhood, being content to wait and see for herself what it was like.

When he spoke of it he called it a castle, but the old defensive structure, perched on the top of a low mound and surrounded by a ditch, had long since fallen into disrepair.

On the lower land beneath stood a new manor house, set in the curve of a river, the land within the loop made into a small, defensible island by a joining leet, the waters from which turned the mill wheel.

Surrounded by the richly verdant fields, the pastures and woodlands which provided its lord with his wealth, the house presented a quiet aspect, but the walls were pierced by narrow arrow slits that overlooked the arched bridge crossing the river from the barbican to the entrance, and battlements dagged the skyline.

It was a house, however, not a castle, despite several towers and a heavy, studded oak door, for it had large mullioned windows glazed by small panes of glass set in lead, like those found in some churches, and tall chimneys rose above the roof with smoke coming from them to drift away on the slight wind. The flow of water around the building appeared to be fast enough to keep the stream clean and sweet.

After Merlinscrag, perched as it was on a windy cliff with pounding waves below and steep hilly countryside behind, Thirkall, surrounded by rolling countryside, appeared as a haven of rural peace. The contrast between both the buildings and the locations could not have been greater.

Yet Robert had come to love Merlinscrag for its very wildness and she expected to love Thirkall as a warm, welcoming place to spend the winter. They were, she thought, blessed in their diverse choice of residences.

Nearby, hens and geese, pigs and dogs roamed the village, which comprised a huddle of dwellings each one complete with dung heap and garden, a cow byre and pig sty. A small church, with a house attached and the priest's glebe lands stretching away behind, had been built at its edge.

In the distance, labourers toiled on the strips, a team of oxen dragged a plough, children with slings shot stones at hovering birds to keep them off the autumn sowing. The harvest was in. In the barns, men worked between two large open doors wielding flails to thresh the grain for others to winnow. Clouds of dust rose from the great shallow pans being whirled to make the lighter husks fly off. None of this activity marred the scene. It was part of the rhythm of the land.

Genevra's gaze, drawn by a shrill whinny, moved to a field where several mares grazed while their foals skipped and jumped and chased each other for the sheer joy of being alive.

She patted Chloe's neck as her mare's ears pricked and she answered the sound. Robert was watching the animals with a satisfied expression on his face.

'The brood mares have done well,' he remarked. 'Let us hope we have hay and oats enough to feed them through the winter.'

'You will have planned it so,' said Genevra with a smile.

'Aye. The barns should be full. But we shall have to kill most of the cattle and sheep. The ground, as yet, does not yield enough to feed them all when the grass ceases to grow. Though, as you can see, at the moment they are nibbling the stalks of the cut crops and dunging the ground at the same time. Mayhap, next year, we shall have a larger yield and more barns to store it in.'

'At the convent, the nuns were trying to improve their methods of farming. You are interested in doing the same?'

'Practices vary and I hope to use the best. My new land steward has made a study of them. Between us, we hope to make the fields more fertile.'

They were almost at the barbican. The watchman and Herald exchanged blasts and they clattered through to cross the bridge and trot sedately along the bridleway leading to the house.

His family knew they were coming for, of course, he had sent word ahead. So it was no surprise to see the great entrance gates flung wide, giving access to the courtyard round which the house and some outbuildings had been built.

Horns sounded, banners flew. Their lord was returning with his wife and heir and doing so in grand style. He wore no armour, though the protective helmets of his escort shone in the low-slung sun and the thick leather

jerkins they wore provided a sensible precaution
against attack.

Genevra rode beside Robert, through the gates and
across the courtyard, to dismount before the entrance to
what must be the south and main wing. A group of
women waited there, two richly clad and obviously
ladies of rank.

As Robert took her hand and led her forward the elder
of the two women, a stiff, thin lady of some sixty years,
extended her hands in greeting.

'Welcome home, my son,' she said. Like her letter, her
voice lacked the warmth Genevra would have expected.

Robert moved steadily towards her, still retaining hold
of Genevra's hand. His voice when he spoke was
also cool.

'It is a pleasure to see you again, my lady, and to
present your new daughter to you. Mother, this is
Genevra Heskith, my wife, Lady St Aubin.'

The dowager Lady St Aubin took a hand of each and
reached up to kiss Robert briefly on the cheek before
turning to study Genevra. As though satisfied, she leaned
forward to kiss her, too. Her lips were shrivelled, her
chin whiskery.

'You are welcome. I have long awaited the day when
my son would bring his heir home.'

The words, sufficient in themselves, lacked the tone
of true conviction. But Genevra's thoughts were diverted
from her mother-in-law by Robert's quiet voice, which
had become suddenly warm with affection as he moved
from Genevra's side to greet his sister.

'Alida.' He took her in his arms. 'God's greetings,
my sister.'

She put up her hands and touched his face, tracing the
contours. 'All is well with you now?' she asked urgently.

'Oh, Robert, how could I have been so stupid?'

I wish he would look at me like that, thought Genevra, suppressing the shaft of jealousy occasioned by the love and tenderness on his face.

'Hush, my dear. 'Twas no fault in you that caused me so much anxiety. Rather, I should blame myself for it, since 'twas I. . .' His voice trailed off. 'But you must meet my wife.'

He made the introduction. His sister was perhaps ten years older than Robert. Possibly more. There must have been other children in between, who had died or been still-born. Then had come Robert and finally Drogo.

Robert's sister had a sweet smile; her face was line-free and gentle. If she resembled either of her brothers in looks, it was the soft-featured Drogo rather than the hard-sculpted Robert.

Alida said, 'May I read your face, sister?'

'Of course.' Genevra knew what to expect, having seen how the blind woman had touched Robert.

Alida's fingers felt like thistledown on her smooth skin and yet Genevra knew that the sightless woman was forming a picture in her mind of her wide jaw and prominent cheekbones, her high-bridged, narrow nose and the brows arching above her eyes. How could she be so foolish as to be jealous of this woman, who was his sister?

'What colour is your hair?' asked Alida.

'Brown, lady.'

'Please call me Alida, or at least sister! And your eyes?'

'Grey.'

'Green,' came Robert's voice from beside her.

'Well, grey-green,' admitted Genevra with a laugh.

'I think you must be beautiful,' said Alida.'

'She is,' confirmed Robert.

Genevra said nothing, but her heart glowed. Robert had sounded genuinely proud of her.

'An you make my brother happy, I shall love you dearly,' promised Alida softly.

The Lady had not interrupted her daughter's inspection of the young, new Lady St Aubin, but now she demanded, 'And where is my grandson, pray?'

A groom had taken the cradle from Chloe's back and the nursemaid had lifted the baby out. Genevra beckoned the girl forward, took Will from her and held him up for his grandmother to see.

'He's a bonny child.' There was admiration in the Lady's voice. 'But you had all better come inside! The wind is quite chill.'

And so Genevra entered Thirkall manor house with its heir clutching at the neck of her cloak to keep himself upright on her arm. Robert's mother led the way and Robert followed, guiding Alida, though Genevra suspected that Alida knew every step of the way and could probably move about a place as familiar as Thirkall without anyone to help her.

The other ladies, clearly trusted servants and companions, brought up the rear, Meg and Sigrid in their midst. Meg had her own nursemaid, who carried in the twins.

There were, Genevra discovered, two halls at Thirkall. An impressive entrance hall, from which stairs led up in a square enclosure, which rose higher than the main roof and ended in a lantern, set within defensive battlements, to give light and air. And, on the left a Great Hall which was, by comparison to others she knew, small, though it reached high to the rafters.

Genevra exclaimed over the huge hearth set in one wall in which a cheerful fire of logs burned brightly, the smoke being carried away up the chimney. No one was expected to sleep here, she was told, but this was where meals were eaten, guests entertained and the manor court held. On a dais at one end stood a long, pedestal table and carved chairs and benches on which the lord and his lady and important guests would sit.

Having inspected the main chamber of the residence, she was ushered upstairs. The staircase, built around a small open well, was wider than any she had previously met and easier to mount. She had yet to see the parlour and the ladies' bower, on the right of the entrance hall, or the library, the steward's office and the bedrooms, which extended round into the building on the west side of the courtyard.

The servants' quarters, stables for the most prized horses, numerous outhouses and storehouses, were all situated on the fourth side, facing north. The men of the garrison and retinue were housed in the towers on each side of the main entrance gate. The kitchen, a separate building possessed of three impressive chimneys, was situated beside the Great Hall and reached by a covered way leading from the rear of the entrance hall.

Robert, naturally, occupied the State Bedroom. It proved to be a large, well-lit room with a solid oak-framed bed hung with heavy blue brocaded material that matched the drapes at the windows, and was situated above the parlour and bower. It had a room with a privy attached, much like the garderobe at Merlinscrag. The main chamber looked south, where a pleasant garden containing small trees and shrubs as well as beds of plants, the flowers long since dead, stretched between the building and the river, skirting the kitchen.

Meg, Sigrid, the squires and Robert's servant were accommodated nearby. The pages had a dormitory of their own but at some distance, near to where Will, with his nurse, was accommodated in a room overlooking the old castle, which obscured any sight of the mill to the west. His nursery chamber lay beyond rooms occupied by the Lady and Alida and their attendants. Genevra fretted and Robert told her not to be so silly.

'He is surrounded by those who care for him, wife. We left him being coddled by my mother and sister. He will be looked after well.'

'Meg has the twins with her,' protested Genevra. Meg had been allocated a room to share with Sigrid, where the two women and the nursemaid could look after the twins. Poor Meg would have to organise opportunities to be alone with Bernard, although now, as Robert's Deputy Master of the Horse, he commanded a small private space above the stables. They would sorely miss the cottage built especially for them at Merlinscrag.

Mayhap, soon, Sigrid could be found another place to sleep, then Bernard could join Meg whenever he liked. But that was not the problem exercising Genevra's mind at that moment. 'I would prefer Will to be here with us,' she insisted.

'This is not some old-fashioned castle, badly built and poorly planned, sweeting. We have no need to share our chamber unless it pleases us so to do. My father, for all his faults, was far-seeing and employed an architect to plan this manor house in the latest style, one that would allow him to live comfortably but be defensible. Which means that everyone else can enjoy a degree of comfort, too!

'His intention was to build something that would be the envy of all his peers, and I think he succeeded. You must surely agree?'

'Oh, I do. I have been nowhere so light and airy and

yet so warm. Why, there is a fireplace with a chimney even in here! His architect was inspired. But I still wish that Will were to sleep here with us. The dogs have been allowed in!'

'But they are merely dumb animals. They cannot eavesdrop when we talk or hear us when we couple. Will can be with you as much as you like during the day; an he sleeps here, his nurse will have to sleep here, too.'

'They did at Merlinscrag.'

'Aye, there was no choice there. Here, there is, and I choose to bed my wife in private.'

That pleased Genevra, as he had known it would. She raised no further objections to leaving Will to the care of his nurse at night. The girl had proved herself loving and competent. And Meg was ever vigilant.

Over the next days, Genevra explored the house and the estate surrounding it. She quickly grew to appreciate its modern conveniences, not least the way the sewage, mostly emanating from what the servants and retinue termed the jakes tower at the corner of the north and west sides, had been channelled into a culvert to discharge into the leet at a point below the mill, so that it flowed downstream and away from the house.

The days were spent in her husband's company as he showed her his entire domain, which included the fields being cultivated by the few remaining villeins, who had been offered their freedom in return for a small payment, and imported day labourers. He was justly proud of his own demesne lands, his stud farm and kennels.

Eventually they visited the village and the church. There he introduced her to the clerk in minor orders who ministered to the villagers, though a distant priest came occasionally to say mass. Genevra then thought she understood why Robert had brought Father John with him, leaving the priest's assistant clerk to minister spiritually to the people of Merlinscrag, and Old Mariel to see to their ills.

'You want Father John to remain here?' she challenged him afterwards.

'I wanted him with us on the journey. The choice will be his as to whether he returns to Merlinscrag or not. An he does not, then I shall engage another secular priest to serve there. Did you think I would rob Merlinscrag to gain advantage for Thirkall?'

The question was put mildly but Genevra flushed, for she had thought it, and was ashamed of herself.

'For a moment I did, husband. Forgive me, I should know you better than that by now.'

They were isolated together for an instant. 'What can any human being truly know of another?' wondered Robert aloud, eyeing her with that in his expression which spoke of a search for reassurance.

Genevra edged Chloe closer and reached out to touch his hand, where it rested on his pommel. Mayhap this was her moment to convince him of her own honesty.

'We can know enough to be certain of the essential goodness or evil in a person,' she told him softly. 'I spoke without thought. I do know that you care for all those you rule and deal with them fairly. Therefore I should have realised instinctively that you would not rob Merlinscrag of its priest simply to obtain his services here.'

His mood changed in an instant. His eyes vivid blue, he smiled, wiping the lines from his face, a transformation that happened with increasing frequency. She was, she thought, winning her argument—he was progressively becoming convinced of her virtue and her honesty.

And she was certain that he was, without acknowledging it, beginning to love her. Actions spoke louder than words. He had brought her Whimsy, currently busy sniffing among the gravestones and crosses, and her every need was met with generosity and alacrity. Bed was a haven of joyous intimacy. His concern for her safety appeared almost obsessive.

Whimsy seldom left her side, and growled at any stranger who approached her mistress. There had scarcely been need of the retainer Robert had stationed outside their chamber at Ardingstone, and who had escorted her everywhere were Robert himself not with her. Sigrid, too, had stuck to her side and Genevra suspected that she had received instructions so to do, unless Robert or Meg were with her.

Genevra had not been upset by the watch kept on her. Ardingstone was vast; all kinds of people wandered its courts, galleries and corridors. Robert wanted no mischance to befall her while she was there.

Here, there seemed to be no reason for him to take such precautions. Yet a man-at-at arms was always present, not only outside their door, but also outside Will's chamber.

She had remarked on it. 'Surely, husband, in your own fief, you are not fearful of mischief?'

'There are those here who have a certain loyalty to Sir Drogo, my sweet. Or who may be paid or blackmailed to do his work for him. I am happier when certain of your safety.'

She had believed him. It was not so much distrust as anxiety which made him so careful of her.

Because of Robert's eagerness to show her Thirkall in its entirety and to present her to his people, it was several days before Genevra found herself alone in the ladies' bower with his mother and sister. Alida, she sensed, wanted to make a friend of her. The Lady, while outwardly welcoming and pleasant in her manner, treated both Robert and his wife with reserve.

Both women, as a courtesy, had appeared for supper in the Great Hall on the day they arrived, but the Lady and the lady Alida preferred to eat in the small parlour, which was how Drogo had been able to get away with his lie as to the state of the Lady's health. Genevra could understand why Alida should wish to eat in private, for she must be conscious of fumbling and making the occasional mistake while feeding herself, and this was confirmed by Alida herself.

'You have not always been blind, I believe?' Genevra asked.

'Nay, I had seen some twenty summers before the accident that blinded me befell.'

'A piece of nonsense, for which I blame Robert,' said the Lady abruptly.

'You should not, Mother. I have told both you and Drogo, time without number, that it was entirely my own fault, but Drogo will not believe me and still holds it against Robert. And because you do, too, though not so violently as does Drogo, who at the time was too young to understand anyway, Robert blames himself.'

'And so he should. He was sent to serve Northempston because he was uncontrollable. But even your accident did not deter him from future devilment.'

'He was a high-spirited child, Mother, full of fun and courage. Father did not understand him and made his life a misery. He was, I think, happier with the Earl.'

'He was,' affirmed Genevra. 'I have heard him say that Northempston treated him more kindly and with more understanding than he did his own sons. Robert's own father being so unsympathetic, he found the Earl's treatment of him a vast improvement and has always been grateful to him. He was proud to belong to Northempston's affinity. But how did the accident happen, Alida?'

Alida smiled. 'Robert was always mad for horses, could ride before he could walk, almost. He was home on a visit when he found a hedge it would be a challenge to jump, since there was a ditch with water in it behind and almost immediately beyond that a stone wall, the remnants of a disused building. 'Twas a difficult combination of obstacles but he was confident he could do it and I was equally confident of my own horse and capabilities. I agreed to the challenge with my eyes wide open—'

'And never saw another thing again,' said the Lady grimly.

'No. But, Mother, I was ten years older than Robert, 'twas my fault entirely for agreeing to allow him to make the jump and then to follow him over. 'Twas exciting. There were a couple of grooms in attendance, but no one who could say me nay.'

She broke off of her own accord, her blue eyes, blank now, staring into space but seeing only the events of the past. 'He took his horse over like a bird. It looked so easy. I put my Noble at the hedge, he took it well, but the wall beyond was too much for him. He stumbled. I fell and hit my head on the stone of the wall. I thank God that I am still alive. Robert, of course, received a thrashing.'

'Which he soundly deserved. You were condemned to live the life of a recluse here at Thirkall, with no chance of a husband.'

Alida chose to ignore her mother's remarks. 'I could not return to Court, that is true. But I still ride, with an escort, and I have not been entirely without suitors. That I am not wed is of my own choice. I am content.'

'You were at Court?' asked Genevra, immediately interested.

'Aye, my dear. I knew your aunt.'

'My. . .aunt?' Genevra was puzzled, since she had no aunt that she knew of, unless—but Alida could not possibly mean Hannah?

'Yes. Baron Heskith's daughter, Margaret. Of course, he is dead now and your father is the baron—'

'You mistake, lady. I am Margaret's daughter, not the present baron's. Did you not realise? Did Robert not make it plain? I was born a bastard.'

A choking noise came from the Lady. 'He most certainly did not! So my son has had the gall to produce an heir whose mother is a bastard, is that it? Trust Robert to do the most outrageous thing he could!'

Genevra felt her temper rising. She knew now why the Lady had not been invited to their wedding or told precisely who it was he was marrying. She was, apparently, always severely critical of her son's actions, and would have made a scene. Yet, despite this, he held his mother in affection and esteem. Why, otherwise, should he speak of her as he did and rush to her when he thought her to be ill and asking for him?

'He did it, my lady, at the request of the Earl of Northempston,' she said. 'At the time neither of us knew it, but his lordship has since acknowledged that he knows me to be his granddaughter and has followed my progress with interest. Despite my base birth, he is prepared to leave all his possessions to me. And has requested the King to bestow the earldom on Robert at his death.'

Genevra had kept her voice level with an effort. Even
so, she could not quite keep the note of triumph from
her voice at the end. To her delight, the Lady looked
properly astonished and deflated. Words, clearly, failed
her. Alida, on the other hand, leant forward, her face
alight, her hand reaching out towards Genevra.

'Margaret's daughter? Oh, my dear, I knew she was
pregnant, of course. But have you believed, all these
years, that you were born outside wedlock?'

'Aye, Alida. My mother never said otherwise.'

'I can tell you that you were not!'

'Aah!' Genevra closed her eyes and let out a deep
sigh of satisfaction. 'Everyone thought me a bastard. My
grandfather, Baron Heskith, was always kind to me but
my uncle's wife had me sent to a convent the moment
he died and Uncle Gilbert inherited. Only recently have
I come to believe that my mother may have entered into
a secret marriage with my father.'

'Who was?' demanded the Lady urgently, having
recovered her voice.

'Lord Northempston's younger son, Arthur, my lady.'

'And they were wed, Mother! I was one of the Queen's
ladies, too, and Margaret confided in me. A priest performed the ceremony in a church near the Palace of
Eltham, where we were in residence at the time. They
made their vows at the church door and then took part in
a nuptial mass. The Church must recognise the marriage!
Margaret told me all about it afterwards, though she did
swear me to absolute secrecy.

'Northempston was indeed severe on his sons and
Arthur was terrified of rousing his ire. He depended upon
his father for his allowance and, of course, could have
been prevented from gaining control of his inheritance
an he displeased his sire—'

'Aye,' said Genevra. 'His lordship has confessed to all this. He regrets his harshness now he has mellowed with time, I believe, but had either of his sons stood up to him as your brother did, he would have been better pleased.

'He was—mayhap still is—a man who believes it right to treat those he loves with harshness, but does not expect them to cower before him. If they do, he can no longer respect them. He could not bear to see the effect his severity had upon his sons. I imagine it made him feel guilty. And, in consequence, he became even more harsh. I pity him.'

'But do you like him?' asked Alida.

Genevra considered, but only for a moment. 'Strangely enough, yes, I do, though I cannot say that I love him. He used to visit the Convent of the Blessed Virgin, where I was sent as a pupil and where I was left to moulder until I was one-and-twenty! My uncle, Lord Heskith, made no attempt to find a match for me, since he stood to lose the revenues from Merlinscrag either on my marriage or on my attaining the age of one-and-twenty. He wished to keep them for as long as possible.

'The Earl, though, made the Convent gifts and spoke to all the sisters and pupils. I sometimes wondered why he seemed to spend more time talking with me than with the others, but it never occurred to me that he had a personal interest—not until I discovered that he had promoted the marriage between Lord St Aubin and myself.'

'And my son accepted the match, knowing it would offend me?'

'I fear so, my lady. You see, above everything, he wished to please the Earl of Northempston, who had stood to him as a father. He owed him loyalty and obedience. I do not pride myself that it was my status or person that persuaded him to agree.'

'But, my lady mother, do you not see? You have no grounds for your objection to the marriage, because Genevra is not base-born!'

'But can she prove it?'

That was a question Genevra could not answer.

Robert, told of what had passed, first of all made it quite clear to the Lady that his choice of wife was entirely his own concern and none of hers.

Afterwards, in their bedchamber, with only Alida present besides themselves, he questioned his sister further. Only then did he propose taking immediate action to try to prove the legitimacy of Genevra's birth.

'For your sake and for our children's,' he told her gently. 'I wed you, not your pedigree, but we live in a world that sets great store by rank and legitimacy. Therefore, if the marriage can be proved to have taken place, I shall rejoice.'

'I should rejoice for your sake, Robert. I know the Golden Eagle did me, a supposed bastard, great honour by taking me to wife, and only did so at the behest of the Earl of Northempston.'

Robert smiled. 'I considered the union only because he asked it of me, that I confess. I knew he must have good reason for suggesting it. But once the Golden Eagle had seen you, sweeting, it would have taken a great deal more than your supposed base birth to make him forego the match.'

'Really, Robert?'

'Really, Genevra. Now, to business. We must seek out the church and the priest who wed your parents.

Doubtless there will be a written record but, if not, the priest's sworn word will suffice.'

'He may be dead, Robert. 'Tis over twenty years since the wedding took place.'

'Aye, some two-and-twenty years, an we are not mistaken. When exactly did it take place, Alida?'

Alida scarcely had to think. No doubt all the events of that time had been brought back to her memory. 'At the end of November in the year fifty. When were you born, Genevra?'

'At Lammas-tide the following year.'

Alida turned her serene face towards the sound of Robert's voice. 'There you are, then, Robert. Your wife was not only born, but also conceived, within wedlock!'

'My dearest Alida, you must know that it makes not one jot of difference to me when or under what circumstances my wife was born! Genevra is Genevra, and is my wife. That is enough for me and should be for everyone else, too.'

Astonished by this declaration, Genevra could not help but wonder whether Robert truly meant what he said. If so, it took a great load from her mind and made her extremely happy.

'But it will please the Lady to know that there is no blot on your heir's pedigree! I wondered why we were not invited to attend your nuptials, my dear, but now I understand.'

''Twas not only that, sister. I did not wish to involve you or our mother in a long and tiresome journey.'

'That sounds most thoughtful of you, brother, but I know it for an excuse! I for one would rather have been present. I am not an invalid, you know, just because I cannot see.'

'My dear one, I know it. 'Twas more than just an

excuse. You are blind because of my recklessness and I cannot bring myself to risk you again. You are too precious to me.'

'Stuff! I have explained to Genevra that it was no fault of yours that I chose to take that jump. I should have said no and, for your own sake, forbidden you to attempt it. Then we would both have been undisputedly safe. But I, like you, enjoy risk. And so I followed you over the hedge.'

'If you enjoy risk, why have you never risked marriage, sister? You say you are content as you are, but you would surely be happier with an establishment of your own. And children.'

'Having children has never worried me, Robert, I lack the mothering instinct. It must be so,' she added quickly, hearing Robert take a breath to dispute the statement. 'Otherwise I should have forbidden you, a ten-year-old, to take that jump! But an establishment of my own— perhaps. Especially now you are wed. I *am* content, and yet—'

Robert took her hand. 'Yet what, Alida?'

'There is a knight, one of your vassals, Robert, a comely man, so I am told, who has asked me several times to wed him. He is a widower with children, two almost grown, two still young.'

'How old is he?' asked Genevra, picturing some elderly greybeard.

'But five years older than I.'

'Which fief?' This was more to the point, so far as Robert was concerned.

Alida told him.

'He holds one of my richest tenancies. Of course I know Sir Matthew. I had no idea he was interested in you, my sister. You would make any man a perfect wife.

Well, if it is your wish, I shall certainly not oppose the match. I have always found him a pleasant, honest fellow. And you will receive a substantial dowry.'

'Thank you, Robert.' Alida patted the hand holding hers. 'I was certain I could rely on you. I have not quite made up my mind yet, but the idea has a certain appeal. I do not find his presence distasteful. In fact, I have allowed him to kiss me. After all,' she blushed and went on quickly, as though to stifle criticism, 'I cannot see him, so I must feel. And he feels most. . .pleasing.'

'We shall be very happy for you,' murmured Genevra. 'But you must not think that you have to leave because I have come. I shall not always be here and Thirkall will need a chatelaine in my absence.'

'Mother will no doubt still be here and Robert has installed an efficient steward. I shall not be needed. So mayhap I shall be better off somewhere else, where I am.'

They left it at that. But Genevra had little doubt that, despite her protestations of contentment, Alida would welcome an escape from her mother's constant presence.

# *Chapter Fourteen*

Father John, apprised of the situation, expressed himself delighted to undertake the task of searching out his brother in Christ and, through him or in any other manner, obtaining a copy of any record of the marriage between Arthur Egerton and Margaret Heskith made at the beginning of the season of Advent in the twenty-third year of the reign of Edward III. He set out the next day, with a small escort of men-at-arms, vowing to make as much speed as he was able.

A messenger was dispatched to Ardingstone with a letter telling Northempston of the new information and of Father John's mission.

Genevra was forced to practise patience, which proved easier than she might have anticipated, for she found so much to interest her at Thirkall.

She spent more time outdoors than she did in, to the Lady's evident disgust.

''Tis not your place to be forever out hunting or haunting the stables and the kennels,' she admonished her daughter-in-law. 'Your place is in the bower, since it is too cold to sit out in the pleasaunce at this time of the year. There is plenty to occupy you indoors. Your duty is to breed children for your husband, not horses and dogs.'

Genevra flushed uncomfortably, but was determined to stand her ground. 'My lady, I was confined in a nunnery for ten years of my growing life. Now I am free to do as I like, subject only to the lord my husband's approval. He encourages me to hunt with him and to take an interest in the breeding of the horses and hounds. In addition, it is necessary for us to ride out together so that I can meet with his vassals.'

'They should be summoned here,' objected the Lady.

'I prefer to see them in their own homes. My lady, when I breed again, my activities will necessarily be limited. I intend to make the most of the periods in between when I am able to be fully active.'

The Lady still did not approve of her, despite the fact that her birth was virtually proved to be legitimate, and that she was the acknowledged granddaughter of an Earl. Sometimes she thought that nothing she or Robert did would ever please the Lady.

Yet she doted on Will and, at mention of other grandchildren, her face softened.

'William should have been born here,' she said as she stroked the child's golden hair, unable to unbend enough to forgo criticism. 'I trust you will endeavour to be in the right place when future progeny are born. Are you not yet again with child?'

'No, my lady.' She was a couple of days overdue, but Robert would be the first to know if her pregnancy was confirmed, not his mother. If only the Lady had been as welcoming and loving as Alida!

Her mother-in-law's attitude was the only thing Genevra found fault at Thirkall. She lived in the hope that, one day, the Lady's frame of mind would change. If she tried hard, she could sometimes detect a slight thaw in her manner. She would be glad to give birth here if the Lady's hostility ceased. If it did not, then she would rather return to Merlinscrag and the reassuring ministrations of Old Mariel.

Mariel was a strange creature, yet Genevra's confidence in her and her prophesies was growing. She had given birth to a son and Meg had produced healthy twins. She began to believe that she would mother four more healthy children in due course. Two more sons and two daughters. In what order and over how long a period remained to be seen.

As for Mariel's other predictions, well, she had discovered who her father had been and her legitimacy was well on the way to being proven. But the thing which struck her most when she realised its significance, was the fact that the information that might result in success had come from a blind woman. Alida had told what she knew from the darkness of blindness. Could that be what Old Mariel had foreseen?

Two weeks passed and Genevra's courses still had not come and she had developed a slight queasiness in the mornings. She felt it time to admit her hopes to Robert. He had not, strangely, seemed to notice her missed period.

Yet that night, when, in the cosy security of the bed, she confessed to her suspicions after they had made love, he merely grunted.

'I thought you must be breeding again, my love. Did you think I had not noticed the lengthening period since your last indisposition?'

'You knew? Oh, Robert—' she hit him gently on the chest '—you never remarked!'

'I thought I would leave it to you to be certain, sweet-

ing.' He drew a deep breath and gathered her naked body
in his arms again. 'But my rejoicing is unalloyed. Will
will have a sibling, and as long as you survive, I shall
be overjoyed, whether it be a daughter or another son or
even should the child be still-born. You are the most
important person in my life, my wife. Without you beside
me, I should not find it much worth living.'

Genevra could scarcely believe her ears. Robert was,
in so many words, declaring his love.

She touched his cheek with her fingers as she tried to
reassure him. 'I believe I shall be safe, Robert. You know
Old Mariel, of course. You no doubt also know that she
has the gift of sight. I did not tell you that she looked
into my future, for I scarcely knew whether to believe
what she saw or not, but she did and so far everything
she prophesied has come about.'

Robert, unexpectedly, withdrew slightly—so slightly
that only she would have recognised the minute change
of the tension in his muscles. 'What did she say?'

'That I should discover who my father was. That my
child would be a boy and that Meg was bearing a boy
and a girl. That happiness would come to me from the
darkness.'

He picked on the one thing that was not plainly a fact.
'The darkness?' He sounded sceptical. 'What could she
have meant?'

'For a long time I wondered, Robert. But, do you not
realise? Alida is blind and she has given me the hope of
being able to prove my parents' marriage existed. Old
Mariel did not know what she meant at the time. Only
that out of the darkness would come my light.'

She did not repeat Old Mariel's mention of the distrust
between Robert and herself. Nor did she mention death.
Darkness and death, Old Mariel had said. Genevra pre-

ferred not to contemplate what that might mean.

'Was that all she said?' His voice reflected his continuing scepticism.

'Not quite. Husband, she said she saw me with a brood of children, three sons and two daughters. So, you see, I am quite convinced that I shall survive this next childbirth.'

Suddenly, his arms tightened again and he buried his face in her neck. 'I pray her sight is God-given,' he murmured, 'for the prophecy, were it fulfilled, would ensure my future happiness, too.

'Genevra, my love, I have been selfishly suspicious of your honesty in the past, but I want you to know that that shadow has quite lifted from my mind. Seeing you here, at Thirkall, and noting the regard my dearest sister holds you in, has convinced me as nothing else could. Will is mine, I know it now. Can you forgive my past doubt?'

The tears were tricking from the corners of Genevra's eyes to run across her temples into her hair. She shifted to entwine her legs and arms about him. 'There is nought to forgive, my husband. 'Tis Drogo who needs to seek God's forgiveness for all he has made you suffer over the years. But I doubt he ever will.'

'Drogo is vicious, he will try to cause trouble in the future, but I do not think him evil enough to attempt to kill to gain the inheritance. So as long as we have trust between us and work together. . .'

'He can cause us no real harm,' Genevra finished for him.

'We must never allow him to gain influence over the children.'

'No.'

\*     \*     \*

Robert picked up the crawling Will, long since out of his swaddling bands and into skirts, to sit him on the back of Abel, as though the huge hound were a horse. Will clutched at the wiry fur and crowed with delight as his father urged the dog to walk.

''Tis the first time my lord has taken a real interest in him,' Genevra murmured to Meg and Sigrid, both sitting by her side sewing in the Great Hall. It was, in truth, unusual for Robert to be present in the Hall during the day, except to break his fast.

'Men are never drawn to babies,' observed Meg. 'Wait until Master William is old enough to learn to ride and to hold a toy sword in his hand. Then see your lord's interest grow!'

Genevra laughed and Robert looked over.

'He'll make a good horseman.' He smiled, lifting the child from the patient hound's back. 'Won't you, my son?'

Will reached out his arms towards Abel and struggled to make his father understand that he wished to sit on the dog's back again. Robert, with an expression of real affection on his face, obliged his son.

Genevra watched with joy welling in her heart. When she was not outside herself, she preferred sitting in the Great Hall rather than in the ladies' bower, where she found Robert's mother's presence oppressive, or even in the parlour. Both those rooms were in any case too small to allow the pages and other children, not to mention the babies and their nursemaids and the dogs, to be with them.

Now that she was breeding again, if Robert were prepared to remain indoors on occasion, she had another reason to prefer the Hall. He would not be comfortable in the ladies' bower or the parlour.

The Lady often commanded Will's presence, sometimes in her own chamber, but was not prepared to tolerate the noise and bustle of having so many children about her. The nursemaid took him to his grandmother, who did not keep him with her for long.

Alida often left her mother's side to sit with Genevra and her ladies in the warmth provided by logs burning in the massive fireplace. She loved to hear the children's voices and to sit with Will on her lap.

Genevra would miss her sister-in-law sadly when she wed Sir Matthew. The match had been agreed and the wedding arranged to take place in the spring. For Alida, 'twould be the best thing. She would be happy and fulfilled with her husband and her new, ready-made family.

'I shall have to learn my way about my lord's house and demesne,' Alida remarked, as though reading Genevra's thoughts. ''Tis the thing that most concerns me about the move. I know this place so well I need no guide and no stick unless I venture beyond the water.'

'You must visit Sir Matthew often in the next few months,' suggested Genevra. 'Become familiar with your new home before you move there. I'm certain it could be arranged.'

'Of course it could,' said Robert, joining them after returning Will to the care of his nursemaid. 'I, myself could take you there sometimes. In any case, Bernard or some other groom or man-at-arms could escort you—'

'I have never lacked an escort to go wherever I want, Robert! An I can gain Sir Matthew's consent, I shall do exactly as Genevra suggests!'

Robert laughed. 'I had forgotten how independent you are, sister! When next he visits you here, I will indicate that the plan would meet with my approval. You may be older than I am, my dear, but I am still head of this household and, until you are wed, stand in the stead of your father!'

'Nonsense!' cried Alida though she, like Robert, was not serious. 'However, since Sir Matthew is a most courteous and correct gentleman, I am sure he would be easier in his mind over entertaining me in his house an he knows you have no objection.'

Genevra had seldom been so happy as she was in the days that followed. The certainty of her pregnancy grew, as did Robert's demonstrations of affection towards both herself and Will.

He could almost have been called light-hearted as he went about his duties in the courtyard, directing his men, whistling to the dogs and calling them cheerfully to heel.

'You have brought my brother true happiness,' Alida said one day, 'and I thank you. 'Tis no more than he deserves. I do wish that he and Drogo were on better terms.'

'How can they be,' demanded Genevra, 'when Sir Drogo insists on carrying on his pointless feud against him? He set out to ruin any chance of happiness we had in our marriage. I thank God that he was not successful.'

'I pray for him every night,' murmured Alida. ''Twill upset Mother an he does not come to Thirkall for Christmas.'

'For her sake, I expect Robert will allow him to join us.'

Genevra did not look forward to the prospect. But she had little chance to brood over the problem.

The following day, an exhausted messenger arrived from Ardingstone.

The Earl had remained in residence there after his

royal guests had left. He had seemed in unusually good spirits, had spent most of his days out hunting, returning in the evening tired but happy. And then, suddenly, he had been taken by a seizure, fallen from his horse and died.

'He must have had a premonition.' Genevra dabbed at her watery eyes. She had scarcely known her grandfather, but she could not hear of his death without real regret. She had been looking forward to seeing him often, of coming to know him well.

When Robert began to prepare in great haste to attend the funeral, she had still not entirely grasped the fact that she was now a rich woman and that by marrying him, she had enabled Robert to command her fortune, as had been Northempston's intention. Even were he not granted the honour of Northempston and did not inherit Ardingstone, the Earl's other possession were considerable.

It had all happened so quickly, the promise and the realisation of her inheritance.

Being in the early stages of pregnancy, Genevra did not even contemplate attending Northempston's funeral. Just as childbirth was women's business, so death was largely men's. She was unknown and her presence would create a deal of speculation and curiosity she would rather avoid.

'I shall not be away long,' Robert promised as, with Alan—Sir Alan—at the head of his retinue and Robin, now his only squire, in attendance, he mounted Prince in the courtyard.

'God speed you on the journey, husband. I shall await your return with impatience.'

He quaffed the stirrup cup she had offered him, bent from the saddle to kiss her hand, shouted an order, and trotted from the courtyard, his retinue streaming behind him.

As the husband of the heiress, he must arrive in style. Neither of them had mentioned the possibility of his being granted the honour of Northempston. That depended upon the whim of an elderly, senile king. If not on him, then on his council. The Duke of Lancaster would do his best to procure the title for Robert, Genevra felt sure, but his voice could easily be ignored or overruled.

They must wait and see.

Robert had been gone two weeks and more when a slow-travelling party was seen making its way towards Thirkall. From the battlements above the main entrance gates, little could be seen at first but a group of men, a litter and a string of sumpter mules. Then someone among the few soldiers left to defend Thirkall realised that the men wore helmets. And that one of the horsemen wore a long black gown.

Next moment someone shouted, ''Tis Lord St Aubin's pennon!'

'Father John is returning!' cried another.

'Nay, 'tis Sir Drogo's device,' contradicted the man in command of the guard, and immediately strung his bow, drew an arrow and lifted the weapon. 'Prepare to repel his advance! By his lordship's command, he must not be admitted!'

'Call Lady St Aubin! She must say yea or nay!' cried someone else.

Genevra had heard the commotion and ran out into the yard.

'What is it?' she demanded of the guard's captain, who was emerging from the jakes tower.

'I'll find out, my lady,' he panted, dashing towards the gatehouse stairs.

Genevra decided that it would take too long for him to go up, ask his questions, take a look and come down to report. She mounted the stair in his wake.

By the time she emerged on the roof to peer through a crenellation at the advancing party, the guards had made up their minds.

'They are flying both pennons, my lady,' she was told.

There was no sun. She peered into the distance, straining her eyes to catch a glimpse of Robert if it were indeed he who was coming.

'I told you so!' shouted one of the men, who had come with them from Merlinscrag and knew the priest better than the others. ''Tis Father John!'

'Then who is in the litter?' demanded the Captain.

Genevra scanned the group but could see no one dressed in the flamboyant style favoured by Sir Drogo. Yet his pennon was indeed flying.

'Sir Drogo, I imagine,' she said quietly. 'I will go down and be ready to greet them at the barbican on the far side of the bridge. An he is truly ill, we cannot refuse him entry. But you, Captain, will detail three men, in turns, to keep him under constant guard until we are certain that he intends us no ill.'

As she turned to descend the stair, she remembered Drogo's brilliant approach to Merlinscrag. Was this subdued advent a ruse to get past her guard? Why, oh, why did Drogo have to come yet again while Robert was away? It seemed almost like history repeating itself, except that the message from Ardingstone had, without question, been genuine. But Drogo would not scruple to take advantage of Robert's absence. . .

The responsibility was hers. And it seemed that he

was returning in the company of Father John, who knew what had occurred at Merlinscrag. If it was Drogo in the litter, mayhap he was sick.

In any case, the Lady should be able to keep her younger son in check. She must be called.

Genevra sent a messenger to the Lady the moment she reached the courtyard. Then she walked through the main gates, along the bridleway and across the bridge to arrive at the barbican. She missed the reassuring presence of Alan of Harden at her shoulder, but had two stalwart archers at her back.

Father John led the procession and slid from his tired horse as he reached her.

'Greetings, Father. You bring Sir Drogo with you?'

He made obeisance. 'My lady! I met Sir Drogo and his retinue on my way back and since he is, I believe, mortally wounded, I thought it my duty to bring him here, where he can be tended by his family.'

The litter had been slung between two mules and the men leading them brought it forward. Genevra lifted the canopy and looked at Drogo. His sunken face was pale, except for the signs of high fever staining his cheekbones. Sweat beaded his forehead. He moved restlessly, although unconscious. There could be no doubt of his condition being genuine, especially as Father John had vouched for it.

She stepped back. 'Very well. He may enter so that his mother may tend him. But not his escort. They will return to his fief and wait there for news and orders. Who is in charge of them?'

An aggressive man stepped forward, pushing Father John to one side. 'I am, my lady. But we cannot leave our lord unprotected!'

'Why not?' demanded Genevra. 'Think you that Sir

Drogo's mother will allow further harm to come to him?
His personal servant may remain with him, but the rest
of you are to go on your way and wait quietly for orders.
I do not forget the trouble your behaviour caused at
Merlinscrag.

'Should news of any ill-discipline reach my ears here,
you will all be expelled from Lord St Aubin's lands,
which includes Sir Drogo's fief. Now, be on your way.
My men will lead the litter in.'

Sullenly, grumbling under their breaths, they wheeled
their horses and a couple of the sumpter animals, which
carried their personal possessions, and rode off. The rest
of the procession followed Genevra and Father John
across the bridge and into the courtyard where, once
again, the Lady and Alida waited.

The Lady was suddenly transformed. The colour left
her face at the sight of her son, but her inner strength
was revealed. She issued orders and, without hesitation,
took charge of his care.

At her word he was carried to her chamber and
installed in her bed. She, she announced, would occupy
the small chamber where, normally, an attendant slept.

Genevra dismissed the guard she had ordered. Drogo
was in no state to sit up, let alone make mischief.

Father John tended Drogo's wound, poulticed it with
herbs and rebound it. Genevra, watching with the Lady
and ready to assist, could not contain a gasp of horror
when she saw the putrid flesh surrounding a deep wound
beneath his right arm. The sight convinced her that Father
John was right in his prognosis. Drogo stood no chance
of recovery.

Alida, standing nearby, heard her gasp and asked
urgently, 'Is it bad?'

Genevra's voice shook as she answered, 'I fear so.'

'There is no hope?'

'I fear not,' said Father John, washing his hands in a bowl of water.

Alida felt for a stool and sat down.

'How did it happen?' she asked Father John.

'I did not see,' said the priest. He folded the towel he had used and set it aside. 'We found him lying at an inn one night. His men were taking him home, but without assistance they would surely have failed to get him there alive. I tended his wound and offered to accompany them, to bring him back here. They had little choice but to accept.'

'But the wound,' persisted Genevra. 'Did he fight a duel?'

Father John looked uncomfortable and glanced at the Lady. 'Not a duel.'

'Do not mind me, Father,' said the Lady grimly. 'Tell us what you know.'

Father John spoke reluctantly. 'According to his retinue, 'twas the result of a drunken brawl. Swords were drawn. . .I believe there was a female involved.'

'Fighting over a strumpet,' said his mother, half in disgust, half in pity, as she patted her son's burning forehead with a cloth wrung out in cold water. 'Do not think I do not know what my son has become, Father. He had no luck in his life.'

'He had the luck to be born a St Aubin, my lady!' protested Genevra. 'Had he overcome his jealousy of his older brother. . .rejected the vicious hatred he nursed in his bosom instead of allowing it to fester and grow. . .'

'He won his spurs,' put in Alida softly. 'My poor brother. He should have taken his knightly vows seriously. He could have made a name for himself, as Robert did.'

'Robert was always there before him,' said the Lady gruffly. 'And then there was you, my daughter. He never forgave Robert for making you blind.'

'You know how wrong he was over that, even if you will not admit it and so cause Robert to feel unwarranted guilt. Drogo has never shown deep affection for me in any other way. He has,' said Alida bitterly, 'used me to betray Robert. No, Mother, my accident was simply an excuse for him to show openly the enmity he felt for his brother. And you encouraged him.'

The Lady snorted. 'I did no such thing, my girl!'

'You could have shown him that you did not agree. You should have tried to mend the rift—'

''Tis not unusual in a family for brothers to war against each other. Drogo never set his men on Robert—'

'No,' agreed Alida. 'He had some vestiges of honour left.'

'But he would have killed Robert in a duel without scruple,' burst out Genevra. 'I saw murder in his eyes at Merlinscrag. While Robert,' she went on softly, unconsciously revealing her tender feelings for her husband, 'could have killed Drogo twice over, but refrained. For your sake, my lady.'

'Humph,' said the Lady, but a flush of what Genevra could only imagine to be discomfort crept into her face. 'Leave me with my son,' she ordered brusquely. 'You may all sit with him later, an you so desire. I will call Father John should there be the need.'

In the turmoil of Drogo's return, Genevra had thrust from her mind her anxiety to know whether Father John had been successful in his quest. As all but the Lady left the chamber, the priest hovered without the door and, as she passed, touched her arm.

'May I speak with you, my lady?'

'Assuredly,' said Genevra. 'I am most anxious to know what befell. Come to my chamber.'

She led the priest in and sat him on a stool by a small table that held a flask of hippocras and a drinking horn.

'Refresh yourself with the spiced mead,' she invited.

John poured a measure into the horn and drank.

'Thank you, my lady. Now I must explain. I was returning with good news when I found Sir Drogo at the inn.'

John spread his long black robe about his dusty feet. To an impatient Genevra, he seemed slow to carry on.

'Good news, Father?' She clasped her hands together in her lap. 'You found the priest who wed my parents?'

His skirts spread to his satisfaction, John looked up. 'I did, my lady. First of all I made enquiries at the Palace of Eltham. There are those still there who remember the time when Margaret Heskith waited upon the late Queen. They could speculate instantly on the identity of the lady Margaret's lover, but knew nothing of a wedding—it must have been a well-kept secret. However, they told me the name of the priest who was responsible at the time for ministering to those residing there. He had retired to a monastery in Kent, they thought.'

'Nearby?'

'Some five leagues distant. So I took to the road again and found the place, where he still lives, quietly and peacefully, an old man of some seventy years.'

'He remembered my mother?' demanded Genevra eagerly as Father John paused to sip again at his cup.

'Aye, my lady, and your sire, too. A most attractive and worthy young gentleman, according to Father Simon. He wed them in a nearby church porch and celebrated mass afterwards. He vowed to tell no one of the ceremony without their permission.' He grimaced and took another pull at his drink. 'In fact, I had to convince him of their deaths and of your need to prove the legitimacy of your birth before he would speak!'

'But he did! Oh, Father, thank you! I am so happy! Do you have proof, or only his word?'

'He gave me a signed statement, my lady. Here.'

He handed Genevra a piece of parchment, which she quickly read. The expression on her face changed to one of relief and happiness as she took in what it said.

As soon as she had finished, John produced another document from beneath his robe. 'But I have here a copy of the record itself. It is there, in the church rolls, and can be seen at any time.'

Genevra took the second piece of parchment with a shaking hand. Tears of relief and joy gathered in her eyes as she perused it.

'So there can be no doubt,' said Father John quietly. 'You were born in holy wedlock, the union blessed by the Church. You are the legitimate heir to all Lord William Egerton's possessions excepting only Ardingstone and those properties tied to the Earldom of Northempston.'

As he finished speaking, Genevra dropped to her knees before the priest and grasped his hands. 'Thank you, dear Father John! How can I ever repay you for all you have done for me? You know that we shall never willingly allow you to leave us! Whether you choose to remain here or to return to Merlinscrag, you will never lack for a living.'

John smiled. His weariness seemed to have gone. 'I have enjoyed my travels, my lady but, when I have recovered my strength, I should like your permission to return to the people I know. I shall be waiting for your visits, eager to see you and Lord St Aubin return with your family. But I have prayed about this and the people there need me more than those here, I think.'

'Then of course you must go. You cannot know, but Lord Northempston has died and my husband has gone to attend his funeral. That is why he was not here to receive you on your return.'

'The Earl is dead? I am grieved to hear it. But it makes you, my dear, a very rich woman!'

'Whatever I have is my husband's. I have sent a message to him to tell him of Sir Drogo's arrival, though he may be on his way back by now.'

'He will be saddened by his brother's death,' said Father John, 'but will rejoice in the news I have brought.'

'Indeed he will. It is a pity my grandfather did not live a few more weeks so that he might have been told of your success, Father.'

'He would have been made very happy. But he was certain in his own mind already. So do not distress yourself over that, my lady.'

'No. But will you give thanks with me, Father? I should like to thank God for all his mercies.'

'Let us pray,' said Father John.

# Chapter Fifteen

The following day Genevra went back to the Lady's room, where Drogo lay. Having sat up all night with her son, the Lady had left Alida to watch over him while she retired to the bed in the adjoining chamber. Although Alida could not see, she would sense any change in Drogo's breathing, hear any new restlessness the fever might bring, and send the young serving-wench sharing her vigil to fetch help.

Genevra went chiefly to take Alida refreshment. She had no wish to sit in sisterly attendance on a man who had tried to rape her and in consequence caused so much heartache to both herself and Robert, but on the other hand she could not ignore his presence completely.

She murmured a greeting so that Alida would know who had come in, trod softly across the rushes and placed the tray of bread and ale where Alida could reach it.

'You may leave us. Wait outside,' she told the girl before softly asking Alida, 'Is there any change?'

'I do not think so. Mother says he was restless and rambling in the night, but he seems quiet now. Look at him for me, Genevra.'

Genevra went to the bed and held aside the curtain.

He was, she found, conscious, his eyes open and staring up at the tester.

His gaze moved slowly to her as light spilled in through the parted curtains. He stared back at her with feverish incomprehension until recognition slowly dawned.

'Why,' he croaked, ''tis my dear brother's wife. Where is Robert, my dear? Has he abandoned you again? Why don't you come closer? Were it not for this devilish wound, I'd finish what I began at Merlinscrag.'

Amazingly, he seemed lucid. Genevra choked back the angry words which rushed to her lips. 'You would have no more success now than you did then, Sir Drogo,' was all the reply she made.

'But your hounds are not with you now, are they? 'Twas a pity you proved so difficult to seduce, sister. A word from you even then and they would have lain quietly by while we entertained each other.'

'Entertained!' snapped Genevra. 'Is that how you would describe rape? You must have known that the thought of having you near me made me want to vomit!'

'Such flattering words, sister! Would I had the power to make you pay for them. As it was, your misplaced loyalty to dear Robert prevented me from revenging myself on him once more.'

Genevra's tone was fierce. She clutched the curtain in a tight grip to prevent herself from shaking the invalid until his teeth rattled. 'What has he ever done to you that you should hate him so?'

'He was born five years my senior.'

'And for that you have soured both your lives?' cried Genevra disbelievingly. 'He could not help it! But because of it you cuckolded him with his first wife and gave him a bastard to bring up as his heir. You guessed that he would be ready to believe that you had achieved the same object with me. What was your aim?' she demanded. 'To ensure that your son would inherit Thirkall, not his?'

'You are clever, my dear sister.' Drogo's voice had weakened and slurred but he managed to invest it with venom. 'My aim was to cuckold him again, to plant my seed in your womb so that *my* son would inherit what should have been mine were it not for an accident of birth.'

'Your mind is twisted, Drogo. You had no right to the barony at all.' Genevra leant over him, commanding his clouding gaze with hers, and asked, 'And had I given birth to a daughter?'

'Why, then I should have had to cuckold him again, dear sister.'

Drogo slurred the words out, but they were said with such malicious intensity that they still carried to the sharp-eared, silent witness of this, his declaration of intent.

He may not have known of Alida's presence behind the curtains or, if he did, he had forgotten or did not care. Her small moan of distress went unnoticed by him. His clouding consciousness was focused on the cold, beautiful face caught in his feverish gaze. Genevra disregarded the sound. It held no meaning for her while her attention was centred on the man in the bed.

'But you failed, Sir Drogo,' she declared forcefully.

'Aye, my lady, thanks to you, my intention was thwarted. But I'll wager I caused him no little disquiet, and that he doubts whether his heir is his own son.'

'No, he does not. Not now. I'll not deny that you gave him pain, as you wished. I hope the knowledge makes you happy and that you feel ready to meet your Maker with such a vile action on your conscience.'

Genevra, seeing Drogo's eyes lose their focus, thought he was probably sinking back into confusion. She felt a presence by her side and knew that Alida had come to join her by the bed. But she went on urgently with what she had to say. He might still understand.

'He no longer even suspects that,' she insisted. 'So, in the end, your scheming counted for nought. He has a true heir and is certain of it.'

She spoke with a conviction she did not entirely feel. Robert had protested his belief in her fidelity and she valued his declaration above everything. Only the smallest cloud still remained on the horizon of her mind, in case he was not absolutely and completely convinced. But she desired above everything to persuade Drogo that he had utterly failed in his design.

'Robert was always the lucky one,' he muttered, his words difficult to decipher. He wandered on, scarcely aware of what he was saying. The words came from the deepest recesses of his brain, the place where his brooding, twisted mind had cherished and inflated them. 'Inherited the title, distinguished himself in battles, won tournaments, charmed the best women. Won you for his bride, a great prize even though you are a bastard.'

Now Alida's gasp of outrage did reach Genevra. But Drogo had sunk back into delirium. His gabbled words now made no sense at all.

'How could he?' cried Alida, her arm encircling Genevra's waist. 'I would never have believed my brother so evil. And to call you bastard to your face!'

'I do not regard that now,' said Genevra. 'Father John returned with the proof of my legitimacy.'

'How happy that news makes me! But Drogo! I knew he harried Robert, tried to hurt him, to make him jealous,' went on Alida, her voice anguished, 'but I never guessed the full extent of his perfidy. . . Robert never said that Jane—that his son—'

'Did you not count up the months, Alida? He was abroad when that child was conceived.'

'They were in London,' whispered Alida. 'Jane remained there for years while he was away. We did not see her. . .'

'Robert covered up her unfaithfulness, then. He did not cast her and the child off. But it was a blessing they were taken by the plague.'

'Indeed, it was. And he suspected you. . .when Drogo visited Merlinscrag—'

'Drogo did his best to cause mischief between us, to make him believe that history was repeating itself. And succeeded for a while. But it is over now, Alida. We have come to trust each other.'

'I thank God for it! But I fear for Drogo!' she cried in distress. 'We must impress upon Father John that the moment Drogo is lucid again he must make his confession and receive absolution. He must receive the Last Rites. I could not bear for his soul to go to Hell!'

'Nor I,' said Genevra. She could not wish that fate on anyone, even Drogo.

Whether Drogo confessed to his sins, what he told Father John, no one ever knew, for the secrecy of the confessional was absolute. But the priest assured them that he had administered Holy Unction, had anointed him with oil he had blessed. He had received the Last Rites and could die in peace.

Two days later Drogo breathed his last.

Robert had left Thirkall to attend a funeral. When he returned it would be to attend another. Genevra had

sworn Alida and Father John to silence over the matter
of her legitimacy. She wanted to tell Robert before the
fact became general knowledge. Even the Lady was not
informed. In any case, she was so distraught by Drogo's
death as to be prostrated.

Alida spent much time with her mother. What she
told her of Drogo's confessions Genevra did not enquire.
Genevra knew that she would not broadcast the matter
beyond her mother's chamber, for to do so would serve
no good purpose. The Lady had spoilt her second son
from birth and deserved much of the blame for what he
had become. She should be told.

Genevra waited impatiently for her lord. She had so
much news to impart and so, mayhap, had he. Besides,
she had missed him and longed to be in his arms again.

Three days after Drogo's death, the messenger she had
sent to find Robert returned, his horse lathered, to say
that Lord St Aubin was not far behind him. He had
met up with the returning party on the way and had
immediately been charged with bringing back the news
of his lord's coming, most probably the following day.

Genevra ordered Chloe to be saddled ready. As she
donned her riding gown and stepped into her leather
breeches, she smiled to herself over the memory of
Robert's expression when he had first seen her wearing
the originals. Surprise had given way to amusement, but
he had not scolded her or tried to stop her from wearing
them. In fact, he had arranged for a new pair to be made,
which would fit her better. He was, she considered, the
perfect husband.

And she would ride out to meet him. In vowing Alida
and Father John to silence, she had forgotten the likelihood of John's escort having picked up some hint of his

discoveries. Few in the household had held Drogo in any affection, but even so it was strange that a subdued air of excitement should pervade the house in despite of the deep mourning imposed by his death. She intended to reach Robert first, before rumour could.

She waited impatiently until his train appeared in sight and then set out, alone. When he saw her approaching, he spurred ahead, galloping to meet her. And so they came face to face with no one else within earshot. They brought their horses alongside each other, nose to tail.

'Sweet heart,' he greeted her, his eyes vivid with pleasure, 'how I have missed you!'

'And I you, Robert.'

Their hands met in mutual warmth and joy. Genevra wished they could kiss, but that was impossible.

'The messenger said that Father John brought Drogo home wounded. Did he bring more welcome news?' asked Robert.

'Yes, he did, he has the documents to prove my parents' were wed. But, oh, my dear, such a time we have had! Sir Drogo is dead. Father John could not save him.'

She gave him the news baldly. There seemed no way to break it gently.

He nodded, the pleasure wiped from his face. 'I had feared as much,' he said grimly. 'And my lady mother? How has she reacted to his death?'

'Badly,' admitted Genevra. 'She has taken to her bed.'

'A pity.' He did not sound too upset. In fact, he smiled. 'But all else is well, it seems. Your parents' marriage is confirmed?'

'Indeed it is.'

'You know, of course, that the circumstances surrounding your birth make not the slightest difference to my regard for you?'

'I hope and believe so, lord. But it makes a difference to me. I am glad to be able to bequeath a true and noble ancestry to your heirs.'

He smiled and squeezed her hands again before releasing them. 'In that respect, and in that only, it pleases me, too.'

His retinue had caught up, Sir Alan at its head, but it waited a respectful distance behind. She waved a greeting to the young knight before she turned Chloe and they began to ride back side by side.

'But what of you, Robert? Was the funeral, though a sad occasion, a splendid one, as befitted the Earl? Who was there?'

'It was, and most of the nobility attended the service in the cathedral at St Albans. Lancaster was present.'

'He was?' Genevra did not wish to appear too eager, in case disappointment awaited her, but she had to know. 'What of the earldom, Robert?'

He could no longer contain his exuberant happiness. He gave a great shout. 'It is mine, wife. You are now Countess of Northempston!'

Genevra's joyous laugh rang out. 'How grieved Hannah will be! My uncle will owe you allegiance!'

'Is that all you can say, my love?' His face was set in disapproving lines, but his blue eyes danced.

'No, of course I am delighted for you, Robert, but I cannot help wishing to crow over Hannah! She caused me so much grief as a child.'

'It is out of her power to hurt you now, my love.'

'As it is out of Drogo's power to hurt you, my dearest husband.'

Robert sobered. 'Aye. Is the funeral arranged?'

'The churchmen are seeing to it. The house is swathed in sombre materials being made into mourning gowns.

Drogo will be buried with his ancestors in the churchyard
and with full knightly honour, little as he deserves it.
But 'twould distress your lady mother too much to forbid
a procession led by his horse bearing his spurs
and sword.'

She paused to guide Chloe round a pothole, then
glanced sideways at Robert, seeking his approval. 'His
retinue are at his hold. I refused them entry to Thirkall.'

He nodded briskly and flashed her a smile. 'A wise
decision, wife. They may attend the funeral, of course,
but after that I will split them up and post them to various
garrisons under my command, where they can be disciplined by the castellan. If I dismiss them as a body, they
may form a masterless, disruptive band and become a
scourge in the countryside. They have to live.'

'I shall be glad to see them leave the district,' admitted
Genevra. 'We want no lingering influence of Drogo's to
remain.'

'I had cast off Drogo's shadow some time ago,
my love.'

The words were spoken so sincerely that Genevra had
to believe him. Besides, his entire attitude had changed
over the last weeks. He had become the happy, cheerful
man she had glimpsed beneath the stern, disillusioned
knight she had agreed to wed.

'Aye, my husband, so you had.'

It seemed that all the shadows which had darkened
their marriage were dispelled. As they passed through
the barbican, over the bridge and into the courtyard,
Genevra saw Thirkall through new and appreciative eyes.

She could be very happy here. Merlinscrag would
remain dear to her, but Thirkall would become her home,
however grand the other castles and dwellings they might
now possess. Ardingstone could never become a home.

As in her grandfather's time, it would be a place for jousting and banqueting when the Earl of Northempston entertained.

The first thing Robert did on entering the building was to visit his mother's room, where Drogo still lay. He stood for a long moment regarding the body of his brother before he lightly touched the cold brow.

'For myself I can forgive you, brother,' he murmured. 'But not for the harm you did Jane and tried to do Genevra. May God see fit to give you rest.'

He passed through to the chamber where his mother lay abed. She was asleep.

Alida, sitting by the window, turned her face towards him.

'Robert?'

He strode across to kneel at her feet. 'Aye, sister.' He kissed her hand. 'You are well?'

'Quite well, Robert. Father John has given Mother a draught to aid her rest. She was much distressed by Drogo's death and I made matters worse by telling her how dastardly had been his actions toward you, my brother.'

His hand tightened on hers. 'How much do you know? What did you tell her, Alida?'

'I was in the room when he spoke with Genevra not long before he died. Not to apologise for the way he had behaved, but to regret that he had not been successful in his plan to ensure that 'twas a son begotten of his seed which inherited the barony of St Aubin. He failed first of all because Jane and her son died, and then because of Genevra's loyalty and refusal to betray you. You do believe her innocent, do you not, Robert?'

'Aye, Alida.' He paused. 'Confirmation of my belief

does not come amiss, but I am glad I came to trust her completely before the proof was offered me. 'Twas your love and trust in her that first made me realise how stupidly blind I had been. But somehow Drogo's spite had so crept under my skin that I could believe him capable of anything, of being able to bend anyone to his will.' He kissed her gently on the cheek. 'He is no loss, Alida.'

'No,' his sister agreed quietly. 'We should mourn what he could have been rather than what he became. But go now, Robert. You must not dally with me. You have been sadly missed by your wife and son.'

'You will join us for supper in the Hall? We shall be celebrating my elevation to the honour of Northempston.'

'Robert! How wonderful.' Her pleasure was whole-hearted. 'Yes, I shall certainly be there.'

'Twas not until after they had supped and the entire household had drunk to the health of the new Earl and his Countess that Robert had a chance to open the letters that had arrived during his absence from many of his scattered manors.

Both were already prepared for bed and their servants, ladies and squires had been dismissed for the night.

'I must just see what my stewards have to report,' said Robert, picking up several letters lying on his table. 'I shall not be long, my love.'

Genevra wished he would come quickly to bed, for she longed to be held fast in his arms, to celebrate the passing of so many shadows from their lives in the way she most enjoyed. But Robert had new and fearsome responsibilities and so she must learn not to complain if he felt compelled to attended to them first.

In fact, he broke the seals and just glanced quickly at

their contents. One, though, he perused more carefully. He gave an exclamation, more a laugh than anything, and tossed the missive on the coverlet for her to read while he scanned the last of his correspondence.

The report was from Martin, at Merlinscrag. As Genevra read the rather pedestrian details of his stewardship, she wondered what had brought that reaction from Robert. Then she saw it.

Old Mariel had sent a message for the lady Genevra.

*She says she sees nothing but light in her cauldron now, my lady*, Martin had written. *She wishes you to know that she would be delighted to deliver your daughter should you be here at the time of her birth.*

Robert had finished with his letters. He came and slid into the bed beside her.

'What does Old Mariel mean?' he asked, taking the parchment from Genevra's hand and holding it to the candle to read it again.

Genevra settled into the crook of his arm.

'When she told me of my future, she gazed into the infusion in her cauldron. 'Twas there she saw the darkness and death that would bring me happiness. Alida's darkness, Drogo's death. She saw the truth, Robert. Neither Alida's affliction nor Drogo's death has brought us anything but relief from shadows from the past. Now she can see only light ahead for me.'

'And this offer to deliver you of a daughter?'

'She has seen that our next child will be a girl, Robert. I believe her. She was right before, she will be right this time.'

Robert moved his hand down to rest it on the curve of her stomach.

'Welcome into the family, Alida,' he murmured. Then, 'Do you wish to return to Merlinscrag, sweet heart?'

'No, Robert.' She felt it safe, at last, to say it. 'I love you, husband. All I desire is to please you. Our children will be born wherever you choose.'

Robert reared over her to look down into her eyes. 'You love me, Genevra?' he asked in wonder. 'How can that be, when I have treated you so badly?'

'I fell in love at our betrothal, when you smiled at me.'

'That long ago?'

'Aye, husband. You were sad, disillusioned, wary of marrying me. I hoped I could bring you happiness, Robert. But the love I felt then was based on hero worship of the Golden Eagle.'

'And now?' he queried softly as she hesitated.

'Now that love has turned into a true affection grown stronger and deeper over time. I love you with my whole heart and soul, my husband.'

'You did not tell me,' he chided gruffly.

'No. I feared to tell you. It slipped out once, but you did not even notice. I knew that you did not love me. Had I told you again, you might have been embarrassed.'

He lifted his golden brows. His eyes gleamed in the candle glow. 'Embarrassed?' he asked, and laughed. 'But now you no longer fear to tell me? How can that be, wife?'

For a desperate moment Genevra wondered whether she had judged his emotions wrongly. Then she saw the expression in his eyes. She blushed hotly. 'I thought . . . nay, I hoped that you had come to love me, too,' she admitted rather breathlessly.

'I cannot imagine what gave you that impression,' returned Robert severely. 'You are presumptuous, wife.'

'I know how much you loved your first wife, Jane . . .' she whispered.

'Yes, I did,' he admitted grimly, 'until she betrayed

me. That was why I was so afraid to allow myself to fall
in love with you. I vowed I would not.'

'Oh,' said Genevra dimly. She shivered. 'Yes, I was
presumptuous.'

'So I would not admit, even to myself, that I had fallen
even more deeply in love with you, my wife.'

He had been teasing her. Genevra, suddenly alive as
she had never been before, cried, 'You wretch!'

His hands were busy exploring her body. His lips
curved into a smile before they descended to take her
lips in a deep kiss that finally resolved all her doubts.

His words, when he uttered them, were scarcely
necessary.

'How could I not love you, sweeting? You captured
my heart long ago. Which made it so much the worse
when I thought Drogo had seduced you or mayhap
raped you.'

'Truly, Robert?'

'Truly, my beloved wife. My heart is yours now and
forever.'

'As mine is yours,' whispered Genevra.

# FREE!

## FOUR FREE
## specially selected
## Historical Romance™ novels
## PLUS a FREE Mystery Gift
## when you return this page...

Return this coupon and we'll send you 4 Historical Romance novels and a mystery gift absolutely FREE! We'll even pay the postage and packing for you.

We're making you this offer to introduce you to the benefits of the Reader Service™ – FREE home delivery of brand-new Historical Romance novels, at least a month before they are available in the shops, FREE gifts and a monthly Newsletter packed with information, competitions, author profiles and lots more...

Accepting these FREE books and gift places you under no obligation to buy, you may cancel at any time, even after receiving just your free shipment. Simply complete the coupon below and send it to:

MILLS & BOON READER SERVICE, FREEPOST, CROYDON, SURREY, CR9 3WZ.

READERS IN EIRE PLEASE SEND COUPON TO PO BOX 4546, DUBLIN 24

## NO STAMP NEEDED

Yes, please send me 4 free Historical Romance novels and a mystery gift. I understand that unless you hear from me, I will receive 4 superb new titles every month for just £2.99* each, postage and packing free. I am under no obligation to purchase any books and I may cancel or suspend my subscription at any time, but the free books and gift will be mine to keep in any case. (I am over 18 years of age)

H7YE

Ms/Mrs/Miss/Mr_____
BLOCK CAPS PLEASE

Address_____

_____

_____ Postcode _____

# *Historical Romance*™

## Coming next month

# THE NEGLECTFUL GUARDIAN
## *Anne Ashley*

Miss Sarah Pennington had taken matters into her own hands! If her guardian, Mr Marcus Ravenhurst, was not prepared to acknowledge her existence, then she would leave Bath and stay with her old governess. For propriety she became Mrs Armstrong, but her travels were cut short by snow and she found herself stranded in a wayside inn!

She didn't know that Marcus was hot on her trail. He might not have visited the chit, but he'd given her everything her companion had requested! Then the weather foundered him too, and he walked into that same inn, unaware that the delicious young widow called Mrs Armstrong was his missing ward—or that she had a marked propensity for getting into trouble...

# THE BECKONING DREAM
## *Paula Marshall*

When her brother Rob was held for seditious writing, the only way Mistress Catherine Wood could ensure his release was to accompany supposed merchant Tom Trenchard—pretending to be his wife!—to Holland on a spying mission. With roguish charm Tom made no bones about wanting Catherine in his bed—after all, Catherine was an actress!—but she was determined to hold him at bay. It surprised her to realise how hard that was, more so as they travelled into danger and depended upon one another, needing all their wits about them...